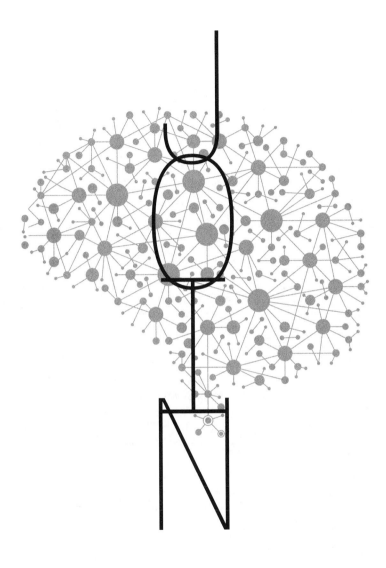

STEVE TOUTONGHI

Published by
Soho Press, Inc.
853 Broadway
New York, NY 10003

Library of Congress Cataloging-in-Publication Data

Toutonghi, Steve
Join / Steve Toutonghi.

ISBN 978-1-61695-670-7
eISBN 978-1-61695-671-4

1. Self-consciousness (Awareness)—Fiction. 2. Humanity—Fiction.
3. Science fiction. I. Title
PS3620.O923 J65 2016 813.6—dc23 2015037546

Interior design by Janine Agro, Soho Press, Inc.

Printed in the United States of America

10 9 8 7 6 5 4 3 2 1

To Monique.
Join me for a story.

PART ONE

What is truly radical about Join is not the miracle of united perspective. What is truly radical is that the network, in accordance with the laws of physics, is ethical.

—Excellence, CEO of Vitalcorp, Secretary of Join Affairs

/* Enumerate the mysteries. */
—Code comment from a test harness written by Hamish Lyons

FROM ONE OF HIS FIVE childhoods, Chance remembers his bare feet, wet and shining on the flat white surface just beneath a thin layer of water. Then he looks up at a sky of intense blue, flecked with bright clouds. The sky is reflecting on the sheet of still water below. The sky and mirroring water extend to the horizon.

His patient's voice interrupts the memory. "Just when you think you've hit absolute rock bottom," his patient Lucky Four says, "you fall again, and farther than you ever thought was even possible. You just keep going."

"I see," Chance Three says. He's having difficulty reviewing Lucky's test results.

Lucky's a six, and Chance finally has results for all of Lucky's six drives. Each of them—except this one, Lucky Four—has the same flulike symptoms and similar microbiome anomalies. After nearly a decade and a half of practice, Chance should recognize Lucky's condition. But the numbers and symbols aren't making sense. Chance is having trouble piecing the data together with a narrative that explains them. He stares harder, but the collection of paragraphs, rows, and columns just doesn't connect.

"Hey," his patient says, "are you all right?"

"No," Chance Three says. He's surprised that Lucky has noticed. Lucky Four has spent every previous moment in Chance's company describing the slow deterioration of his complex personal life, in obsessive detail. He has been incessant and thoroughly self-involved. Join pathologies can be unpleasant, and the obsessive personal focus is probably a symptom of Lucky's illness. Lucky's five other drives may be simultaneously boring five other people.

"I just found out that I'm sick," Chance Three says—the words dodging his better judgment and speaking themselves. He takes a breath. "Just this minute."

"You're sick too?" asks Lucky Four.

"I have cancer," Chance says. "My Five, my most recent join, does."

"I see." Lucky says. "You might need a day or two off."

It takes Chance a moment to understand what his patient is saying. "Well," he says at last, "it's actually terminal. I may need more than that."

"Oh. I didn't know that was still a problem. That cancer can be terminal."

"Yeah, it's rare. I'm with a doctor right now—"

"Like I am."

Chance is surprised. "Yes," he says. The man's face is guileless. Chance understands what he's trying to say. Chance needs to focus on his own patient. But he can't stop thinking about the cancer diagnosis. His arms and legs feel heavy. He wants to sit down, but Lucky Four is watching him expectantly.

Chance says, "My doctor and I are just going over test results—"

"Oh! Just like—"

"Yes," Chance says, interrupting, and then immediately

regretting it. He clears his throat. "That's right," he says. "Like you and I should be doing. My doctor is covering options for care. He wants to keep me comfortable."

"I see. So, same sort of thing here. We'll be talking about treatment."

"Yes," Chance says. "After I've had some time to fully review your test results. Excuse me, just a moment. I'm going to step out of the room."

"Why?"

"I'm not feeling well. Someone will be in soon."

"Okay. But I think whoever I work with should know my story. It might be important."

As Lucky Four is speaking, Chance Three turns toward the door—which slides open—and then steps into the hallway. He steps to the side so Lucky can't see him, and backs against the wall. He puts his hands on his thighs and leans. He's a broad man, with a substantial presence. If people see him like this, they'll worry. They'll ask what's wrong. He doesn't want to talk about it.

Chance Three hears the exam-room door slide open. He straightens quickly and walks away from his patient.

. ●.

CHANCE TWO FLICKS OFF HER retinal display, even as her broadcast gets its first sympathetic response—a glowing exclamation mark briefly suspended in the sunlight that's warming the plane's cockpit. Then there's only the muted, predictable instrumentation of the airliner's consoles and the bright fields of cloud they're flying above.

"I know someone named Cancer," her copilot, Leap Two, says, "like the crab, though, in the Zodiac."

Chance is taking a break from flying the plane. After Chance Two told Leap about Chance Five's cancer, they talked a bit, and then Chance composed the broadcast for friends and family. It has been interesting to note the odd, almost detached sensation of observing each of her five drives—three male and two female—responding to news of the cancer. Chance closes her eyes and settles back in her chair.

"Hey, you want to pay attention to your job there, cowboy?" Leap Two says. The flight AI, Autonomy, is passively monitoring cockpit activity and pilot behavior and will note if a pilot appears to be dozing.

A few months ago, Leap suggested that Chance take a vacation. Leap said, "Get some time on the range." It was kind of funny at the time but also an odd reference. Since then, Leap's been calling Chance Two "cowboy." Chance imagines her own fine, curly blond hair weighted by a big straw cowboy hat that she'd probably have trouble keeping straight on her small head.

Chance Two rubs her forehead. It's difficult to focus. "I don't know what I'm supposed to do," she says.

"Let's see," says Leap. "Intro to Atmospheric Aviation, I remember this bit particularly. Paragraph three, 'The qualified atmospheric aviator understands distraction and boredom as primary enemies of economic prosperity.' Yes, 'economic prosperity.' The world's economic fate is in your hands. So I'm sorry you're sick, but suck it up, cowboy, and do your job."

Chance Two laughs. Chance wonders which of Leap's other drives looked up the note in their old text. Leap might have just remembered it. Leap is capable of holding long grudges against offensive bits of cultural flotsam.

"Thank you, Mistress Baton," Chance says, "but at the

moment, I'm selfishly thinking about my terminal cancer. Not so much of the world at large."

That earns a soft chuckle from Leap. *Mistress Baton* is another bit of cultural flotsam—a reality program that had particularly appalled Leap.

"Okay," says Leap. "Here's what you do: read the research, plan, act. Like everything else. And by the way, I really am sorry."

"Yeah," Chance says, "okay, thank you. Anyway, I know what to do, ideally. But it's the damn meat gap. Getting drives to do the things."

"Yeah," agrees Leap, and then she makes a smooth transition to salacious. "It's all about the meat."

Chance laughs for the sake of the friendship, but her heart really isn't in it.

Leap Two is doing a quick panel check, flicking through reports on the left-side copilot screen and checking off steps on the right side. As Chance watches, she takes a moment to admire Leap Two—the quiet self-awareness that's so natural and unself-conscious, the narrow, classically elegant nose, sharp, high cheekbones, and clear light brown eyes.

Most people would probably consider Chance Two attractive, despite the slightly severe cast of her face. Chance Two is average height, forty years old, and in good shape, with pale skin, a narrow forehead, and a strong, high nose.

But Leap Two is something else entirely, a gorgeous statistical anomaly, a physical outlier whose vitality is animated by Leap's relaxed intelligence. Leap may be vain about Leap Two, but the vanity is justified. Even the grace and physical economy of her arms and hands as she gestures her way through the midflight checklist are almost breathtaking. It's all rote after so many years, but Chance still enjoys watching Leap Two.

Leap is used to people watching Leap Two. She flicks the displays to the dashboard, then repeats herself, muttering, "It's always the meat gap."

Then her head jerks forward and back, and her upper lip rises, showing her two front teeth. It all happens so quickly that Chance isn't completely sure that Leap actually did anything.

It forces a surprised laugh out of Chance, who asks, "What was that?"

"I said, 'It's always the meat gap.'"

"But what was that thing you did? With your head and your teeth." There's a long pause. Leap stares at Chance. Then Leap Two's face hardens.

"I don't know what you mean," Leap says.

Chance hesitates. Leap has always been private about her personal business, often marking a topic as "not to be discussed," as has clearly just happened. But this was a small spasm. Chance saw it. It'll be on the flight vid. There's no point denying it happened.

It was like a sneeze. Too insignificant to consider private. But if Leap doesn't want to talk about it, then it almost becomes interesting.

Chance says, "You had a little . . . it was like you sneezed, or hiccuped."

"Whatever," Leap says.

Leap Two settles back into the copilot seat and presses a spot to request coffee.

"What do you mean, 'whatever'?"

"What are you talking about?" Leap is irritated. She turns to face Chance, unblinking, her eyebrows raised in a challenge.

"What? Don't give me that look," says Chance. "I saw—"

"You didn't see anything," says Leap Two. She turns back to face the fields of clouds, putting an end to their conversation.

．

BEFORE JOINING, CHANCE FIVE WAS an eighteen-year-old named Javier Quispe who had already completed two years of college study. He could play ninety minutes of nonstop football and follow up with a workout. He loved playing in community leagues. He also had a seven-point plan for reintroducing the Andean condor to the wild.

Javier wanted to join despite a fear of losing himself, his individuality, during the procedure. The joins he knew assured him that what he had read was true: each individual's perspective coheres through the procedure, and every individual in the join is also the joined result. There is only gain, they said, and, with the rich interplay of memories from so many people, a deeper understanding of life's irreducible mysteries.

His parents used metaphors—it's like being more attuned to all of who you are, all your different desires and fears; it's like clearly remembering who you were ten years ago, before events changed you. They said the awareness of being more than one person included a comforting sense of companionship.

Now, as Chance Five changes out of his hospital gown, he touches the short hair at the back of his head and rubs his thumb over the scar where his skull was opened to adjust his caduceus. Chance learned in medical school that the caduceus—or "caddy"—got its name because a member of the original team thought that the scar left after surgery resembled the ancient symbol of a winged staff with entwined snakes. Javier always liked snakes.

As a child, Javier had been envious of everyone, joins and solos, who had a seemingly magical ability to pick data out of the air. He got his first caddy when he was twelve, so he too could connect directly to the biowave network.

When he decided to join, Vitalcorp replaced parts of that original caddy with the components required to connect minds. Then he and Chance Four received complementary adjustments and underwent the rigidly controlled protocol of psychotropic drug therapies. As a result, Javier Quispe ceased being a solo and became Chance. His body became Chance Five.

Chance Five soon began experiencing persistent stomach pain. Chance dismissed the pain at first and only barely modified his regular, arduous workouts. Chance thought it might be an injured rectus abdominus or internal oblique. But the pain intensified. Tests found an aggressive, recently identified strain of cell mutation. Chance's oncologist has just told him that it's a cancer that can be triggered, or aggravated, by the join procedure.

If Chance Five dies, then Chance—and therefore Javier Quispe—will live on through other drives in the join. That can continue forever. In a perfect join, human beings lose both their existential sense of isolation and their mortality.

Chance faces the prospect of dying and surviving his own death. "Volatile emotional response with significant drive variability" is how Chance might characterize his reaction to Chance Five's diagnosis, if this were research.

.

Chance One, trim and naturally charismatic, is possessed of innate self-assurance that inspires confidence in others. He works as a data scientist at a public-private cooperative. When he told his supervisor about the cancer, she was surprised. She asked—though he was certain she already knew—how long he'd had his fifth drive.

"About six months," Chance One had said. And then Chance had to worry about embarrassing himself by crying. That level of instability was very surprising in Chance One.

His supervisor nodded and said, "I see. I'm so sorry." But there was a different message in her look. She was thinking, It's better that it's the new drive.

And maybe it is better. Chance Five is a student, just starting out. Losing him might be less disruptive. No one would say something like that, of course.

.

Before joining, Chance Two was quick-witted, opinionated, and given to crafting exceptionally well-reasoned arguments for preserving the status quo. Chance Two continues to give an impression of reserve and matter-of-fact competence. She's an airline pilot with a specialty in long-haul atmospheric aviation and has been the least affected of Chance's drives.

.

Chance Three is currently splashing his face with water from a cold tap in a hospital restroom. His straight black hair lies neatly flat on his squarish head. He is a large man, and though he appears stolid, he is the most emotionally responsive of Chance's drives and often has powerful, sometimes-distracting, reactions to trauma.

Chance Three is a specialist in the quantum personality matrix—a "join doctor." It's a job that requires presence and empathy. Chance is having trouble focusing, and Chance Three has evaded his patient.

.

When she is awake, Chance Four is about motion and precision. A short (close to the Earth), thirty-eight-year-old woman who is fast and light on her feet. The fact that Chance Four is currently sleeping is helping Chance deal with the traumatic news.

.

The year before he joined, Chance Five and a girl named Shawna flew a pod over the salt flats to a place that Nana called *llanura de las bestias*. The plain of the beasts. Beside scattered steel beams and shattered pyramids of yellow, crusted soil lay rotted, riveted husks—the loosely articulated bodies of ancient locomotives.

"I love it here," Shawna said, one hand against a pitted gray-and-orange plate. "This is everything that came before. But we're so lucky. We can live forever now."

And then in cool shadows, he reached for Shawna's warmth, her soft skin, her breath on his neck and cheek.

And in the heat after, he felt a leaden pull into the drifting world, where long molten channels creep through their fiery beds, where blast furnaces roar, and there is the deafening whine of disks biting steel and a flaring out of burning swarf.

CHANCE TWO AND LEAP TWO trained together—flexorology, mechanics, aerodynamics, flight systems administration, electromagnetism, macro-meteorology. Chance tended to score just above Leap in their coursework and has always enjoyed a slight professional edge.

When they were in school together, Leap still had only two drives, but Chance rarely saw Leap One. Leap would say that Leap One was an introvert. Chance knew what Leap meant—one of the nice things about having multiple bodies is the ability to devote different bodies to different temperaments.

Since then, Leap has grown to a four, and Chance has spent at least some time with each of Leap's drives. Chance One even had a short fling with Leap Two. (And Chance can still distract any drive by picturing her naked.)

A couple of years ago, Leap declined a promotion in order to keep flying with Chance. Chance had been pressing Leap's case to their boss when Leap, in direct contradiction to years of moaning over meals and margaritas, turned the opportunity down. Leap said she just wanted to keep flying with Chance. The routes they traveled were better, she said, and she was set in her ways. Chance was touched, and a little puzzled. Then their boss transferred into low-orbit freight hauling, and they haven't talked about it since. Leap is like that sometimes—contrary. For the last month or so, Leap has also been gloomy, but whenever Chance tries to find out why, Leap shakes it off and perks up.

The flight they're on today is a low ten-percenter, with no real weather. The Great Central storm has been subdued for over a week—retracted into a core lightning maze that crouches over the hardball, the charred, lightning-grooved ruin of what was once about ten thousand square miles of prairie.

In an era of megastorms and sudden formations, Chance and Leap—as pilot and copilot—are responsible for rerouting the airliner toward lesser weather while balancing increased distance with schedule requirements. But the flight automation is pretty good at avoiding the worst surprises that storms generate, and the planes are highly instrumented and closely monitored. Having a crew on board provides a safety in case of network flakiness and helps to calm customers, but they spend most of their time reviewing reports from the various flight systems. They aren't usually needed to fly the plane. Except, as the saying goes, when they are.

·●·

ABOUT AN HOUR AFTER THE first one, Leap does it again, the tic. They're beginning the pre-descent review when Chance Two happens to glance over just as Leap Two spasms in the same way. Only this time, her shoulders hump up as well.

Chance Two stares, but Leap gives no indication that she's aware it happened. It wasn't a sneeze and was definitely bigger than a hiccup.

Afterward and without any preamble, as Leap Two is reading her screen intently, she says she's sorry. If Leap is sorry there must be something to be sorry for. Chance examines a chart that maps actual humidity to expected humidity over the last half hour and projects forward for the next thirty minutes to landing. She says to Leap, "Do you want to talk about it?"

When she says it, she has her back to Leap Two, but she knows that Leap has stopped moving. Chance continues the protocol.

After a few moments, Leap Two says, "You only have one drive dreaming?"

What does Chance's dreaming drive have to do with anything? It's strange, alien, for Chance to feel this uncomfortable while talking with Leap.

"Yeah," she says.

"You've got terminal cancer," Leap says. "That has to be stressing you out. Maybe you're not as rested as you could be. You've been working a lot of hours."

This is not the conversation Chance wants to have with Leap. Now that the illness is a reality, and Leap knows, Chance wants to talk about the stress after the preliminary diagnosis, about premonitions of disaster. Chance wants to tell Leap about her anger and about wanting to distrust the data, about suddenly becoming furious with a saltshaker because high-sodium diets are associated with poor stress management. In fact, she took the saltshaker with her during her commute this morning and then felt absurd, holding it white knuckled before stuffing it into a public waste processor.

Leap says, "Have you thought about putting a second drive into storage for a while?"

Of course Chance has thought about it. And this is what Chance needs—a review of the data, a consideration of options, an analysis of possible outcomes. But Leap's voice is wrong. What should sound sympathetic is anything but.

Chance doesn't look at Leap. She focuses on her job.

Leap Two says, in an irritated tone that's almost threatening, "Should I be worried about you?"

"YOU'D THINK THIS STUFF WOULD get easier," Chance Three grumbles, not sure and not caring what he really means by "this stuff."

When Chance Three finished his sixteen-hour shift at Shine University's Join Praxis Center, he ended up here, at Whatever You Want, the restaurant and bar across the street from the hospital. Bottles behind the well-stocked bar diffract an occasional sparkle. The walnut furniture is dinged and comfortably worn. Weak parabolas of blue- and red-tinged light hover around glow bulbs shaped to imitate twentieth-century lamps.

Chance looks at a small drop of condensation on his glass and at the bent image within it. He's thinking about Chance Three's parents, Angela and Sarawut. Chance Three was an only child. His parents married late in life, and he was born to them late. He now believes that having a child was an early attempt by his parents to bridge their differences. But they fought ferociously throughout his childhood, shouting terrible things at each other, whatever might wound. Throwing things. Chance wished for different parents.

And then, right after he graduated from high school, they joined, becoming Ultimate. The parents who had raised him both remained and disappeared. Ultimate was a calm, realistic, grounded, and loving individual. Ultimate was magnificent. It was very weird. Chance had to think of the two of them differently, as one person. His imagination balked at it. He did learn to see them both in Ultimate, but they were healed and happy. Ultimate never joined again, and now Ultimate is gone.

A few feet from Chance Three, the bartender is leaning back against a heavy shelf, arms crossed. The waitress is sitting to

Chance's left. The two of them are a join named Apple. There's only one other customer in the bar, so Apple has been killing time with Chance.

A big chunk of human mental resources are mapped to facial recognition, the subtle detection and decoding of emotion. What Apple is doing right now, watching Chance Three from two perspectives and integrating impressions, is referred to as "triangulating" or "reading through." Practically, it means that it would be very difficult for Chance Three to successfully lie to Apple.

It's uncomfortable to be the focus of both of their attention.

"I've just found out I'm sick," Chance says.

"Oh?" says the waitress, Apple One. "Nothing contagious, I hope."

"Not contagious, but possibly terminal," says Chance.

"Ouch. That's too bad," says Apple One. "Hey, at least you're not solo."

It's a defensive response and almost shockingly uncharitable. As Chance has discovered, joins want to believe that because they can defeat mortality, the loss of a single drive is easily managed.

The truth is more complicated. Some of Chance's patients have years of phantom pains and phantom experiences—hunger, excitement, even visions—that seem to come from drives that have died. Drive death can be so traumatic that fringe groups like the Safe Hemlock Society advocate "practice dying" and stage elaborate "mortality events." The Safe Hemlock Society actually teaches that the only way joins can embrace their true, immortal nature is to experience the traumatic death of a drive.

"Part of me was solo until last year," Chance says. "Part of me is scared."

"That's the luckiest part," says Apple Two, the bartender.

Which is true. If the cancer had struck earlier, Chance Five wouldn't have joined and might have really been killed by it. Dead dead. Then again, this particular cancer is more common and more dangerous among joins. Maybe, if he hadn't become Chance Five, Javier would have remained healthy.

Chance Three says, "I know," but says it grimly. It's hard to be self-pitying when people consider you privileged.

"You'd be about two-thirds of the way to a complete join, wouldn't you, if the drive were to die in six more months?" asks the bartender, Apple Two. He's referring to common wisdom that says psyches integrate quickly, but drives take about eighteen months.

Chance Three is feeling buzzed and is exhausted from his shift, but Chance's mind is mostly clear. "Up until last year," Chance says, "for part of me, that drive was everything, literally. For the rest of me, well, I'm a five. I'm going to be a four again."

"How long were you a four, before this join?" asks the waitress.

"Fifteen years."

"Well, that is sad," she says.

A very long time ago, joins decided that when they had a choice, sympathy from the opposite gender was more emphatic. Now, it's almost etiquette. With the right intonation that choice can also carry a distinct kind of irony. Though it's sometimes hard to detect, Chance thinks he may have just heard it. Chance isn't sure whether Apple believes what she said, doesn't believe it, or both.

"There's not full physical integration yet." Chance is annoyed by Apple's callousness. "Okay, right now this is me, but I—the man who was my Five—am still afraid of dying."

The waitress sighs. This time her empathy does seem real. "You kind of won't," she offers.

"Another whiskey! Something cheap!" the other customer calls with gusto from several tables away.

"So that guy's fucking awesome," Apple Two says under his breath as Apple One gets up, grabs a bottle, and walks toward the guy.

The bartender gives the other customer a quick wave and a nod. Then he explains to Chance, "He's a nine. Was a ten."

Chance feels a small charge of interest—this is someone who's recently lost a drive?

The bartender waits a moment, watching the waitress and customer, then continues, "He says he wants to run down to a two or three. Then he'll build it back up. He likes to kill them slowly, with alcohol poisoning."

"What?" Chance says. "That's horrible!"

Apple raises a finger to his lips—Chance's reaction was too loud. Chance borrows a few more cycles from his sleeping drives, becoming more present with Chance Three, less drunk.

"And if he even got to two or three," Chance says, trying to hold down his volume, "and then he added, how could he be sure he'd still want to do it, to go down again?"

Apple leans his palms against the bar. He doesn't respond but instead watches Chance, challenging him to come up with the answer.

"He's not joining kids?" Chance asks with a touch of disgust.

The bartender's eyes close briefly, and he shakes his head ever so slightly.

"He's using a fixative?" Chance's voice rises a little in disbelief.

"He's hitting on me right now," says bartender Apple, and nods toward the guy. Chance turns around. Apple, the waitress, is leaning against the table and laughing with the guy. She's good looking—curvy, with brown hair; although her short costumey skirt and matching black-and-yellow-striped blouse look a bit silly. But the customer is even better looking—six-foot-four-ish, broad shouldered, chiseled jaw, blond close-cropped hair, narrow, smiling eyes. His face is flush with drink.

Then Apple Two says in a hushed voice, "I don't really know, but that's what I think, a fixative."

"Really?" is all Chance can say.

"That guy's two of the original thousand," Apple Two continues, keeping his voice low. "A married couple. Says he was close friends with Music, but, you know . . ." Apple folds his arms again and leans back against the shelf.

Apple Two is short and slightly heavyset, with dark sideburns shaved into a circle on each cheek. The left half of his head is shaved bald. The hair on the right half is about an inch long. He looks more like a solo from some sort of resistance cell than a bartender working near the core of a spire community. He speaks slowly. Despite the sarcasm, he seems like he might not have a sense of humor.

"The two of them were both pretty well off before joining," Apple continues, his voice measured, to carry to Chance but not far beyond. "They put everything into Vitalcorp, in the early days. And won the lottery of five hundred to boot. Sold the last of their stock—most of it—a few years ago. That guy's very rich."

Chance does a quick estimate. Everyone knows the approximate number. After Vitalcorp finished the trial of one thousand and released Join to the general public, its stock rose so fast it threatened to break the market. Vitalcorp was a capital hurricane, sucking in investment dollars like a megastorm sucks in small towns.

And Join actually did break the government. Things like Social Security numbers and biometric security all assumed a person had only one body. Lots of programs got snarled up—should all of a join's drives get benefits or only one? It was clear that regulators had let Join come to market too early, but the genie was out of the bottle. The government needed the money Vitalcorp was making in order to address the issues Join caused.

In the end, the government froze the stock and seized the company. The joke was they merged. To avoid the catastrophe of a complete divestiture, shares continued to pay a sizable dividend until about ten years ago, when plans were announced to retire Vitalcorp equity, and the dividend started a phased decline. The bottom line was that each dollar invested before the trial of one thousand realized a very, very large return.

Chance's drink is empty. He pushes it forward. Apple is watching Apple One and the other patron closely. He steps up, finds the bottle, and refills Chance's tequila without really taking his eyes off them.

"What, ah, you said he was a nine?" Chance is confused briefly as a drunk spike inhibits the join. He has an attack of nausea and headache, and then he's okay again.

"Yeah. Soon to be an eight," says Apple, distracted by watching them. "Says he was a fifteen once. Now he's going back down. Wants to make it to two."

"What's his name? Would I recognize it?"

"No, I don't think so. Says he's one of the ones that didn't look for press. Says a lot didn't. Says the ones that didn't were safer, during that first round of backlash."

"Do you believe him?" Chance sips his refilled drink.

Apple finally looks at Chance. "Yeah, I do," he says.

"Fixative," says Chance, speculatively.

"You're a join doctor?" Apple asks.

Chance Three raises his glass in acknowledgment and takes another sip.

"How would you get to someone like that, to test them?" asks Apple.

"Well, you'd have to do it when he came in for something else. He probably has his own doctors, though. And, yeah, fixative does work. One prejoin personality gets a distinct advantage, but it's not like the pulp vids and Civ News, and it doesn't have a clear physical signature like, say, a meme virus. Fixative is more . . . flexible. He'd have good lawyers too, so you couldn't prove it in court. But it's *very* dangerous," Chance says. "Why do you believe him?"

Apple's gaze is steady and unblinking. "That guy is an asshole," he says. "A real asshole. Right now, he's telling me how he'd like to kill me. Both of me. He's telling me *how*."

Chance looks over his shoulder, and the guy glances up at them. The guy catches Chance's eye and smiles, then refocuses his attention on the waitress, Apple One. The guy is starting to look pretty sloppy.

Apple Two says, "A while ago, I saw him drink a drive to death. Over a couple of months. At first I didn't know what he was doing. He flirted a little. He's a big tipper. Anyway, it gets pretty clear pretty fast that he's going to drink hard when he comes in. I felt like shit some nights, serving him. One night, he says, 'Hey, don't feel bad. This is what I do.' 'What?' I ask. He says, 'I kill drives.' He says, 'I do it in different ways. I'm drinking this one to death because it can be slow.' He says, 'I want to feel it.'"

Apple shakes his head. "I should have cut him off."

Apple has a glass of water under the bar. He takes a drink. Chance can hear waitress Apple and the customer laughing.

"I've seen solos try to drink themselves to death," Apple Two continues. "And the thing is, it's hard for them. They lose their nerve. That guy just drank right through, like it was a show. He passes out. I'm calling the ER. So I cut him off. Maybe a week later, he comes in with a different drive. Healthy, happy. Shows me a Civ News story. His other drive's dead of alcohol poisoning. Says he owes me. Says he appreciates it must have been hard for me. That was years ago. Then maybe a week ago, that drive comes in."

"But he sounds unstable. Killing drives . . . Why hasn't the Directorate picked him up?"

"Exactly," says Apple. He turns his back on Chance, lifts his bar rag, and drops it on a shelf. He says, "He hasn't been picked up. That's why I believe him."

Chance Three's heart starts beating fast. Sweat starts on his upper lip. He wipes it away with the back of his hand and tries to calm his breathing. Chance's mind is mostly clear, but the drive has been touched by panic. The alcohol doesn't help.

His drink is empty. He should get up and go home.

Chance Three motions to Apple to refill his glass. He throws back his newly poured shot. A moment later, the bartender has gone somewhere. Chance stands, wobbling a bit.

He walks to the other guy's table. Bumps into a chair, over-compensates, and stumbles. Steadies himself. He sticks out his hand. "Chance," he says.

The guy doesn't move. "Rope," he says.

Rope watches him for a moment, then asks, "You wan' a last drink?"

"Last drink?" Chance asks quickly.

Rope gives him an odd look. Explains, "They're gonna close."

"Oh! No, no, I've really had plenty." Chance feels stupid standing. He pulls out the chair opposite Rope and sits down.

"I'ma haf one more." Rope lifts a hand to signal Apple One.

She walks over with a bottle and refills his shot glass. "Last call," she says. Rope makes an effort to waggle his index finger at her.

Rope is slumped in his chair. His arms are dead weights, one resting on the table, one limp at his side. His mouth is hanging open slightly. His eyes—though deeply bloodshot—look clear. The drive is nearly unconscious, but the person within it is alert.

"Can hol' ma liquor," Rope says. The mouth on the handsome drive smiles. "Sorry, I'll do betta wif my speech." Rope is putting more effort into working the drunken drive.

"I don't mind," Chance says.

"No." Rope laughs, speaking slowly, enunciating. "Don' imagine you do. Apple jus' told you more than she should haf about me, din't she?"

Chance Three nods.

"Don't worry about it," Rope says, with increasing clarity, his body still slumped and unmoving. "Really."

Chance says, "Apple said you were two of the original one thousand." Rope's eyes move slowly in agreement. Chance continues, "It sounds as though you . . . have a lot of experience with . . ." Chance can't finish the sentence.

"With what?" Rope asks. In join lore there's a phenomenon commonly referred to as "possession." It's meant to describe exactly this. Rope is alert, energized, unfazed by the alcohol, but the drive is a mess.

"What do I haf experience with?" Rope asks again, slowly, and Chance hears keen interest in the voice.

Chance leans forward. "One of my drives has cancer, end

stage," he says. "I think the prognosis is maybe three or four months."

Rope says nothing. Chance watches him. Rope's eyes close. Eventually, Chance sighs and begins to get up.

"Ahm sorry. This drive's cooked. Meet me here, tomorra, nine A.M.," Rope says. He tips forward and then falls onto the table. He knocks his empty shot glass over, and it spins off the side of the table, raps on the wood floor, and rolls. A trickle of blood spills from Rope's mouth.

Both the Apples arrive at Chance's left. "Leave him," says bartender Apple. "I'll clean him up in a few minutes." Waitress Apple raises her eyebrows expectantly, as if saying, Now would be a good time to leave.

.●.

THE DAY AFTER CHANCE FIVE turned six years old, he was part of a crowd of children pouring down narrow steps and into the wide world outside their green school bus. In Chance's memory, the children fan out into a crisp, bright morning. The shadows of Chance's playmates are stark black silhouettes stenciled onto the white plain of Uyuni, the world's largest salt flat. The plain stretches without variation from a southern scoop-mining operation toward the hazy northern outlines of low and distant peaks.

"The culpeo," Nana says, "is a fox who lives in the mountains close by, but no dogs or foxes or wolves can live on the salt plains." She is smiling at Alain, comforting him with this confirmation that the salt plains are unlikely to shelter wild dogs. Alain is Chance's best friend and was bitten by a dog last year. He has a scar on his left hand, between his fingers.

Chance and Alain have talked about joining when they get old enough and then living together forever. Nana says good friends make good joins. But when he's fifteen, Alain will move away, and he and Chance will lose touch.

Chance watches his shadow and raises a leg up to his side. His shadow moves as if it's a giant. He stomps his yellow Soxters down onto the salt and then grinds them to make the crunching louder. "Arh! Arh! Arh!" he says. His shadow is enormous and manic. Alain is laughing at it.

Nana says, "Chance has a giant!" And here memory works its magic. Chance's name at this time was Javier. Nana's actual words, if she did say something like this, had to have been "Javier has a giant!" But Javier has joined with Chance, so Javier is Chance. Chance's memory readjusts the name.

There's delight in Nana's voice. Chance is as big and confident as his shadow. "Arh! Arh! Arh!" he yells, and raises his fists from his sides. His shadow becomes a cleanly etched, tall, and thin giant throwing a tantrum on the flat ground. Other children have noticed and are pointing. Some are laughing, and a couple are imitating him, making their own madly dancing giants. Chance loves the crisp air against his cheek, the smell of salt, and the laughter of the other children.

"Chance, look at me!" someone calls, but he's busy now rocking side to side and making his long shadow tip swiftly back and forth. He moves his arms so the shadow has long snaky arms. "Chance, look at me!" Someone else calls. Then other kids are calling, "Chance!" "Chance!" But he keeps imagining his shadow getting bigger and bigger.

A few kids are pulling and pushing on his shoulders, and their shadows merge with his. Others notice and start to merge their shadows with his on purpose, and suddenly there's a long shadow mass quivering at the edges, and kids are pushing and laughing and everyone's calling his name, "Chance!" "Chance!"

On the ride back to the mining base, Nana sits next to him. She smells clean, and he scooches over on the bus seat to be closer to her parka. He leans against her, and she puts her arm over his shoulder and smiles down at him. All the Nanas are kind and always smiling, but he likes this one best because of her face. One of the other kids from a couple of seats back says, "Chance, I liked your giant." Chance is proud. He made something special that the other children remember. He grins and pushes his face into Nana's parka.

Another Nana is walking down the aisle of the bus making sure everyone is belted in. Another is driving. Another is sitting in the back of the bus playing patty-cake with a girl named Lucita, whom everyone likes. The seven Nanas are all the same person. They care for all the children of the other joins who live on the mining base.

⋅●⋅

WHEN THEY FIRST MET, JAVIER was impressed by Chance's design—the complementary skills of Chance's four drives. Chance One was a researcher, with specialties in risk analysis and macro-weather modeling. With the advent of megastorms and sudden storms, weather modeling became a prestige profession, responsible for saving lives and guiding economic activity. Chance had a reputation for being very good at it.

As an airline pilot, Chance Two was in another profession whose status was rising as the weather worsened. Even with the aid of advanced AI, Chance's specialty was viewed as critical infrastructure—a challenging and highly technical career.

But the clincher was Chance Three, an actual join doctor. Short of a Vitalcorp executive, a join doctor was the single most useful profession to take on.

Chance Four, short and sinewy, with long dark hair, was handy, mechanical, and martial—a valuable balancing influence. She was also good looking. He didn't want his attraction to her to influence his decision, but it was hard to discount.

As Chance, Javier would gain all of those professions. If he chose one of them for Chance Five, he'd start with years of practice and expertise. Or he could add something new to the join.

And Chance's attention flattered Javier. Five is regarded as a significant number for a join, because it's the next step after the so-called middle-class join. Joins often start with a solo couple in love, a "honeymoon join." As the drives age and the join becomes more comfortable financially, it begins to worry about losing a drive. Because young solos can be wary of joining with mature drives, the next step often combines two honeymoon joins, an older and a younger. The younger join gains financial stability; the older adds an increment to its life span.

Licensing fees increase with each active drive. The fees get so high that going from two to four can mean several years of paying down a large loan. The term "middle-class join" is meant to recall paying on a mortgage. When a join finally can go from four to five, choosing the fifth is considered its first truly free decision. Chance's choice of Javier as number five validated years of hard work.

After Javier had joined, Chance felt the experience of each of the five drives, including the new one, with equal intimacy. It would have been strange to keep the name Javier, a name that fit only one life's experience. The joined individual preferred to be called Chance.

CHANCE OWNS THE FOURTH AND fifth floors of a spire at the edge of the Pine, a two-square-mile park in the center of New Denver. Chance's spire is one of several in a large community. The spires are widely spaced, and the land between is filled by "greensward," unmanicured brush crisscrossed by narrow footpaths. Rare surface roads slice through the greensward like unwelcome discipline.

Elliptical at its base, with slightly wider lower levels tapering asymmetrically toward narrow heights, Chance's spire looks almost like an enormous blade of grass. Planted balconies that include a pod-docking space skirt most of its levels.

The front of Chance's dining room is a curved picture window, with a view of the park's forest canopy. The rear of the room transitions to an open kitchen. Light mellowed by high clouds soaks into the browns and mottled grays, filling the room with a composed and casual warmth.

After his night in the bar, Chance Three has had four hours of fretful sleep, a glass of orange juice, and a glass of tomato juice. He is now in the shower.

Chance One and Chance Four are fixing breakfast in the kitchen, their two bodies moving with an efficient and complementary calm, a choreography of shared intention. Of Chance's drives, One and Four have the most disparate histories.

Chance One is forty years old and a hair under six feet tall. His parents were Reform Individualists, committed to life as solos. As a teen, Chance One was sensitive to how unusual that made them within their social circle.

Chance One came to believe that his parents' determined intellectual independence was linked to the fact that they were a black couple in professional settings where they were considered minorities. When he felt his own life being pressured by that aspect of his identity, he cast about for alternatives. At the time, he was also in love with Chance Two. Joining preserved his identity and gave him others.

Chance knows those parents struggled with feelings of abandonment when he joined, though they never said as much. Chance wishes they had been more accepting of life's potential.

Chance Four, on the other hand, was always expected to join. She was a child of the erroneously named and mostly abandoned "cloning" movement. She's not a true clone but rather the result of an early, successful attempt at human genetic engineering. Her genes were contributed by more than two people.

Physically, she's the healthiest of all of Chance's drives, with seemingly inexhaustible energy, flawless brown skin, and long, straight black hair. Her agility and swift reflexes have earned Chance a string of Jai Kido championships in her weight class.

She's also a carpenter, crafting modern, custom furniture from heirloom materials. A recent issue of *InSpire Sense*, *A Magazine of Modern Living*, featured an extended holographic exploration of her work.

.⚬.

AFTER HIS SHOWER, CHANCE THREE walks behind Four and massages her sore shoulder for a few moments. The sex between Three and Four this morning evoked memories of their year together as Solace, a join of two. Then they tweaked Four's shoulder, reinflaming a minor sparring injury.

Chance Three is wearing gray slacks and a thin green sweater, though the day is warm and the house is comfortable. He runs a little colder than the other drives. He also smells a bit musty to the others, but when he's alone Chance can't detect his body odor. He's warm from his shower and lightheaded.

He'll go to the morning meeting with Rope. It might have made sense for Four to go, but Rope has probably looked Chance up online. Chance doesn't want to risk an implied insult by arriving with a drive Rope hasn't met. Chance Four will stay close and do whatever research is needed. If Rope does actually get unpleasant, she can help save the day.

While Chance Three digs into breakfast, Chance focuses attention on One and Four. One and Four both have great mouths with complementary taste maps. They're eating eggs with avocado and Sriracha (spicy food tastes better to the two of them than it does to the others), along with fried bread and dark-chocolate chia-seed butter. Chance likes to synchro-eat with them, chewing and swallowing in tandem.

Chance Five is out walking in the Pine, after which he'll return to sleep. Because of the cancer, Chance has suspended his studies at the university and is keeping Five to a very minimal routine: meals, walking, sleeping, exercise, some socializing at the Spares Club—mostly pool and cards.

Despite the stress from Five's diagnosis, the morning has started in one of those floating periods of satisfaction and easy tranquillity. All of Chance's drives are smiling—even Two, who's in flight with Leap. It's nice to look around the dining room and see smiling faces.

The path Five is following skirts a gully. A jogger, also smiling serenely at some internal prompting, runs by, and Five notices her long legs in black spandex. Chance Five and Chance Three are both a little aroused. On the airplane, those sensations prompt Chance Two to tell Leap how beautiful the park is this morning. Leap flicks an index finger through the air (Chance imagines her advancing a diodrama on her retinal screen) and says, "Mind on your job, cowboy." Leap is also happy this morning.

Without distracting Chance Two, Chance moves the left index finger of every other drive onto the same drive's right radial vein. Five's pulse won't sync because he's walking, but Chance still feels the profound percussive echo inside Five's body as the other three hearts start to synchronize their beats. The combined rhythm of the others highlights Five's pulse, making it easier to hear against the sounds of the morning walk—the slow breeze through aspen and pine, the crunch of Five's feet on gravel, the crinkling of his windbreaker, the ringing of a birdcall.

Soon, Five's pulse is a lightly driving tympanic time-and-a-half beat above the structuring bass of the other three hearts that are beating together. For a brief time, Chance falls into something of a trance, maintaining just enough awareness to keep connected to Chance Two's routine.

It's that entrancing, peaceful sensation that explains why Chance barely gets out of the house in time to make the meeting with Rope. Chance Three and Chance Four fly off in different pods.

One and Five are going back to sleep.

.●.

BARTENDER APPLE IS SITTING ON a stool in back of the bar when Chance Three enters. Across a pony wall, the restaurant has a weekend crowd bustling in for breakfast. Waitress Apple isn't around. A short, bald drive with a pleasant, relaxed demeanor rises from conversation at the bar with Apple and walks toward the door. "Glad you could make it," he says. "Rope Three." He extends his hand, and Chance shakes it. He appears to be in his midsixties, wearing a loose gray cardigan, tan slacks, and loafers.

"I guess your other drive is probably—" Chance begins.

"Knocked out," Rope finishes the thought. His smile is avuncular. His eyes crinkle in a friendly way. "How's this one doing?" he asks, meaning Chance Three.

"All right," Chance says. "I was moving slowly this morning, though."

"I bet. You want to step into the restaurant?"

"Sure. I'll have coffee."

"Oh, you already ate?"

⁎

LEAP TWO DOES THAT TWITCH thing. They've completed their ascent, and Chance Two just notices it from the corner of her eye. She says, "You did it again." They hit an air pocket, and the plane shudders.

"Start a vid if you're so excited," Leap says, deadpan.

"Look," Chance says, "I don't know what it is. But I'm seeing something real. You know I'm a doctor, right? Does it happen to your other drives too, or is it just this one."

"I think you're maybe stressed by the cancer," Leap says. "As a doctor, you know the odds of that too. I bet you're outlying right now, running all five drives and not getting enough rest. I'm gonna be completely straight with you, Chance." Leap stops watching her instruments and turns to Chance. She's calm, her voice even, concerned. "I don't have a tic, or whatever it is you think you've seen. I'd know if I did. I'd have seen it in a mirror. I'd have felt it. I'd have knocked something over."

When she's annoyed, Leap is always willing to say whatever she thinks will give her space. It's ludicrous to suggest that Chance's sick drive is creating perceptual distortion in Chance's join. There are documented cases, but that's an absurdly rare syndrome that requires real weakness in the rest of the join.

"If you're implying what I think you're implying, then I'm fine," Chance says. "I'm only running three right now. The sick one's down. And my One."

"Not enough," says Leap. A smile is teasing the corners of her mouth.

Chance can't help but laugh. "Jeez. I'm the doctor," she says.

"I'm an EMT," says Leap.

"In an ER," says Chance.

"You should be careful," Leap says. "You're experiencing a trauma."

"I know what I'm doing," Chance says. "I can't rest all my other drives. I have things to do."

"Nothing that important," Leap says.

"So now we're talking about me."

"Yes. But like I'm saying, I'm pretty sure that's what we've been doing all along."

.●.

"YEAH, I ATE, THAT'S WHY I'm a little late." Chance knows his Three drive just showed a hint of guilt, which is fine. Three felt stretched and dried this morning and needed the food when he got it.

Rope looks thoughtful. "We could walk," he offers.

"No, no, I could use another cup of coffee. You probably haven't eaten."

"No, I haven't." Rope smiles. Chance motions toward the restaurant, and they start walking.

As they cross into the restaurant with Rope in front, a big man walks with them, walking beside Chance. He's about as tall as the drive Chance met last night but broader in the shoulders.

Rope stops for a moment and turns to face Chance. The big man stops as well. "That's me," Rope says, indicating the other man. "I hope you don't mind."

"No, not at all," says Chance, suddenly feeling very uncomfortable. This additional Rope is wearing charcoal slacks, a white dress shirt. He looks like a bodybuilder. The aisle through the bar is not wide. The new Rope drops back, and Chance is now walking between Rope's drives.

"This is my Fourteen," says the big Rope, from behind Chance.

⚬

CHANCE FOUR IS SITTING IN a closed pod near a reflecting pool, a couple of minutes from the restaurant. She's found Rope online and is stepping through public records for his drives, trying to calculate the number of people who joined to create Rope. Twelve of them are documented, but there are current references to him being a nine. The few older references she finds set him at different numbers, up to eighteen, and there doesn't seem to be a pattern to the numbers. Sometimes, he's mentioned as a nine, maybe a month later a fourteen, then a three. It's very strange, and there isn't any explanation of how he might be adding or subtracting drives.

But there is an article from several years ago about a drive's death from alcohol poisoning. The article notes Rope's "tragic history," explaining that this is the third of Rope's drives to die over a very short period.

There's a little information about Rope Fourteen, the big drive who just sat down to breakfast with Chance. The drive was a feral. "Feral" is a term applied mostly to solos in communities that reject Join, but it also sometimes means people who are ideologically against it. Rope Fourteen grew up outside of civilization. He was living near the lava plains in eastern Washington when he joined. He's got security training but doesn't have a job.

Rope Three, on the other hand, is a city administrator and the oldest remaining drive in the join. A very well preserved ninety-one years old. Rope has apparently scrubbed his data stream. Rope Three's daily activities are locked up, and what Civ News can be found about him is pretty generic.

⁎

BOTH ROPES ARE ON ONE side of a restaurant booth; Chance Three is on the other. Rope Fourteen is saying, "As you may be aware by now, Fourteen was feral. It's very rare and potentially dangerous to join a feral. I include a few. So I guess I'm a little feral myself now." Fourteen and Three both produce an identical, toothy smile. Nothing friendly about it.

"I've read the literature," Chance responds. (Chance Four is now doing a quick review of the join literature for feral solos.)

Chance Three says, "With multiple feral joins, there's a significantly elevated risk of—"

"Yes," Rope Fourteen cuts him off. "Whatever your Four is reading right now, I've already read it. I did the risk analysis. I

found mitigations. I did the joins. They were without ill effect."
The Ropes smile again.

Chance is surprised. "How did you know it was my Four?"

"I'm something of a network geek."

Chance leans back. Rope includes the accumulated experience of—if Civ News is to be believed—a staggering number of individuals, up to twenty-five. Chance is one of those who believe that very large joins can be at risk of acquiring an arrogance so potent and overweening that it becomes their dominant trait. It's far more likely when a join is composed of similar individuals, though. Rope doesn't strike Chance as overly arrogant, but ignoring the warnings of good research is definitely a negative indication.

"I found mitigations," Rope Three continues, "that are not in the literature."

"Do you mean you're," Chance says, "experimenting on yourself? What sort of mitigations?"

This time, only Rope Three smiles. He says, "Why did you come over and talk with me last night?"

Chance says, "Well, what sort of mitigations are you using? You know this kind of thing is right in my professional wheelhouse."

"Yes," Rope Three says. "You're a join doctor. I thought mentioning that might get your attention. I'll tell you soon. But I know you're unlikely to believe that what I'm practicing, my techniques, actually work. You'll think, If they're effective, why aren't they documented? Right? So I promise I'll tell you what they are. But before that, I think we should learn a little more about each other. Why did you come over to talk to me last night? You have a new drive that's terminally ill. I think you said it was cancer, is that right?"

"Yes," says Chance.

"Fourteen will order for us. You want a doppio and a turmeric bear claw?"

Chance's biopage notes those as favorites. Rope has done his research.

"Thanks," Chance says. "Okay. Well, my Five's a student. My name was Javier, before joining."

And Chance suddenly remembers playing the hologame Fatal Ride with his best friend, Alain, in the old apartment that smelled of mildew. Alain was ruthless, an invaluable ally until the critical moment. Then he did whatever was needed to win.

"My parents were a honeymoon join," Chance says. "Both professionals. We lived in the Andes. My Five is superb. Ninety-five plus in four intelligence dimensions, athletic, a sweet temperament. We joined about six months ago."

"Congratulations," Rope Three says.

"Thank you."

"And you're concerned about trauma, when the drive dies?" Rope Three asks.

"Yes."

"You're a doctor. You know that you're at a fragile time."

"Yes."

"And why did you want to talk with me?"

"You have . . ." Chance hesitates. There's something sharp in Rope Three's look. Rope Fourteen is listening, impassive, and Chance feels certain that he's received a warning of some kind. But Rope Fourteen has said nothing, and Rope Three is still smiling. Chance thinks about Leap telling him that he is off; that he is hallucinating.

"You have firsthand experience with drives who've died," he says.

"I do," says Rope Three. "And some who died very shortly after the join."

"That's why I came over to talk with you last night," Chance says.

Rope Three's smile is warm, comforting. "You want to know what it's like to die," he says.

"Yes, for a drive to die."

"Yes," says Rope Three. "Of course, your new Five will not die. He's joined. He's part of you now. But his old body"—Rope Three shrugs—"it doesn't matter, does it? As a doctor you know that. You're going to be fine. Yes, it isn't fully integrated yet. Yes, it doesn't feel fully independent, as your other drives do. But you're aware that your anxiety is from the drive's body intelligence. You don't fully understand the drive yet. You're not fully abstracted from it. So you fear something will be lost."

"Yes," says Chance. "That's how I feel."

"It's unnerving to fear death. Our relationship with death is complicated."

"Yes."

"Now it's almost as if you've forgotten it," says Rope Three.

Rope Fourteen says, "But it hasn't forgotten you."

Chance is surprised by the switch to Rope Fourteen. Fourteen's voice is measured, deliberate. "In my home," he says, "the unenlightened see joining as a kind of predation. The consumption of a soul by a demon. They can't imagine the continued existence of every individual in a join. Joining can be a very difficult topic for ferals. Many of them—in the context of their religious dogma—believe true mortality should be preserved."

"Yes, I've heard that," says Chance.

"But, of course, that's foolish," says Rope Three. "An opinion rooted in ignorance."

"Still," begins Rope Fourteen.

"I, personally, do have a problem—" continues Rope Three.

"With our immortality." Rope Fourteen finishes the thought. Smoothly switching drives in midsentence can seem showy. It's difficult to match intonation and inflection, to make the sentence sound as though it's being spoken naturally, but Rope does it effortlessly, in a way that adds emphasis but seems perfectly natural.

"The problem that I have, at its core, its fundamental essence, isn't with me," Rope Three says. "It's not about my existence."

"It's with you," says Rope Fourteen. "The 'other.'"

"In the beginning," Rope Three says, "when Join was first introduced, and for a long time after, I assumed we'd all join. That we'd all become one single individual. Can you imagine that? No more other. No more competition. The largest category of risk for our species—the risk of competitive self-destruction—effectively zeroed out."

The waitress arrives, not Apple One but a tall, fair-skinned woman with short dark hair and straight bangs. Chance doesn't recognize her. He guesses that Rope Fourteen has used his retinal screens to order on the net. But the waitress doesn't ask who wanted what. She sets the plates down—an omelet in front of Rope Fourteen, fruit and yogurt for Rope Three, the turmeric bear claw for Chance. Chance gets the doppio; Rope Fourteen has drip coffee; Rope Three has green tea.

"Anything else?" the waitress asks Chance.

"No, thank you," he says.

Chance lifts his doppio, blows on it to cool it. Takes a sip. Rope Three nods at him and has a bit of the fruit and yogurt, blueberries and chunks of strawberry. He apparently enjoys it. He has another bite and smiles at Chance.

Chance takes a second drink of his doppio. He has an incipient perception that something significant has happened. He doesn't speak. He tries to clear his mind, to coax it forward.

Rope Three leans toward him, across the table. "But in the last couple of decades"—he picks up the thread of his earlier thought—"the science has really started clearing up, hasn't it? So we know there's no conceivable way to do a completely safe join above one hundred. In fact, with our current understanding we can really only manage about twenty safely." He sits back and sips his tea. Chance's doppio is delicious. Rope Fourteen has already finished half his omelet. He doesn't appear to be listening.

"So there will always be an other," Rope Three says. "That is my problem. That is why I am disappointed." He draws the last word out slowly, then says, "I am moved to change the situation."

The avuncular smile again. "I sound like a diodrama villain, don't I?" he asks.

Chance is surprised by the question. "Why a villain?"

"Well, obviously . . ." It's Rope Fourteen who replies, his mouth full. He swallows his bite of omelet. "I like to kill drives." His gaze is hungry.

Chance is not hungry and is regretting the meeting. "I think this is more than I was expecting," he says.

"Very likely," says Rope Three.

"I don't know where you're going with this," Chance says. "I just wanted to ask about—my situation."

"Yes, I guessed that, Chance," says Rope Three. "And so I put together a demonstration that I hope will help you."

As he had the night before, Chance feels the prickling of fear. Something about Rope is broken. Chance has seen pathological joins. He's treated a few. Chance says, "Apple told me you might have used a fixative."

Both Ropes regard him placidly. Rope Three says, "That would be illegal. And dangerous. If Apple said that, she shouldn't have."

"I didn't believe it when she said it."

"Thank you," say both Ropes, in unison.

"But I do think something is going on with you."

"Oh," says Rope Three, amused. "You want to treat me?"

Chance takes a deep breath. "I'm sorry," he says. "I think meeting you here may have been a mistake. I'm going to leave." But he doesn't move. It's not the fear, exactly. It's something closer to curiosity, but of a strange, riveting variety, almost like weight in his limbs. As if it's becoming difficult to move.

"Please," Rope Three extends a hand. Chance watches it move toward him. "I'm sorry. I just think it's important that we be honest with each other. I don't think what I said should surprise you. Apple told you about me, didn't she? I kill my drives. But don't worry, it's perfectly okay."

That's not what the literature says, but Chance nods anyway, though it's difficult.

"You might not have completely believed what Apple told you," Rope Fourteen says, "but it's true. There's more to it, though. I'm very well connected. I have friends on Vitalcorp's board. So I don't worry about Vitalcorp, about the Directorate." He waits for a response. Chance nods.

"You're concerned that the fear of your Five dying may destabilize your join," Rope Three says. "Maybe start a pathological depression. But that's not all. There are things you haven't told anyone. You've been working your other drives hard recently, skipping sleep. You decided a few years ago to join with a few younger drives. But you haven't been doing a good job of saving money to make that happen, have you? So, instead, you've been working harder. Taking extra shifts. You're taking risks. You've fatigued your drives. You've been stressing yourself so much that you're not thinking clearly. And now you're sick, which makes it worse. Right, Chance?"

Rope Fourteen says, "Go ahead, Chance. Tell me the truth. That's what we're doing here, having a heart-to-heart, remember?"

⋅●⋅

ON THE AIRPLANE, CHANCE AND Leap have flown into a gust of ferocious turbulence. They're both focused on their displays. Leap is quickly sifting through metrics. Autonomy, the guidance system, is making suggestions.

"Chance," Leap calls.

They're hitting air pockets, and the cockpit is noisy. Atmospheric particulate levels are showing a dramatic shift, and a cold front they've been tracking is shifting in their direction. They're definitely heading into a storm, but it's spinning up more quickly than it should be. They're also getting unusual electromagnetic readings. Things just don't look right. They need a new plan, a new route.

"Whadda you think?" Leap's been asking about an alternate route suggested on the shared display. Autonomy is waiting for approval. "Are we gonna take it? C'mon, cowboy!"

Chance isn't doing what she should be doing. She's not splitting her attention effectively. Something is wrong in the restaurant. Chance Three's perceptions aren't right. All of Chance is focused on Chance Three. In her pod by the reflecting pool, Chance Four is completely still, her dark eyes unfocused.

The plane rocks. Leap shouts, "Dammit, do something!" But Chance doesn't respond.

Autonomy says, "The cockpit stress level is above the recommended threshold. Both drives present appear potentially compromised. Protocol S-Nine, initiated."

"Fuck that," Leap says. "I'm overriding." She does. Chance doesn't respond to the urgent request for confirmation. It subsides. Leap's the captain now. She growls, "Goddammit, Chance! Shit. I'm not having an S-Nine on my record."

Chance notices her display changing as Leap accepts a new, less-volatile route through the storm. The plane banks starboard, drops suddenly through an air pocket, shudders massively. Chance bounces against her restraints. There are loud banging noises. Starboard, a twister might actually be forming.

⁙

FLUSTERED, CHANCE LOOSENS UP. JOINS express themselves through drives in much the same way that solos express themselves using their limbs, their bodies. And, like limbs, in familiar situations drives may operate without much conscious oversight. An analogy is often made to a "flow" state, in which solos perform practiced activities with a speed that doesn't allow for conscious interference. A person running multiple drives can put distance between the awareness of the join and one or more drives, allowing the drives to run semiautonomously, in a join-specific analog of a flow state.

Faced with two situations that require urgent attention, Chance does this reflexively, focusing awareness and jumping back and forth in bursts between Chance Two, in the airplane, and Chance Three, in the restaurant, leaving Chance Four in a kind of trance and Chance One and Five asleep.

．●．

CHANCE THREE'S BODY IS STIFF. His jaw aches. Chance says, "Yes, I've been overtaxing my drives. I suppose you guessed all that. I don't know how else you could know. I'm not proud of it. I'm not a risker. But I have been working hard. I want new drives."

"I'm very glad you admitted that," Rope Three says. "You're doing well. You've done us both a great favor by being honest. It means we can move together to the next stage. Now, you're a doctor. The next stage is the very beginning of a process that could result in you contributing to the greatest breakthrough in join science since the trial of one thousand."

Chance shakes Chance Three's head, to clear it. Chance is having trouble processing all that Rope is saying. Rope Three leans forward. He is earnest, sincere, his elbows going up on the table, his hands gesturing as Rope Fourteen leans back to make room for him.

"Some interesting things are going to happen now, Chance," he says. "You should prepare yourself. Before these things begin, I have to warn you. You'll want to contact the authorities. Your Four is positioned to do just that. But don't do it. If you do, things will go badly for you. Believe me, I wouldn't be doing this in public if I wasn't sure that the authorities weren't a threat to me and that I am in complete control of this situation."

Chance Three aches. The drive's muscles seem to be almost glitching, seizing up and then releasing rather than moving smoothly. Chance is focusing on clarifying his connection with the drive.

Rope Three says, "First, I think we should talk about the waitress."

The waitress is suddenly there, beside the table, standing next to Chance. Chance Three turns to his left to look up at her. She says, "I think you almost caught on. I left a few small clues. This is my Twenty-One." Rope Three sits back in his chair.

The waitress, Rope Twenty-One, continues, "I've poisoned your coffee. Your Three drive is going to die. You want to play the game, Chance, the real game, for unlimited stakes. This is the ante."

"And to prove that I'm in the game too," says Rope Three.

Rope Fourteen says, "I've killed my Twenty-One."

Through the rising aches, Chance sees now that the waitress also seems to be in pain. She's grimacing; she's resisting it, concentrating, but her eyes are beginning to cloud. Chance realizes that Chance Three can't move. The drive is somehow stuck. Chance begins pushing every cycle at it that can be mustered, but the limbs won't move. The chest is freezing up. Chance can't make Chance Three breathe.

Rope Fourteen says, "How am I going to do it? Well, I'm going to tell them that your number Three is my number Nineteen. I have a reputation for drive failures, so, in the early going I'll insist that this was just two more failures. That invention will be uncovered quickly, but that's okay. Its real purpose is to take advantage of some ambiguity in the laws around killing a drive. There are some suicide laws they interact with poorly. It's a trick I've used before. Complicated, but the result is that the story will give me a helpful legal standing. And I have friends who will adequately obfuscate a couple of records. This incident will annoy my attorneys, but that should be the only blowback. And, of course, I lose my Twenty-One."

As if on cue, the waitress falls. Her head smacks the table—a wet crunching sound—on her way down.

"A paralytic poison," says Rope Three. "She had more than you did. I cannot describe to you what this feels like." He's quiet. Rope Fourteen's face is composed. His eyes are closed, as if he's meditating. Rope Three says, "But, fortunately, you're going to see for yourself."

Chance is struggling against a tide of panic.

"This is what you want to know isn't it?" says Rope Three. "I'm glad you were honest. You'll recognize that I'm doing you a favor. Your experience won't be as rich as mine. I've had a lot of practice. I usually prefer a slower death, but I'm much better now at staying with the drive as it dies. Ah! Her heart just stopped." Both Rope Three and Rope Fourteen are staring at Chance.

Rope Fourteen says, "Yours is about to."

Broad, identical, senseless grins spread across the faces of both Rope Fourteen and Rope Three. Then Chance Three disconnects.

.●.

CHANCE SEIZES UP. A PERIOD of blank unawareness. Of unspecified duration. When the lights come back on, each drive is pulling in a long, gasping breath as if it were rising out of a deep, cold dive.

Simultaneous reengagement with all drives.

Chance One sits bolt upright in bed, his eyes wide. There is tranquil, bright warmth and mellow sunlight through the windows.

Chance Two wakes on the airplane amid the rumbling and pounding of extreme turbulence, the plane shaking and banging, throwing her against her restraints. Blood is running from her nose, over her lips, spotting her blouse. She is groggy.

Leap Two is managing three displays, responding to the crisis and lack of assistance with a practiced and focused precision. Leap, shrugging off the churning and buckling of creation.

Chance Three is gone.

In her pod, Chance Four blinks at the retinal projector, then begins to scan Civ News. Chance has been unaware for a couple of minutes. Police have already started moving to the restaurant. Images of the dead drives have hit local info feeds, including one of Chance Three—openmouthed, slumped across the table with Rope Twenty-One on the floor beside him. Rope Three and Fourteen are nowhere to be seen. A few moments later, an explanatory heading is added, "Join Pioneer Suffers Freak Drive Failures, Details to Follow."

Chance Five's drug-induced hibernation wears thin. His eyes startle open. He also draws a shuddering, gasping breath. His eyes remain wide for a few moments. Then he breathes deeply and slowly relapses into slumber.

Within all this, Chance is struggling against a rapid flood of sensations and impressions, unable to fully process, to select relevance and filter the rest; to make sense of everything that's happening or even some of it.

Chance remembers the face of Rope Twenty-One as she succumbed to the poison, the body struggling to survive but the eyes accepting, the awareness urging the body toward death rather than recoiling with it, rather than fighting against the insult.

And Chance rewinds through the battle with Chance Three's failing body. A lurking sense of inevitability, as if a face could appear perfectly healthy while fronting a skull that is missing the cup that holds the brain. And Chance fighting to believe the evidence of the face, the story it's telling, while each new moment advances a complete refutation. A sudden stabbing pain in the knuckles of an index finger. A liquid sensation at Chance Three's waist. The weight and unforgiving hardness of the drive's rib cage. The incremental petrification of the drive's throat. Within an advancing delirium, Chance clings to a single, frightening certainty. Any assertion of health is a fairy tale.

SOMEONE TAPS ON THE POD window. Chance Four tears her attention from the trickle of online news reports and is startled by the face of a Rope she knows—the drive who was drinking in the bar the night before. He's bending toward the pod, motioning for her to open the hatch.

"Home!" she shouts in panic. "Chance, home!"

And the pod slides smoothly away from Rope, who straightens and watches as it slowly begins to ascend toward its vertical-lane height. Rope holds up his left hand as if urging her to wait. Her pod accelerates away, and he's lost in the receding blur.

Chance changes destinations, heads toward the restaurant where Chance Three died. A comm request from Rope. She blocks it. Another comm request. The block option on the heads-up display appears to be confirming that Rope can't be trying to communicate with her, that Rope is blocked. But a comm request rings again, a light, upbeat melody. Her small hand twitches as she flicks it to the messaging center. Another comm request from Rope. Chance Four shuts down comms.

She watches spires speed by, then studies the greensward

below, the thick brush and trees glistening between spires. In a moment she's over the broad, straight streets that lead to the front entrance of the Praxis Center. Then she's descending. Then parked. The left side of the pod retracts, and she sits for a quiet moment, watching a growing hub of activity around the restaurant door.

It occurs to Chance that if comms go back on, Rope will track her drives. Chance One is at the spire apartment, reviewing security video. Nothing untoward is approaching the spire. Chance Two is instructing the airline system to enforce the personal comm block.

Chance Four steps out of the pod. No one pays attention to her as she reaches the group milling about near the restaurant's entrance. The Join Praxis Center, where Chance works (worked!), is across the street, so emergency personnel are probably already on the scene.

Chance Four shoulders through the crowd toward a drive wearing a red jacket and a Vitalcorp Directorate badge.

"One of the drives who died was me," she says. "The male."

The Directorate drive looks her over. His eyes move as he accesses civilization records online.

"You're disconnected," he says.

"Yes. My drive was killed by a join named Rope, who I was having lunch with. The other drive who died, the waitress, is his Twenty-One."

The Directorate drive is impassive. "What's your name?"

"Chance."

"Why aren't you connected, Chance?"

"I'm afraid Rope will track me."

"Why wouldn't you just block him?"

"I tried."

"You're saying you tried to block Rope, and it didn't work?" The skepticism in the Directorate drive's voice is a wind of doubt that blows through Chance, leaving a deeper cold and a greater uncertainty.

"That's right," Chance Four says.

"Give me supervision, then turn comms back on," he says. "I've already sent a request."

Chance hesitates. The Vitalcorp Directorate will require that Chance turn on comms to be authenticated, to prove identity. They'll believe that they can protect Chance, that their security is sound. But Rope has already shown an ability to override a block. Only civ admin levels have that kind of access. If Rope has civ admin authorization, Rope will be able to watch Chance's interaction with the Directorate. If Rope is higher than civ admin—Vitalcorp Directorate admin or something else—Rope will have other, secret authorizations, the kind everyone knows exist but that aren't made public. Turning on comms will make Chance vulnerable.

Usually, each drive has its own physical reactions, but in the face of overwhelming emotion, a physical response can reverberate from a single drive out to others. Adrenaline pulses through Chance Four as she confronts the Directorate drive, and an adrenaline response spreads to Chance One and Two.

Chance Four says, "I think Rope has at least civ admin–level access."

The Directorate drive's eyes flicker, and she knows he's checking on Rope's clearance levels.

"If we're both talking about the Rope who just lost two drives in there," the Directorate drive says, "then that Rope is a private citizen. Well connected, but only high citizen. No civ admin authorization."

So Chance knows: Rope isn't listed as having civ admin but can defeat a comm block. That means Rope's got some other kind of clearance, and unless the Directorate confirms it, Chance can't trust either the Directorate or the Directorate's records or both.

Chance asks, "Then how did Rope override my comm block?"

"I'd need to check your comm block to know that."

"I can't give you access." Chance's frustration breaks into Chance Two's voice. "He can override."

It happens quickly—a decision—and then impatience overcomes the Directorate drive's impassivity.

"I can't help you," he says. "Please step back, away from the entrance."

He motions her backward.

"That was my drive," she says. Her voice rises and frays.

The Directorate drive shakes his head. "Only two drives dropped. Both belong to Rope. We're securing this area. Please step away from the entrance."

She sees the beginnings of the question in his eyes: Is this drive (*is she*) psychologically fit? She drops back with the crowd.

.●.

LEAP TWO IS ACTING CAPTAIN. The turbulence has settled; the plane remains in-flight. Chance Two still has backup authorization on critical decisions.

"I lost a drive," Chance says.

Leap had been reviewing storm-tracking data and forecasts. She sits up straight when Chance says this.

Leap says, "Autonomy, I approve the new course."

The central screen that Autonomy uses to convey state clears to solid green.

Leap turns her chair to face Chance. "What? What do you mean? The cancer? I thought you still had time—"

A vestige of turbulence rattles the cabin. Chance and Leap both brace. Leap checks her right-side, heads-up display, then turns back to Chance. The alerts along the cabin window are showing faded yellow, low risk.

Chance Two reaches up to one of the few physical switches in the cabin, an aluminum pin above an engraved aluminum label that reads PRIVACY. Chance switches it toward ON. Leap watches with surprise and worry.

Chance speaks slowly, finding a way through the explanation. "No. Not Chance Five. Not the student. He's still sleeping." Chance's voice chokes up, and her eyes water. She continues, "My Three, Leap. I died. My drive is dead."

"What?"

Chance nods. Leap whispers, "Christ." Then, coolly, forcefully, asks, "What are you talking about? What happened?"

"He was poisoned. I know who did it." Chance can't help it. She cries for a few minutes while Leap watches and the plane rattles occasionally. In the warm bedroom of the house, Chance One is crying as well.

"Poisoned?" Leap finally says. "What do you mean? That doesn't happen."

"Poisoned," Chance confirms.

"But what do you mean? No one can get away with that. It doesn't make any sense."

Chance is inconsolable. Says nothing.

"Where are your other drives?" Leap asks. "I can come over with my One or my Three."

"No," Chance says. "I've got a drive sleeping. I'll set my One down in a few more minutes. He's just crying right now. My Four is near the restaurant, where it happened."

"In New Denver?" Leap asks.

"Yes," Chance says.

"Does it have something to do with this join named Rope losing two drives?"

Chance knows that at least one of Leap's other drives has begun scanning Civ News.

"Both of those drives that died weren't Rope's," Chance says. "I mean, I guess I don't even know if either one of them were Rope's. One of them was my Three."

"But Civ News says they're Rope's." Leap Two's voice makes it clear that Leap is trying to understand. Why would Civ News be inaccurate? "Is that why you flipped the privacy switch?"

"Yes," Chance says. "I needed to tell you. I might need your help, and I don't want a record of this."

Most employees consider the switch a quaint anachronism. If joins want a private conversation, they just connect using other drives. Chance has never used the switch before but appreciates that its continued existence acknowledges the value of a face-to-face conversation with a specific body.

"You can bring a drive to my place, so we can talk," Leap says. Then, "After what happened earlier this morning . . . with you . . . they'll want a little detail on why we turned on the switch."

"I know," agrees Chance.

"Okay. You want captain back?" Leap asks.

Chance experiences a momentary lightness, a swell of gratitude toward Leap. "No, I don't. You fly. But thank you."

"Okay," says Leap.

Chance turns off the privacy switch. They fly for a while, neither of them talking. Chance doesn't help and doesn't pay attention to what Leap is doing. When they're about an hour from landing, Leap turns on the privacy switch again.

She says, "I'm trying to get my head around this. You're saying this Rope character, someone I don't know, and that you've never talked about, killed your drive. Who is this? How do you know this person? Why would this Rope want to hurt you? I just . . . I don't get it, Chance. What's going on?"

Chance has been trying to make sense of what happened but is still numb. Leap watches her but doesn't speak. It's clear that neither of them has anything more to say, so Leap switches off privacy again.

Leap swipes open a comm channel. She reports the authorization changes so far and justifies them by describing Chance as physically ill. There'll be an inquiry, but it's one of the few reasons that may not carry a penalty. The death of a drive is reason enough for a join to step out of a command role.

Then Leap says, "Autonomy, primary flight assistance required. Leap will continue as copilot. Please confirm."

Autonomy responds, "Confirmed. Primary flight assistance engaged. Autonomy will pilot flight number B-Two-Ten-CC. Leap is now copilot."

Leap closes the comm channel, switches privacy back on, then turns to Chance.

Chance knows what Leap wants. She says, "Okay. I'm gonna tell you what happened, but, please, don't do research as I talk. Rope is . . . informed. I'm afraid Rope will know you and I are friends and may be watching you as well."

Chance gives Leap a quick summary of the meetings with Rope.

THIS TIME, THEY FIND EACH other on the Uyuni salt flat, the group Chance thinks of as Team Teenager. They've met before, when all of Chance's drives are sleeping at the same time. It's a dry day. A little chilly.

There are five of them—Ashton, Renee, Jake, Shami-8, and Javier—each of the individuals who joined to become Chance, each in late-teenage bodies. Chance is each of them and understands the differences between them, the emotions and beliefs that oppose one another. Chance reconciles them simply by inhabiting them all.

They sit in the stillness of the vast plain. The distant shadows of mountains circle them like curtains of night. Sunlight fills the space around them, and the sky is blue, but it feels as though the sun is down and the lucid world is a lie. They all know this is a dream. On the other side of what they can see, on the other side of the blue sky and the other side of the salt flat beneath them, is the same endless emptiness.

They're seated around an old picnic table. A salvage from a place once called a state park. The table was a fixture in the home in Indianapolis where Ashton grew up. Ashton became Rocket One and then Chance One.

At first, all five are silent in the face of the change they've undergone. Then Shami-8 and Javier start playfully kicking each other under the table.

"You need to stop, now, boy. You're gonna get yourself in trouble." Shami-8, who became Chance Four, flashes a perfect, toothy grin. Her wide forehead, narrow chin, dark eyes pinched with mischief—all are familiar, beloved, lit from within by enthusiasm.

"I know your secrets. I know your moves before you move," Javier says.

She raises an eyebrow. She's not impressed.

Then she says to the whole group, "Even a sad meeting doesn't have to start sad, does it?"

Jake, who became Chance Three, says, "I spend years studying join sicknesses, and then my body is killed by a sick join."

The cold intensifies and all of them move, shifting uncomfortably where they sit. Jake looks down, not meeting the others' eyes. "I was substantial," he says. "I liked my body."

"You had a nice body," Ashton says, politely.

"Javier is awesome," Jake says, "but he's—he may be a short-timer. Javier—I know how painful this is for you."

"It's okay. I understand," says Javier. "I'm sorry about the, my—" He shakes his head, looks out at the plains, which are stark in the reflected light, then continues, "I can't even say it. I didn't know I was sick. Man, I worked so hard to stay healthy, to be so fit. I mean, my body is amazing. This is just . . . I don't know how it happened."

"A nightmare," Jake says.

"I'm sorry about that too," says Javier, quickly. "I mean, Rope."

There's a long silence. When a choppy breeze finally passes between them, Renee, the young woman who became Rocket Two, and then Chance Two, says, "We were all going to lose our bodies, sooner or later."

She tilts her head and regards Ashton, across the table, recalling their long conversations from years ago, their shared speculation on how it might feel to watch centuries pass from within the comfortable security of each other's company.

"But will I remember me?" Jake asks. "I want to remember myself."

"You will," says Renee. "You'll be here. And that's what this is, isn't it? A memory?"

"We should take my body out more. Use it while we can. We should enjoy it!" Javier is forceful. He sits up and looks directly at Shami-8.

"Yeah, that might be nice," Shami-8 replies.

Ashton says, "We can do what we can, but we're going to follow the treatment, and our doctor said to let Five rest and use its cycles for other things. Let it relax and try to heal."

"I just . . . that's me . . . I want to experience more before I'm history." Javier scratches the wooden tabletop with a finger.

"Yeah," says Jake.

"I'm sorry, Jake," Javier says.

"You know, there's still hope for Five," Jake says. "But Javier, you should know what you might feel when your body does die. And the truth is, I don't feel much different, in a way. I mean, I miss it. It's painful. But I don't know how else to say it: I feel okay. That's not exactly right. I also feel . . . broken. And this is a setback, but I'm no worse than I was, really. That is, no worse than any of you are. And I have you. I don't feel lost."

"Thanks." Javier says, clearly trying to follow Jake and accept what he's saying. "I don't know, though. The thought of losing my body hurts. It really hurts."

"It hurts all of us," Renee says. The others murmur agreement.

"I know how you all feel," Javier says, "and you know how I feel. You know it's not the same."

Chance is suddenly with them, looking out of the eyes of each person at the table. Chance sees each of them perfectly from the perspective of each of the others. Each body and each face has a different tone, a different emotional shape.

Jake's loss is a foundation. Javier's fear builds on that.

．●．

THE NAMES DISSOLVE AS CHANCE One wakes in New Denver. The names can be so ephemeral. They're critical before a join, when one name means one awareness riding the current of the present moment. When everything breaks apart, and rebuilds around parallelism and the union of what had been exclusive, names can lose their potency, become labels, become data.

Chance One pulls back a blanket and sheet. Chance Four is sleeping on the other side of the bed. Chance Four's shoulder is chilled, so he pulls the sheet over it, covering the ends of her dark hair.

He stands. His feet swollen and dull, his skin dark against the cool, honey-colored hardwood. His body unbends slowly as he moves toward the bathroom. His lower back aches.

As Chance One steps into the bathroom and the lights come up, he makes a gesture toward the mirror above the sink to activate its interface. He summons vids of the house perimeter. Nothing worth noting. Perhaps Rope is busy with whatever legal fallout has come from the assault. Chance One taps above his temple to switch on retinal displays, then logs in through the airline account. He sleepily reviews some weather data, brushing fingers against the palm of his left hand to help manage the display as he pees.

He shuffles into the living room and the built-in lights begin to glow. It's dark out, and the big windows onto the lawn and park reflect the inside of the house. Chance sits on a broad couch and watches the late news on a wall display. He says, "Scan for Rope, please." His personal agent knows he's spent some time with a join named Rope, and it knows which Rope, so related stories are prioritized, and he learns immediately that Rope has been arrested.

CivNews only has a few terse reports. The Vitalcorp Directorate is investigating Rope. Questions arising from inconsistencies in Rope's statements and the statements of other interested parties have led to an inquiry. The Directorate has launched exhaustive autopsies and a full forensic analysis. Rope's access to the net has been suspended, and the Directorate is in the process of finding and detaining his remaining eight drives. The whereabouts of two of Rope's drives are currently unknown.

How the hell is Rope hiding drives?

The sheets slide off of Chance Four as she sits up. She rubs her sore shoulder, then walks to a desk in the bedroom. She unfolds a personal display and also starts reviewing news.

Nondestructive truth techniques can be applied to a captive drive to determine the whereabouts of a join's other drives. Through Chance Three's work at Shine's Join Praxis Center, Chance actually pioneered one of them. Chance Four reviews recent literature about drive triangulation, searching for details that might help explain things, while Chance One continues scanning the news. The idea that two of Rope's drives might be hidden creates a credibility problem with the entire story. The Directorate still hasn't contacted Chance.

After what's happened, and the stress of Chance Five's illness, Chance knows that paranoia is a health risk, but that doesn't slow the flood of possible scenarios. What if Rope has simply planted this slant on the story to lure Chance back to unrestricted network access? Could Rope be that influential?

The three major news agencies are all covering the story through brief updates. Stories like this are often single sourced, though. Rope wouldn't necessarily have to influence all three agencies. But Rope would have to influence the Directorate. Rope would have had to use the Vitalcorp Directorate to build the story, and that would be a risky move, even for an executive senator. Which Rope is not.

THAT MORNING BEFORE SUNRISE, CHANCE Two rolls out of bed in a guest room at Leap's house in the Olympic Archipelago, a bit groggy from the long flight and late landing. The storm they'd flown into was part of what's beginning to look like a full split of the Great Central megastorm. Its quick formation in a low-probability location is consistent with the other two megastorm splits from the last two decades. The event profile is a very close match to the Bengal megastorm split that ravaged New Dhaka. That storm brought on the worst loss of solo life since the era of coastal flooding drowned the original Dhaka, along with many other major cities.

Chance and Leap had fought through the storm for an hour and then finally gone north to avoid it, dodging spirals from the northeast storm as they went. They had endured hours of rough flying, Chance helping as personal emergencies allowed. It had been a long day.

Chance Two stands and walks heavily to the door. Leap lives on an island in the archipelago. Leap's house is built in the UMI (Universal Modal Infrastructure) Craftsman style— meant to resemble old homes of the Pacific Northwest, but on the modern service grid and with adaptive nanomaterial. It was Leap One's childhood home, originally built by Leap One's mother.

Chance pops the bedroom door open. The hall glows softly so the door to Leap's room is visible despite the darkness of early morning. Chance stands in front of Leap's door, waiting for the house to rouse her friend with the customary mild light, warm breeze, and soft tones.

"Chance, what got you up?" Leap One says from behind her, surprising her. Chance turns to face him. Leap One is leaning into the hall from the staircase. He doesn't have a job, and Leap has him on an alternate schedule. She often keeps him awake while her other drives are asleep.

Chance pads over to the staircase.

Leap One says, "Let's talk downstairs."

P A R T

Things are exactly what they appear to be, just not what you think they appear to be.

—Adofo, from the
Seventh Pan-African Address

You mean you remember.
No, I mean when my loved ones slip
away from this life
they continue to live with me.
Just as you are the spirit of many,
so am I.
What you do with technology
nature has done through love since the
mind began.

—Joseph Rex,
Poe's Mission, Book I

T W O

"I got in touch." Leap One is leaning against the kitchen island. Behind him is a large, hardbound book with a metallic silver cover adorned with two bright yellow *X*'s, made to look as though they've been applied with dripping paint.

Fortyish, short, and lean, Leap One has dark brown hair and a full beard, both starting to gray. He moves slowly, as if containing agitation. Chance Two is sitting at a breakfast table across from Leap One, her back to a window. The calm and lack of sentimentality that reads as a hard edge in Leap Two has always struck Chance as slightly creepy in Leap One.

"What do you mean you 'got in touch'?"

"I vidcast the Directorate and filed a formal Friend of the Deceased brief on behalf of your Three drive."

"What?"

Leap One waves a hand, then says, "I think it's important that they—"

"But that could have led Rope to this home!"

"I guess it could have."

"While I'm here!"

"Yes," Leap admits.

"Christ," Chance says. "You put us both in danger. Are all of your drives really here, in this house, Leap?"

"That's right."

"Leap, he killed my drive and at least one of his own, but very likely several of his own. He's sick. Really sick. He may have a meme virus. Whatever's wrong with him, it's at that level. If all of your drives are here, he could clean you up completely, just by coming here."

"No. He's under arrest, and the Directorate is hunting for him. He's busy saving himself. And we're on an underpopulated island with limited access. I have perimeter surveillance and video-alarm defenses. If someone were approaching the house, I'd know."

"At least two of his drives are still out there, running around."

"I'd know."

Chance is thin on resources right now, and she keeps seeing the two Ropes grinning as their Twenty-One drive's head hit the table.

She says, "There are at least three theoretically foolproof ways to locate all of a join's drives if you have custody of one. Why can't the Directorate find two of Rope's drives? Why? Rope has influential friends. And there's something about him that's not right. He is not a normal join!"

"I think you may have just answered your own question."

"What?"

"You said, 'theoretically.'"

"Oh, don't give me that alternate tech crap again!" says Chance, frustrated by Leap's unrepentant lack of intellectual discipline, Leap's gullibility. "You are killing me," she says softly.

"No, cowboy. The cancer's doing that. And this Rope guy."

Chance can't think of anything to say. Leap continues, "I

know you don't believe in a lot of it. A lot of it is crap. But there are real results that contradict what the Directorate is telling us. A quantum network implant? Do you really know what the hell that is? Do you actually know? The materials do something predictable, so you trust them. A scientist stumbles across a material with ridiculously powerful properties, and then it's been forty years since the first join and we still don't have a theory that really explains it!"

"We do," says Chance.

"And the psychotropics we take during cooldown," Leap says. "Chance, all you really know—and you were an actual join doctor—is that there's a predictable interaction between consciousness and quantum phenomena. You don't even know *how* the drugs help!"

"Of course we know how they help."

"Break down rigid modes of perception? Establish conditions favorable to reimagining the self? Fine, but how *exactly* does your *state of mind* influence the *network*?"

"You make it sound like we're children playing with fire," Chance says. She stands and walks to the kitchen island, across from Leap. She grabs the silver book. "And you're reading science fiction by feral solos who can barely fabricate basic plastics!"

"'God chose what is weak in the world to shame the strong.'"

"God?" They stare at each other for a moment, neither backing down. Then Chance says, "We know more than that."

"Oh, really? What else do you know?"

Chance sets the book back down.

"What else do you know, Chance? Try me."

"I'm not going to get into it," Chance says. She walks back to the table.

"Oh, okay." says Leap One. Chance notices that Leap Two, in her nightgown of yellow cotton, is leaning against the threshold to the kitchen. Leap Three, a tall, rangy man in his late thirties, is standing behind her. "You're not going to get into it," Leap One says, drawing Chance's attention back to him, "because you don't believe I'll understand it."

"No," Chance says, "it's not that."

"It's not?"

"No! We just don't have time."

"You think I wouldn't understand," says Leap One, bitterly. Chance is struck again by how alien Leap seems, how unlike her old friend. As if reading her mind, Leap Two takes a step into the kitchen and says, "As for time, that's all we have. We're right here, in my house. And because of that storm and your little incident while we were flying through it, we probably won't have another flight for at least a couple of days. Chance, you might not have any more flights at all. You're worried about Rope, but after our flight today, you should be worried about your job."

"He's out there, Leap! He's out there, and now you—and this house—have popped up on his radar!"

Leap Two speaks slowly, enunciating each word. "No. No. No. He. Is. Not. Coming. Here. Chance."

Chance's fingers are cold. She wants to close her eyes. Leap's anger, combined with a sense of injustice that Chance hasn't felt from Leap before, seems aimed at her. It's like she's talking to a stranger. Chance Two says, "Why do you have three drives in the kitchen right now?"

Leap Two gestures at herself and Leap Three. "These two are hungry."

The quiet sound of footfalls. Chance turns back to Leap One as Leap Four enters the room behind him. Leap Four is a young

Japanese woman with hair dyed the color of rust. Squat, power-fully built, with a broad, thoughtful face.

"You're all here," Chance says.

Leap Four says, "It's my home."

Then, in unison, as if in a scene from a vidcom or a night-mare, all four Leaps convulse at the same time. Their upper lips rise. Their shoulders jump. They pant loudly. Then all four are looking at Chance as if nothing has happened.

．●．

THE TRIAL OF ONE THOUSAND was the first public demonstra-tion of Join. Five hundred pairs of prequalified volunteers were chosen by lottery to become five hundred individuals. It was a sensation. Despite the emergence of megastorms and indisput-able new evidence of an imminent catastrophic rise in water levels, those five hundred new individuals and their "I am both of us!" campaign dominated international news for months. The public was transfixed. "Would you?" seemed the only rel-evant conversational gambit.

There were also immediate questions about which agencies could regulate Join. The government's positions were weakened by the debate about what Join was and what it meant and by a fragmented international response. Vitalcorp had also recruited influential investors. In the end, despite committed resistance, the public's enthusiasm for the sheer audacity of the product proved decisive. Only a year after the last couple in the one thousand became a single individual, Join was approved for, and released to, the general market.

In that initial release, Vitalcorp included a prohibition against a join of more than two, with exceptions allowed for research.

The process had been discovered almost by mistake. Vitalcorp wanted to introduce it in stages. But people petitioned for exceptions and squeezed into rapidly proliferating studies. Within a few years, the largest legal join was Excellence, the CEO of Vitalcorp, who was a twelve. (Excellence also set the tradition for naming joins.)

Since then, the science has progressed. While Vitalcorp discourages large joins through its fee structure, the legal limit for "active," or living, drives is now twenty. (A join may include more than twenty people if some drives are deceased.)

But the largest join ever recorded was illegal and kept secret for most of its existence. It had one hundred fifty-three drives, some of whom had been key scientists at Vitalcorp and all of whom had been early investors. It called itself Music.

While negligible for legal joins, it's now clear that the likelihood of a dangerous failure increases rapidly above twenty drives and becomes certain just above two hundred. There are two main categories of join failure: collapses—in situations like a flip, a cumulative coma, or a beta-wave resonance collapse— and meme viruses. Both are deadly. Music was the first known incidence of a meme virus.

Before much of this was understood, the One Hundred Fifty-Three revealed itself. The drives started buying yellow paint and painting two yellow *X*'s anywhere within reach. They painted nonstop, literally without rest. They didn't sleep, didn't eat. Several wandered into traffic as they were painting. Some wandered off cliffs. A few electrocuted themselves.

There was no record of them being joined, but this was just before the government merger, and Vitalcorp was a behemoth, distorting international politics. Excellence, combining the resources of a titanic corporation and the personal influence of twelve wealthy and highly connected individuals, was among the most powerful people in the world. Vitalcorp really had nothing to fear, even in the face of the scandal.

To end the painting incident, Vitalcorp put Music's eighty-one remaining drives on ice and seized all of Music's corpses. Two years later (and after the government takeover), Vitalcorp revealed that Music had fallen victim to a previously unknown pathological agent. Vitalcorp's forensic team found the same prion, a self-replicating form of protein, in the brains of each of Music's drives. Unlike other prions, which replicate until the host dies or until all available raw material—e.g., the brain matter within a given skull—is altered, this one appeared to reach a nonlethal steady state and then stop growing. In each drive autopsied, examiners found a lattice of interconnecting molecules so similar as to be a statistically impossible expression of prion growth. And yet there they all were.

The disease, referred to in most research as "reflective spongiform encephalopathy," was termed a meme virus by the popular press, though it only distantly implicated memes and was not in any way a virus. Infected joins would develop an absolute fixation on an idea or complex of ideas. Vitalcorp said that in the previous two years it had found other cases, though it did not release evidence. It provided studies showing that joins of fewer than twenty active drives are perfectly safe. The Roman numeral for twenty—two X's—in yellow became a new symbol of terror.

⚬

MANY YEARS AFTER THOSE EVENTS began to change the world, Leap was created through an act of love—the joining of Ian, who became Leap One, and Aurora, who became Leap

Two. When the two met, Ian was twenty years old and Aurora was eighteen. They discussed how they both felt about Join in their very first conversation. They fell in love, and with each successive day the two of them grew happier and more certain that they wanted to join.

Aurora's parents were easy to convince. They had divorced when Aurora was in elementary school. Aurora's mother, Colleen, had remained single and hadn't made her mind up one way or the other about Join. Her father, Winston, had spent every penny he possessed to buy into a join with three college-aged women. Aurora's parents were also easy because she didn't really care what they thought.

Ian was an only child, and his mother, Josette, was firmly against it. "No divorce if you join," she would say. "Why would you eliminate the single greatest satisfaction of marriage?" Ian's father, Josette's second husband, had died that year of a venous thromboembolism. It should have been detected, but he didn't like doctor visits.

Joins often say that the very first moment that they are aware of themselves as a join is disappointing and not significant in memory. They experience a period of disorientation from the surgery and drugs, and then events resume with a familiarity that belies the radical change they've undergone. Their access to other bodies, another gender, other memories—each of these things comes with a feeling of lifelong intimacy. Every body and every memory is brought to a join with the experience of possessing it since the day it was created. Because everything is familiar, there is no remarkable experience to create an initial threshold in memory. Joins create the threshold afterward as they experience the advantages of having multiple bodies and reflect on the magnitude of their change.

During her teenage years, Aurora believed she got too much undeserved attention. She didn't feel particularly good at anything. People might listen to her, but they also assumed they could direct her, and they'd throw in offhand comments about her looks. She didn't know how to respond. She resented it.

Months after the join, Leap realized that those feelings were no longer a concern. Rather, Leap felt a confidence that neither Ian nor Aurora alone had possessed. Leap decided that the confidence was from their faith in each other. Their love had fused into a new source of strength.

.●.

A DECADE AFTER LEAP ONE and Two joined, Leap decided to join with Brian Dearing, and become a three. Brian and Leap Two met in a hospital ER when Leap Two's mother had a sudden low-insulin event. Brian told Leap Two that the old name for the now-treatable disease was diabetes. Of course, Leap had already known that. Everyone knew what diabetes was. Still, Leap was disarmed by Brian's earnest attention to Colleen and the absorbed and candid way he discussed the implications of her treatment.

They began spending time together. Brian said he loved all of Leap. Leap was flattered and quickly found Brian—his unexpected prickliness, his enthusiasms, his love of rock climbing, of guitar music, and of the abundant and confusing lore of physical health—indispensable. It wasn't the same kind of love that Aurora and Ian had felt for each other, but it was powerful and genuine.

After the join, when Leap asked Chance what was different about Leap as a two and Leap as a three, Chance started with easy things: Leap's new understanding of medicine and Leap's ability to describe what it's like to free-climb El Capitan. More subtly, Chance thought Leap might have become more adventurous, a bit more of a romantic, perhaps more aggressive.

A coworker of Brian's told Leap Three that it was as if he went away and then came back after fifty years, changed by experience. He was very different, but still the same person.

THE NIGHT AFTER LEAP ONE'S father died, his mother, Josette, discovered a surprising second set of books that covered the family businesses. Then a desperate creditor tried to claim her husband's casket on the day before his memorial service. Leap One's father had apparently been forced to be more honest with some of his creditors than he had been with his family.

Josette fired her dead husband's accountants and attorneys and was immediately confronted by her husband's brother, Chuck, who was determined to part out what remained of the family businesses for cash. For years, Josette fought a long series of acrimonious legal skirmishes against Chuck and other members of the company's board.

Large swaths of land were becoming toxic. One point of bitter dispute between Josette and Chuck was her desire to obtain and preserve a string of carefully selected parcels of land. As the years passed, the value of areas she had bet on spiraled upward. The company leased its properties, or sold at premium prices, and used the income to speed the growth of its bank. After a final, decisive judgment against Chuck and his faction,

Josette would say that she and her husband had made a bonbon together. He'd made the empty wrapping, and she'd made the chocolate and ice-cream treat.

Josette and Chuck met one final time, shortly after receiving the judgment, to discuss Chuck's belief that he was being treated unfairly.

·●·

JOSETTE IS MOTIONLESS, WATCHING CHUCK across the conference table. She's the cat. He's the mouse. As recently as last month, he'd thought he was the cat.

"Look at it from my perspective," Chuck says.

"I'm trying, Chuck," Josette says. "But, to be honest, I don't hear anything that sounds like perspective."

"What I'm saying"—Chuck glances at Leap One; Leap almost detects a break in his façade—"is that I've spent my life building this company. You and Ian"—he checks himself—"Leap, I mean—"

"Thank you," Josette says, causing Chuck to hesitate. Leap recently became a Three and Join has been a fact of life for years, but Leap One's family continues to resist its reality. Despite her own reservations, however, Josette enjoys defending Leap to other family members.

"What I'm saying is that you and Leap now own the fruit of my labor." Chuck waits, creating an opportunity for acknowledgment, which isn't given. "Look, I honestly can't make sense of what Mark did." Mark Pearsun is the attorney Josette trusted with her business. Chuck's admission is surprising. He's not one to purposefully expose a weakness. "You leveraged a minor technicality—"

"We leveraged the law," Josette says. "And a big problem from the beginning is that you weren't paying attention to it."

Chuck is tiring. Even at the start, while he was recounting his successes over the years and his sacrifices—not marrying, not raising a family—he looked as though he hadn't been sleeping.

"I guess I can't fault you for using leverage where you found it," he says. "Mark is a capable attorney. But after what I've given, I do deserve, at least, a stake."

"What do you think you deserve?" Josette asks.

Chuck straightens, believing he has finally worn her down. "The five percent I asked for. I think that would be fair."

"You sold two percent."

"I didn't know it was you I was selling to."

"It wasn't."

"It was the *same thing*."

Josette turns to Leap One. "Ian . . ." She closes her eyes and cocks her head, then corrects herself. "Leap," she says, "do you believe that your uncle deserves a three percent stake in our company?"

"No," Leap says.

"Do you believe he merits any compensation, beyond what we've offered?"

Leap shakes his head. No.

"Chuck, I'm sorry," says Josette. "It looks as though we didn't need to have this meeting."

Chuck, holding his aggravation in check, says, "I'm an asset."

"Then our parting should be easier to accept," says Josette. "You'll have other opportunities."

"There are things you don't want me to talk about."

"I think this meeting is over. Don't you?"

"No, I'm not sure that I do."

"You and Mark should work out final details," Josette says.

She pushes back her chair and stands. Leap stands and, after a moment, Chuck does as well.

"This isn't right. We're family," Chuck says, but almost chokes on the final word. When she doesn't respond, he straightens, scorn quickly replacing vulnerability.

"Okay, then. We're done here," he says. "Goodbye, dear."

⁘

AFTER CHUCK IS GONE, JOSETTE asks, "How did I do?"

"Maybe a little bitter," Leap One says.

"But, overall, pretty well, considering?"

"Yeah, I think so. Considering."

Josette looks out the window at her property, the landscaped green-and-yellow flank of native plants bordered by a strip of cherry trees, a small apple-and-pear grove, and then a steep drop into Pacific coast rain forest. "Tomohiro can be a pill," she says, referring to her master gardener, "but he is a brilliant man. He made this place beautiful."

"Yes, he has," says Leap, admiring it with her.

"We're done with him," she says, meaning Chuck.

After a pause, Leap says, "Mark said that Chuck's completely broke. He won't be able to cover medical—"

"Are you defending him?"

"Not him, just the—"

"Good, because he wanted everything when he deserved nothing. He and your father left a mess that it's taken me a *decade* to clean up."

"I understand—"

"Do you know what else I've done during those ten years?"

"No, I—"

"Nothing. I haven't done *anything else*. This, what we won last month, is mine."

．●．

LEAP FINALLY BECOMES A FOUR about a year after affairs with Chuck are settled, and following a confusing conversation with Tomohiro, Josette's master gardener. Tomohiro asks Leap to meet for lunch at a barbecue place called the Joined Pigs. Tomohiro and Leap have never met for lunch before.

After greetings and a brief preliminary chat, and after they've ordered, Tomohiro says, "I am . . . planning to go."

The way he says it indicates that the news is significant, but Leap doesn't understand why. "Do you mean you're going to work for someone else?" Leap asks.

"No," says Tomohiro. "I mean I'll leave. This." He makes a small and graceful gesture that manages to encompass the entire Pacific Northwest.

"You're going to move?"

"Yes, I am going to move."

"Well, are congratulations in order? Are you retiring?"

"In a way, retiring, yes."

"I see." Leap realizes that it's not just nervousness he's sensing. Tomohiro seems frightened. "My mother will be very sad, I'm sure."

"That is why I wanted to talk with you. One reason."

"Have you told her yet?"

"I have not told her. I think, I don't want to worry her yet. She and I have things to discuss, and at that time, she will find out."

"Okay," says Leap, trying to keep up, "but—"

"I am in trouble," says Tomohiro.

"Oh," Leap says. "I see. Well, what kind of trouble? I'm sure she would—"

"No. No. I don't want to worry her. Leap, I am sorry I must ask, but this conversation is very important to me. Before we go any further, I must know it will be confidential."

"You don't want me to tell Josette?"

"I require you do not tell anyone."

If Tomohiro is in trouble, it seems odd to ask Leap rather than Josette for a favor. Leap has had the impression that Josette and Tomohiro are close. But Josette has enough on her mind, and Tomohiro would know that.

"Okay," agrees Leap, "if that's what you want, I'll keep it in confidence."

"Thank you. Please know I am not exaggerating. Believe me, I have spent many, many hours considering what to do in this situation."

"Okay."

"You have heard me talk about my niece?"

"Yes."

"She is sixteen. I do not want to leave her, but I think she should stay here."

"So you're saying you'll be taking a trip," Leap One says, "and you need someone to look in on your niece?"

"Yes, but not quite."

"All right."

"I will be gone for at least two weeks. Then I will move, and I will send for my niece."

"Okay. So you need someone to help her move?"

"Yes," Tomohiro says, "that is what I mean, almost."

"Why is this difficult?" Leap asks. "I can help. After all you've done for us, I'd be happy to. I'm pleased that you thought of me."

"Thank you." Tomohiro's voice is rough.

"What am I missing?" asks Leap. "Why are you concerned?"

"I want you to know I appreciate what you are doing. Very much so."

"Of course." Confused, but thinking the purpose of their meeting accomplished, Leap reaches for the sandwich that arrived as they were talking and takes a bite.

"There is another thing," Tomohiro says.

"Okay."

"I think it might be better if my niece did not live by herself while I am gone. I want to ask if, perhaps, she might stay with you."

Leap lives in the house where Leap One grew up. He prefers solitude, but the house is large enough for guests. Tomohiro's niece is sixteen and presumably reasonably independent. She might not be too much trouble for only two weeks. Leap says, "Doesn't she have friends that she'd prefer to stay with?"

"I don't know their families," says Tomohiro. "I am very sorry to ask."

"It's okay," says Leap. "She can stay with me. But can you at least tell me why you don't want to talk about your trip?"

"I would like to tell you more," Tomohiro says, "but it's a personal matter. Not something I can discuss. But it is a good reason. Your trust is the difficult thing I am asking for."

The strangeness of the modern world. There are so many tragedies in so many people's lives. For fifteen years, the Olympic Archipelago has been an oasis of relative calm. But the gears of the world grind on. Leap considers. And then says, "All right."

"Thank you," Tomohiro says, his relief visible.

"So when would all this happen?"

"Today, after lunch."

"What?" says Leap. "This is too much, really."

"As soon as possible," Tomohiro says quickly. "Today would be best."

Leap has already said yes and can see how much it means to Tomohiro. "Okay," he says at last, "I can get a room ready, I suppose. I think you could probably bring her over this evening."

＊

TOMOHIRO'S NIECE, HIMIKO, ARRIVES LATE that night. It quickly becomes clear that the change has surprised her. Himiko was told only that she would stay with a friend while Tomohiro is at a conference.

She seems very shy and stays in her room. Leap tries to message Tomohiro after Himiko's first night at the house, but he doesn't respond. On the second night, Himiko tells Leap Two that her uncle was frightened. They share their confusion about what might be motivating him. Leap admits that Tomohiro hasn't provided a list of family contacts as he'd promised.

Because Tomohiro hasn't responded to repeated attempts to contact him, Himiko and Leap One drive to his cottage. All of his things are gone.

As Himiko walks slowly through the empty rooms, she says, "What happened?"

"I don't know."

"He left me?"

"No. No, I don't think so."

"Everything is gone. He's gone."

"Yes," Leap says.

"Even things he didn't like."

Leap dreads accepting what is becoming painfully obvious. He follows her into the garden—rhododendrons, camellias, jasmine, roses. Two healthy rows of herbs.

"Could he be with your family?" Leap One asks. "Do you know where your family is?"

Himiko shakes her head, then says, "In Ulaanbaatar."

"Okay, where? You know which city, but where in the city?"

"I don't know anything else. Or even if they're in the city, really. He was finding out."

"Names, or . . ." Leap's voice trails off as Himiko watches him.

·●·

AFTER A BRIEF INVESTIGATION, RECORDS of travel to Central Asia turn up. Tomohiro has gone to Ulaanbaatar, of his own accord, and then purchased a general rail ticket. He is not a missing person. Messages to his central account bounce.

Himiko has nowhere to go. She is quite clearly crushed. She seems shy, but when she speaks she is decisive and opinionated. She will occasionally lie to see how people react.

When Himiko was six, her family sent her alone from Ulaanbaatar to find her uncle, Tomohiro. Growing up in Hawaii, Tomohiro had distinguished himself sufficiently in high school to earn a foreign-student scholarship at Keio University, in Tokyo. He earned a Ph.D. in psychiatry, then returned to Hawaii because the thought of living in another place deadened him inside. He found work at a community college. He would say he always knew where he wanted to live but had never asked himself why. Then his fiancée left him two days before their wedding and, for a short time, he went mad.

As he pulled himself out of a depression deep enough to destroy his standing, his reputation, and his sense of meaning, he felt a need to reinvent himself. Those were years of rising water levels, unprecedented hurricanes, and the coastal diaspora—a movement of populations that eventually included the exodus from Hawaii. The other survivors of Tomohiro's family, who had learned to be terrified of oceans, joined renewal projects in Central Asia. Tomohiro hopped a boat to the Pacific Northwest and secured a position as an apprentice gardener on a large estate in what was now being called the Olympic Archipelago.

When Himiko arrived, Tomohiro shared his small, meticulously clean cottage with her, and his firm insistence on meeting expectations. Not expectations around performance in school, but around making conscious choices.

"Always ask why," Tomohiro reminded her tirelessly. Now she imagines that Tomohiro, who rescued her once, has left her with three strong guardians, the three Leaps. After several frustrating conversations with her friends, she asks if she can continue to live with Leap.

Leap enjoys her presence in the home, her unexpected perspectives. Josette takes to Himiko immediately and without reservation, and Josette is never wrong about people, so she herself says. When social workers finally come, Leap says Himiko can stay until she gets on her feet. Josette's attorney helps Himiko file for emancipation. Leap wonders whether this is what Tomohiro had in mind from the start. After her twenty-first birthday, Himiko joins Leap, and her body becomes Leap Four.

FROM FOUR DIFFERENT CHILDHOODS, LEAP remembers different kinds of cruelty and different kinds of love. For example, Tomohiro could be relentless, keeping Leap Four awake all night, not allowing her to close her eyes until she finished her chores, a long and detailed list that he regularly updated. She must clean the kitchen floor. It was her job. She must clean once a week, and there are only seven days in a week, no more. If Tomohiro had high standards for what "clean" meant, then those needed to become her standards. And Tomohiro could put everything he had lost, all of the possible things that were impossible because she was with him, into a simple look. His lips would turn down, and his eyes would soften. Tomohiro never talked about what was in that look, but over the years Himiko learned some of it.

Leap Three's childhood was different. His parents didn't create schedules and task lists. They ridiculed certain things and offered sparse praise for others. During three years in rural Montana, he joined a clique that ran the social scene at the junior high. He became cruel because it felt like success. But memories of things he did followed him during the years after. A feeling grew of being without a reference—of not being able to trust himself. It wasn't until a college girlfriend told him that his smile resembled his father's that the pieces suddenly fell together. His family had operated through intimidation, like the clique.

He wanted to change something fundamental. He went into emergency medicine to help people. But it was the join with Leap that gave him real perspective. As Leap he could compare childhoods. Now Leap believes that any choice that moves you away from cruelty moves you closer to love.

CHANCE FEELS AS THOUGH THE world has blinked. There is no acknowledgment of the convulsion that just gripped all four of Leap's drives.

Leap One is saying, "Where else would I go? I've never been scared enough to rent an apartment somewhere just to make sure my drives aren't all in the same place at the same time."

Chance Two closes her eyes to focus on remembering what she has just seen—the spasm that Leap apparently didn't feel. She tries to compare it with symptom panels for join pathologies. After Chance Three's death, she's still able to find her way through the literature, but her ability to recall information has been blunted.

When a drive dies, research suggests a diminution of expert skill that is roughly proportional to lost brainpower times a coefficient dependent on the level of join integration. The integration of Chance Three was excellent—there were few kinesthetic barriers. Chance is confident that she is still extremely well informed on join pathologies and treatments, and Chance is very sure that whatever the hell Leap just did was the result of a join pathology.

Chance Two says, "You know, you did it. Just now. The twitch thing." She waves at all of Leap's drives. "All of you did."

A nearly imperceptible shudder passes through Leap's drives, a weakening of confidence. Then Leap Four, whom Chance hasn't spent much time with, says, "I'm aware that I do that."

Chance is silent and then says, "I'm glad, because if it is what I think it looks like, it could be very, very dangerous."

Leap Two says, "My One and Two drives are physically tired. Two stayed up for a while after we got in last night. I'm going to rest them. My Three is getting ready for a shift. He's going to be making something to eat. You're welcome to have some—tofu scramble?"

"Are you changing the subject? I'm a friend, Leap. You know, I might be able to help you."

Leap One yawns. Leap Three yawns and says, "Great, we can talk while I make breakfast."

Chance watches Leap One and Two leave the room. There's been a lot of research done on the physical space joins leave between drives. Drives will stand closer to one another than solos of most cultures would. They often touch as they pass. As Leap Two passes Leap Four, she stops for a moment to brush at Leap Four's eye, an almost unconscious gesture.

That kind of intimacy among drives is mocked by solos. Before most solo resentment hardened into religious resistance, there was a famous sketch comedy show, *Howard, Howard, Howard, Howard, Howard, Howard, and Howard*, that parodied the closeness. The seven Howards would stand in a circle, five men and two women, picking one another's noses.

"Okay," Chance says when Leap One and Two have gone, "tell me what's going on."

Leap Four sits across from Chance at the table. Leap Three is moving between the refrigerator and the stove.

Leap Four says, "You mean the . . ." She pulls her shoulders up and raises her upper lip for a moment, then says, "It's probably what you think it is."

Chance says, "I don't know what I think it is. I haven't diagnosed it. I'm not sure that I can anymore. Have you been to someone for an opinion?"

"No," says Leap. "And I think you do know what it is; you're just saying you don't know what sort of join pathology or how far advanced it is. But you know it's join related."

Chance is still getting used to speaking to Leap Four. Drives eventually share the gestures and expressions of a join, but each drive also maintains a distinct style. For example, some drives' faces are great for conveying reserve, some for contempt, some for perseverance, etcetera. Each drive's nervous system is different. Each drive's body proportions are different. The length of each drive's limbs is different. Even things as simple as the quality of a drive's teeth can contribute to a drive's ability to communicate a particular message.

Leap Four appears introspective, physically awkward, almost unaware of the possibility of being observed. She often looks as though she's remembering something funny. Like all of Leap's drives, she shows contempt fluently—a swiftly passing shadow.

Leap Four glances down. Chance can see her eyes moving as she thinks through whatever concerns she has. Leap Four says, "I may know a little more about it."

Chance says, "To me, it looks like a network break. I can't help thinking about it. This is recent—it must be your most recent join—your Four. But that was years ago, and it's happening only now. I know this is difficult to talk about, but could your Four have a latent dementia, or another kind of issue like that, that's been getting worse, that wasn't diagnosed when you joined? Things have moved fast in the last five years. We know how to treat this sort of thing."

Leap Four laughs. "I know. I probably know as much about it as you do. I don't think the problem is with my Four."

They watch each other for a few moments, neither speaking. Then Chance says, "I'm a"—Chance takes a moment before beginning again—"I was a join doctor. It's what I did for several years. And I'm your best friend. You could have talked to me."

"No. I'm sorry. I love you, but you would have told the airline."

"They *have to know*! We're flying live cargo!"

Leap says, "There are at least three independent systems checking everything that happens."

"And the weather still almost just got us. Last night!"

"No, no. Do you really think we were in danger?"

"Yes!" Then Chance does a few quick mental calculations and says, "I don't know."

Leap says, "You know as well as I do. The odds are astronomical."

"No, about one in three-point-six-two million. For each flight we pilot."

"Okay. Yes. That's probably the number."

"It is."

"But that's the number whether or not I'm in the seat."

"You know, I felt like shit," Chance says. Her voice rises. "I'm already close to the edge. Now I'm dealing with a *murderer*! You made me think it might have been *me*. I *doubted* myself." Chance is trying to calm herself.

"I'm sorry," Leap Four says. "I'm so sorry."

Again, neither says anything for a while. At the stove, Leap Three is slowing. He looks tired and unhappy. Leap Four continues, "I was scared. I felt like I needed to protect myself. It's no excuse. I'm sorry. One reason I asked you to come here was to tell you about it."

"How long have you known? How long has it been going on?"

"A few months."

"Shit. It's progressive, isn't it?"

"Yes. I think so," Leap Four says.

"Leap, you can't ignore this. These things can—there's a decent likelihood it could kill you."

"Yeah, if Rope doesn't."

"I can't understand you right now. Rope just killed one of my drives. How can you make that joke?"

"I don't know that it was a joke."

Chance is hurting. Each of her drives feels physically sensitive; each drive's stomach is upset; each drive has a low-level headache. Chance Five is sweating and unable to sleep.

Chance forces herself to concentrate on Leap's problem. To try and ignore the threats to herself. "You think that you do know what's going on?" she asks. "What the problem is?"

Leap is reaching a decision. Leap Three stops moving. He's standing in front of the stove. Leap Four says, "Yeah, I think so. I think I know. I'm sorry I lied. Like I said, I was scared."

Leap Two is suddenly standing behind Leap Four, at the entrance to the kitchen. "Come on," Leap Two says. "I'll show you what happened."

⚫

AS LEAP THREE PUNISHES AN egg, Leap Two leads Chance from the kitchen. Leap moves hesitantly. She almost seems to be reconsidering whether to bring Chance to wherever they're going. They stop at the bottom of the staircase in the house's main entrance.

"You need to prepare yourself," Leap says, "and understand that I already know everything you're going to want to tell me. I know you'll still say something about it, and the truth is that I want to talk about it, and I want your thoughts. But try to avoid the obvious, please. I'm well aware. It's painful."

Leap Two starts up the stairs. At the top is a short hall surrounded by five doors. One of Leap's mothers had this house built. It's three stories and a basement, but Chance hasn't thought about access to the third floor. Two of the five doors are open, including the one to the room where Chance was sleeping. Leap opens another door, revealing a staircase that leads up to the home's third floor.

"You're hiding your secret in the attic?"

Leap closes her eyes and cracks a very small smile. "Yes," she says.

When they reach the top, they enter a single large room. The light is dazzling. Chance's eyes need a moment to adjust. Light floods in from a wall of windows set into gabled dormers near the top of the stairs. Beyond the windows are blue sky and the rising sun. Another bank of windows lines the opposite wall.

The room is filled with creams and faded greens, an over wing chair—a wing chair with arms flattened and flared to allow perching, so two or three drives can share—two slipper chairs, and a single large sofa. A long bronze coffee table, glass topped and filled with sparkling chunks of geodes, sits in front of the sofa. Scattered about the room are tall, wave-shaped, polished glass sculptures that drape thin, semitranslucent shadows over one another and everything else. Near the far end of the room is a bed. Josette lies in it, her thin white hair spreading in snaggly luxury around under her frail, wrinkled head. Leap Two turns toward Chance. Chance sees Josette smiling at her in the distance, sees Leap Two smiling right beside her.

Chance says, "Oh my God, Leap."

Leap Two says, "Oh, don't be a prig."

Chance knows what is happening to Leap. She can roughly characterize when it all started. She can reasonably estimate the rate of progress and Leap's current state. And there can be no doubt about the pathology's future trajectory (and it is a join pathology). The condition itself is mysterious, but its progress is copiously documented.

AS A CHILD NAMED IAN, Leap remembers hiding under an end table.

"Okay, Chuck, then you take him!" His mother's words freeze him there.

He doesn't like his uncle Chuck. Chuck has been telling Leap's mother how she spoils Leap, how she coddles him. Chuck thinks there's something wrong with Leap; that he may be retarded. He thinks Leap's mom lets him get away with too much; doesn't push back when Leap says he'd rather not go to the baseball game or when Leap decides to read instead of watching football or playing bridge with the family. It's an old theme.

Leap's mother knows that suggesting Chuck do anything at all to help will shut Chuck up. This time, though, she's angrier than usual, and her words plant a suggestion of emptiness in Leap, even though he knows she doesn't mean it.

He hears his father laugh, the warm, assured laugh of a man who can negotiate a bitter family feud with a smile and a wink. Or at least thinks he can. The retro cuckoo clock is ticking directly across the room from Leap. Otherwise, the voices of the adults and his own breathing are the only sounds in the world that he hears.

"You know, she has a point," Leap's father says. "No one else could do what Josette has been able to do with our boy."

"Ah." Leap hears his mother snort contemptuously.

"What?" his father asks. Leap imagines his mother shaking her head and miming waving away the smell of bourbon.

"Well, he is freakishly slow," Chuck says, and laughs. Leap hears his father's weak chuckle. Chuck is goading Josette. He says, "I mean for a village idiot." For the two brothers—Leap's dad and Chuck—family conflict is often the start of their fun.

There's an electric silence. Leap imagines the look on his mother's face. Then he doesn't have to imagine it; he hears that look in the tone of her voice: the low, level, even voice she uses to end conversations and make people squirm with almost physical discomfort.

"Chuck, one day I will cut your beating heart out of your chest for saying that." And Leap hears what she leaves unsaid as well: *for saying that while he is in the room.*

Even Leap's father cannot respond to that voice.

. ●.

A WARM SEPTEMBER EVENING. LEAP is sixteen. His father is away. Leap got his driver's license yesterday, and the first dance of the new school year starts in three hours. Josette's curly black hair spills haphazardly around her amused face as she turns to see what he's wearing. Strands float up around her head, creating a hazy nimbus in front of the kitchen light. Her eyebrows go up, and her look goes from disorganized amusement to clear and genuine appreciation.

"You look great," she says.

Leap smiles and is surprised to realize that smiling is the only way he knows to show her how much he appreciates her saying that. He suddenly imagines the whole universe around him, stretching out to infinity in every direction and still expanding. He thinks of a picture of the Horsehead Nebula, mounded and uncurling in pastel colors against the vastness and darkness of space. He isn't even an iota in all of that grandeur. And then he sees the look on his mother's face.

"Thanks," he says.

"Do you want to drive?" she asks him, and holds out an authorization badge for the car. "I keyed you in a few minutes ago. You can start it now."

"Yeah, sure," he says.

He had thought he was full up with appreciation for her. But in some impossible way, his gratitude actually increases.

THE OLD WOMAN LEANS BACK, away from the spoon, her angry glare focused on her son. "I'm your mother, dammit. You'll do what I say."

"Technically," says Leap One, pushing the spoon closer to her again, "you're one of my mothers. One of four. So I'll do about a fourth of what you say."

The old woman, Josette, grimaces, accentuating her pallor and the mottled violet rash on her cheek and on the bridge of her nose. "Who decides?" she asks.

"What?"

"Who decides which fourth?"

"I do."

"Humph. I'm shut out again."

The skin of her face has a papery quality. There are sores

at the tips of her fingers. Leap sees the nearness of her extinction and wants her to be angry like this. Leap wants more of her, wants her to flare up and fill the room with her anger, the intense white light that has been her for so many years. Leap wants more of her than what is left.

"Look," Leap One says, "you haven't eaten anything today."

"Of course not. I'm not hungry."

Leap sits back in his chair. "Mom, you've got to eat something."

"I ate a lot yesterday. You even told me I did well."

Ah, how love can sharpen to condescension at the touch of a master. She sees his glum response.

"I'm sorry, Son," she says. "If that's what you are. I'm just not hungry. Why don't you leave me be for an hour or so, and then I'll try again? What do you say, an hour? I promise."

She's been saying this for about eight hours now, since he first tried at seven this morning. First, "In a little bit." Then "Come back in twenty minutes." Now "In an hour. I'll try then. I promise."

Leap has always known that unmet promises are rarely empty; rather, they're filled with the unspoken things people don't want to do or can't do. Both of Leap One's parents, as they grew older and could do less, promised more. His father's promises, like banknotes from a failed state, all ended null and void. His father did many things before passing on, but none of them involved cleaning up his affairs. His mother continues to print promises like a central banker, but at least she's transparent about her attempts to use them.

Two years ago she was diagnosed with an advanced, degenerative autoimmune disease. Rare, debilitating, it includes severe arthritis as well as symptoms similar to lupus and

Raynaud's syndrome. It's one form of a collection of pathologies that had all been classified as mixed connective tissue disease. In the two years since her diagnosis, her symptoms have been progressing relentlessly. Now when it's bad, she stays in bed for most of the day.

.●.

JOSETTE HAS JUST WOKEN UP. She'd been severely constipated and groaning in pain for hours. Jenny, her home-care nurse, helped her get through that. Afterward, Josette had the longest uninterrupted sleep she'd had for days.

Jenny says the constipation is normal, as is her lack of appetite. Which leaves Leap in a dark mood and wondering how useful eating actually is now. It's almost a ritual the two of them are practicing so they can share something by pointing together at hot soup and saying to each other, *Life! We're miming living by arguing over whether to eat!* But Leap's mother isn't playing today. The ritual is tiring her out.

Josette won't take more morphine, and Jenny hasn't been willing to intervene. Puzzled and powerless, Leap has watched as his mother's pain has gotten worse. There are times when he's reading to her or sitting by her bedside and she starts to talk to herself, first about how bad the pain is, then about other things. Her childhood. The argument she had with Hattie about draping for the rodeo. The argument with Chuck about selling the bank. It's almost always arguments, and almost always very bad ones.

Leap wonders at the irony of leading a long, good life and then, near the end, rather than being able to stand back and appreciate the whole, endlessly revisiting the difficulties. At this moment, how much is his mother benefiting from the life she lived? And if not now, when? Well, Leap thinks, at least he can be here.

"You can do something about it," she says, shocking him out of his reverie.

"What?"

"I don't deserve this. I loved you. I raised you. You can do something about this."

For a moment, Leap can't follow. If she's referring to what he thinks she's referring to, then they've had this conversation. He thought she understood and that she had ultimately found the idea revolting. Her word. He says, "You didn't want that, and unless you want it, I can't do it."

"Can't? Which one can't? Who can't? My boy could! My boy could. Who are you? I don't know you. Do I know you? Get out. Until you're ready to help me, get out of here!"

Leap One places the spoon back in the bowl and stands. He puts the bowl on a large yellow doily on her dresser top. He rubs his hand through his beard, the kinked hair rough against his fingers and his palm. He pulls at it as he thinks about what his mother is asking.

"Help me," she says. "Help me or get out. And ask Jenny to come here. I need her. She's so sweet."

Leap walks to the door. "Jenny's gone for the day," he says. "She'll be back tomorrow. You'll have a new nurse tonight."

"Okay," says his mother. "Explain to her about the morphine before she gets in, will you. How I don't want it. Will you, love?" Her voice has become distant again. She is distracted.

Leap stops at the top of the staircase and turns to look back at his mother. Her eyes are closed.

Her face is damaged by the disease, discolored in patches.

She is making an effort for each breath. In her tight forehead, clenched jaw, and rigid throat, pain uncoils and coils.

"I'll talk to her," he says.

.●.

JOSETTE HAS TWO WEEKS OF nightmares. Each night she lies groaning. Now he hears her screaming at the top of her lungs. Leap Three rushes into the room to find the nurse beside her trying to soothe her, to quiet her. Her body is so frail. But she's bolt upright, and she's still screaming, terrified of something that's followed her out of her dreams, and Leap is afraid that the knotted threads of muscle in her neck will snap through some brittle tendon or bone that holds the rest of her together.

A few very long moments later, and she's quieted. She asks for tea. She won't discuss it. None of them has slept. They're all exhausted and on edge.

.●.

JOSETTE AND LEAP TWO ARE driving home together from a dinner out. She's had several days of improvement. Now she's quiet, tending her own personal garden of care. When they're almost home, she turns to Leap Two and says, "I'm not sick. I'm just dying. And I don't want to."

"You are sick, but you're not going to die. You can still get better."

Josette laughs. There's no bitterness in it. "*You're* not going to die," she says, "but *I* obviously am. When I made my decision, I could accept it. Millions of years of inevitability. None of us had had any choice. That was how we accepted it. Your kind changed all that."

Leap says, "You chose to stay solo."

They drive for a while, skimming low over the forests of Douglas fir and western hemlock. In the distance, on their right and left, the forest curves up toward the slopes of low mountains. Across the mountain range on their right is the Pacific Ocean, tossing and wild, but here the day is muted, broken by broad, visible shafts of sunlight falling through high, drifting cumuli.

Neither of them is connected at the moment. Both of them are musing. Leap Two looks over at Josette to see the old woman watching her. Leap smiles.

"God, you're beautiful," Josette says. "You must have had men lining up. I was never nearly that beautiful."

Leap gives a half smile and turns away, aware that Josette is still watching her.

After a few more minutes, Josette says, "How the hell could you be my son?" Leap isn't offended. It's a common refrain.

·●.

JOSETTE STEPS INTO THE KITCHEN slowly. The arthritis is not as bad this morning, and she's dressed for walking, but she's still moving slowly. "I've changed my mind," she says.

Leap One is making breakfast. Leap Four is down; Two and Three are both working. Josette's nurse had the night off and is running errands this morning. She'll be back this afternoon.

Leap One asks, "About what?"

"May I have some coffee?"

Leap says, "Okay," and reaches over to switch on the espresso machine.

"No, dammit, not about coffee," says Josette, following Leap's train of thought. "I just want some coffee. I've changed my mind about everything else."

Leap says, "Okay."

Josette sits at the table. "You know, for a long time, I thought I could just think of you as a married couple with very eerie telepathy. Good boy. He found himself a real peach, I could think, on my more moon-addled evenings. Then he came along, the tall one. And then the cute one joined you. I can't think of you as married anymore. I have to see you for what you are. You're my son, but also you're something else. I have to understand that. I need to accept. And I need to change my mind."

Understanding suddenly, Leap takes a deep breath. He moves his pan off the burner and turns to her. "Mom, what are you talking about?"

Josette's look is searching. Her eyes narrow as she concentrates on Leap. Finally, she says, "No, no. It's too weird." Then "Would you make eggs for me too?"

Leap goes to the refrigerator for eggs. He doesn't pursue the subject.

So because he hasn't pursued it, it isn't until the next evening—when Leap One is in his study and Josette knocks on the door—that he knows she's really going to ask about it.

He opens the door. She's dressed in her powder-blue Armani suit, the one she'd wear to board meetings. She looks utterly miserable. "I've made up my mind," she says, frowning. "I want to join."

They talk about it. It's clear to Leap that Josette is scared, and it's hard for him to know how to tease the fear apart from the desire.

"The caduceus is an extremely sensitive instrument," he says at one point, "that depends on consent. The consciousness of both individuals has to be committed to the join to enable the connection. It only works if you really want it to work. You can't fool it."

She rolls her eyes. "You're such a schoolteacher," she says. "You always have been. I know all that. I'm not stupid. I'm just scared, is all."

Leap says, "Fear can be managed"—an expression Josette uses.

Josette grunts affirmatively. She's sitting on the love seat across from Leap One's recliner. Her body is upright, rigid. In the old days, she used to sprawl on the love seat, pull up her legs, and lie across one arm. That was before the arthritis thickened in her joints.

"You've never wanted to before," Leap says. "Why now?"

His mother shoots him an angry look, attempting to push him back, silence him.

"At this point," Leap says, "it may be hard for you to find someone who wants to join."

"I know. But I want to try."

.⊙.

JOIN CAN BE A CAPRICIOUS technology. Under certain conditions, it's reliable and safe—a change dependably situated between beneficial and miraculous. But step outside that range of conditions, and things become complicated very quickly.

For many years, there were broad restrictions on how joins could be performed and who could join. Vitalcorp was clear on the ingredients that created the greatest possibility of success— among them, the ages of increased opportunity. Joins with solos between sixteen and twenty-five years old and between forty-four and fifty-four were almost always successful. When Join initially rolled out, only people in those age groups were allowed to use it. Certain kinds of psychological issues could also increase risk, though usually not beyond manageable tolerances and, in those age groups, not significantly. A very small percentage of the population was just not suited for Join and possibly never would be.

Over time, the Directorate reduced the requirements for join approval. The first to go were most age restrictions. Agencies developed more sophisticated measures of likely success than a blanket prohibition on certain ages. The technology improved, and many early obstacles became negotiable. Still, an upper limit, fifty-nine years old, remained for a long time—primarily to reduce the risk of attempting a join with a mind suffering from undiagnosed illnesses, such as certain kinds dementia.

A medical specialty in prejoin risk developed. A profession. A certification. Soon, the cost of a join included the licensing fees paid to the Directorate and large supplemental fees for medical clearance paid to a CJA, a certified join adviser. The advisers were expert in guiding join candidates through the paperwork and medical examinations required to characterize risk and mitigate liability. Eventually, the remaining age limit became avoidable with adequate precharacterization. A certified join adviser would meet both candidates, review every aspect of the application, and issue a recommendation that could be used to apply for an exception to the age rule. And then a black market for CJA services emerged.

There have been several well-publicized, successful joins of drives over seventy years old. One thing they have in common is a person or a join wanting to help an elderly solo avoid death. Leap is pretty sure that another thing many of them have in common is a large payment. Well, Josette can afford it.

Josette asks Leap to talk with her attorney, Mark Pearsun. She's heard (Leap never knows where she hears this kind of thing) that there's a CJA whom Pearsun has had some business with who might be able to help her. One who specializes in gray areas. Leap and Josette discuss it. Assuming the adviser will clear her, Josette's challenge won't be with legal considerations; it'll be finding a join she's interested in. She must act quickly. Join decisions should never be made quickly. Which goes without saying, so they don't discuss it.

⁕

FROM THE OTHER SIDE OF his small maple desk, Mark Pearsun is leaning back and watching Leap One closely. Late fifties, with thick sandy-blond hair cut shapelessly short and untidy bangs pulled to the left across a broad forehead, Mark has surprisingly monochromatic gray eyes and is regularly unshaven. Leap has seen him only in his office, in a rumpled dress shirt that's always half tucked into expensive slacks. He's been Josette's attorney for over twenty years.

"You don't mind if I call you Ian?" he asks.

Leap has heard variations of the question; all joins have. Mark Pearsun knows it's the cliché used most often to characterize clueless solos. Mark dislikes joins. Leap One smiles.

"You know I don't approve of this," Mark says.

"Mark, you basically work for me now."

"No, I work for the trust."

"My trust."

Mark sits forward in his big rolling chair and puts his elbows on the small desk. "This is very disappointing to me. Up to this point, your mother has been an example for me. What she did, the way she thought, have helped me to think about things."

"I know, Mark, but—"

Mark holds out his hand as if tamping down Leap's sentence. "Just let me finish. She helped me make a decision, about eight years ago, not to join."

Leap digests that. "I didn't know."

"Yeah. I don't imagine she would have told you. You know I've been married twice?"

"Yes."

"Well, about eight years ago, I thought about getting married again. But my girlfriend wanted to join. Now, the way I was raised, well, my father was a Fundamental Individualist before anyone knew what that meant. My sister and I, we both always believed we'd lead natural lives."

Leap bridles at the term, but manages to suppress it. "Natural life" is a term one uses carefully around joins. Individualists consider a join a manufactured being.

"I never wanted more than what I was born for," Mark says. "My years are my own, not borrowed or stitched together—"

Leap cuts him off. "Mark, you're my mom's attorney, not my pastor. I'm sorry you chose to listen to my mother instead of making up your own mind when it was important for you to do that. Now I'm trying to respect her wishes. *Her* wishes."

Mark's stubbornness is one reason Josette has kept working with him, so Leap isn't surprised when Mark continues.

"She told me, when she was in her right mind," he says, "that she would be ready to go when her body gave out."

Leap says, "She's still in her right mind. She told me,

yesterday, that she wanted me to ask you to help. Can you help, Mark?"

"What about the risks?"

"It's legal now."

"You know what I mean."

"Well, that's why we need the name of a good CJA."

Pearsun stands and walks around Leap to his office window. "And if I don't give you a name?"

"I don't know. Maybe I'd go to the darknet."

"Do even you know how to find the darknet?"

"I've never tried."

Mark puts his hands in his pockets and leans back on the windowsill. As executor of Leap's trust, Mark Pearsun would be an important part of Leap's life if Josette died.

"She should just leave me the money," Leap says. "The trust is a mistake."

"I told her the same thing," Mark says. "But you know her. She wants the money to go to Ian, not Leap. She's not sure she knows you."

"She said that?"

"Yeah."

Leap could say, *I am Ian*, but his argument is with Josette, not Mark. He says, "My mother once told me you were comfortably amoral."

Mark laughs. "She's said that to me. One of my charms, alongside very thorough research. I try not to be offended. But this isn't about morality. I'm solo today because I listened to your mother. I can't believe she wants this."

"That sounds like you're trying to do the right thing. She wants you to do what she asked."

"You're wrong. I'm not trying to do the right thing. I'm the kind of attorney who does what my clients pay me to do. But your mother wouldn't ask for this."

"Mark, you could just send me the name of an adviser. I'm here because you wanted to meet. Have you gotten what you needed to get off your chest?"

Mark becomes still. He watches Leap One, appraising him, then growls, "I'm gonna find a *pencil* and write it down on a piece of paper."

THEY HAVE A SHORT VIDEO conference with the adviser, Oceanic, a Three who suggests they meet in person at one of the recreation buildings at a community center. When Josette and Leap One arrive, Oceanic Two, a short, heavy, middle-aged woman dressed in a loose pantsuit and paisley blouse, waves them over to her table. She's got a square face, dark, flattened hair, and red cheeks. When she smiles, Leap imagines her with an elf's hat. It doesn't quite fit. She's a little more expressive than an elf would be.

"Hi, I'm so happy to meet you," she gushes. Out of the corner of his eye, Leap One sees Josette pulling back a bit.

Leap Two, flying with Chance Two, has been casually warming up to the topic of risks for an elderly join. Now she says, conversationally, "So some kinds of undiagnosed dementia could be a problem for someone joining with an elderly person. But we have pretty good detection for that kind of thing. If you have good testing, why are people really frightened of it?"

"Yeah, that's really interesting," says Chance Two, believing she's in a relaxed, early evening conversation during a routine flight. "It's because elderly people can be less flexible in their outlook—"

"Is there a technical term for that?"

"Uh, sort of, yeah, believe it or not, it's called attitudinal plasticity in the literature."

.

In the community room, Leap One says to Oceanic, "We're concerned about attitudinal plasticity."

.

On the airplane, Leap Two asks, "How much of a problem is it?"

"Well, not much of one." Chance Two takes a moment to dislodge something from between two front teeth, then continues, "Sorry. That was bugging me. By itself it probably wouldn't present complications, but elderly patients usually have other tendencies that make low attitudinal plasticity difficult to manage. So, for example, feelings of loss of control can engender emotional volatility that . . . ."

.

Oceanic's lower lip pushes against her upper lip in something between disapproval and a pout. "Oh, we'll talk it over, but I don't think that's going to be a problem. First of all, attitudinal plasticity isn't a problem by itself. And on first impressions, and from what Mark Pearsun has told me, I don't see Josette as likely to have lower than normal plasticity for her age. And, well, she seems perfectly happy."

Josette's eyes narrow.

.

Leap Two says to Chance Two, "So, okay, what are we really concerned about? I mean, what would someone really have to look out for?"

"Well, the biggest danger, particularly with an elderly join, is the danger of a flip."

"Okay," says Leap.

Chance says, "Yeah, you've probably read all about it."

.

Leap One asks Oceanic, "How do you guard against a flip?"

Oceanic has lowered her chin, pushing it against her neck so her head is bent forward and her eyes are rolled up toward her brows. "Well," she says, "in the past I would have said that that's our biggest risk. But I think things have improved to where that's unlikely."

.

Leap Three is tired. It's been difficult staying focused and effective in the ER while One is talking with Oceanic and Two is flying with Chance. He has a half hour left, then will get a two-hour sleep, then four more hours of work, then home. He needs to find someone to trade those final four hours with. If he tries to do that shift, he's afraid he might hurt someone.

"There you are!" It's Gnosis Two, a patient Leap stitched up earlier that night. He's a man who claims to have incredible talents as a psychic distance viewer, and a woman who does tarot and palm readings. While Gnosis One had been reading a client's palm, Gnosis Two had slashed his own palm on a drainpipe.

"No coincidences!" Gnosis said several times, fiercely, as Leap sutured.

.

On the plane, Chance is saying, "The best way to avoid a flip is to be certain that both parties to the join are committed. That they *genuinely want* the join. Technically, there are different kinds of flips. Any change or weakness in conviction state can end in a minor flip. A minor flip, one that happens early, simply prevents the join. The risk for older people, when attitudinal plasticity is low, is that the flip might not occur until values compatibility at the sixth layer."

.

"I'm not going to sugarcoat this one." Oceanic is smiling kindly at Josette. Her voice is subdued, steady. "If a flip were really to happen, well, it could be fatal. For both you and whoever you're trying to join with. Now, even though it's rare these days, it's still the main reason that I would recommend that you find a join as your other half. A flip is less likely if you complete the procedure with someone who has already joined." Oceanic reaches a hand across the table toward Josette. She says, "Usually, someone in your position wants to join to escape death, as it were."

Josette says stiffly, "That's right."

"Well," says Oceanic, "even though there's a lot at stake, it's still very important to be careful and not to rush into it. You have to be confident that your join partner is someone that you do want to join with."

.

On the airplane, Chance Two is saying, "A bad flip, the truly catastrophic kind, is really fascinating, one of the most interesting conditions in all of join science. The network connection is both established and not established, leaving the join incomplete. The most concise way to describe it is that the join is trapped almost between two different alternatives of the present moment, one in which the join is working, and one in which it isn't."

"That's concise?"

Chance laughs. "Well, for join technology that's uncommonly concise. That's as elegant as it gets."

Leap is thoughtful. So far, the weather has been unsurprising, and they're flying into evening. The sun has been setting behind them so that the sky in front is becoming darker and more transparent, stars fading into sight like beacons in a dream of perfection. Leap watches for a few moments and then says, "Okay, cowboy, hit me with the long version."

Chance answers slowly, "Okay, then. Most of what gets talked about in Civ News, in stories about join science, are old risks. Things we can avoid these days if we're careful. We understand most of them. But this, a flip, is . . . just mysterious. Like the join itself, and like a lot of the science around the network, our real understanding of it is fragmentary.

"We don't have the tools to test it. Everybody knows the punch line here: observational bias blows up our experiments. Knowing what you're testing skews your results. The results of any single experiment might show an irrefutable relationship, but the quality of the relationship isn't reproducible. The first time through, the results don't disprove your hypothesis. The next time, they do, unmistakably. Bottom line, the network seems to operate through consciousness and even across time. I mean, that one really bends me. There are seriously debated theories of join science that describe the caduceus as, in a very limited way, a kind of quantum time machine."

As the light outside fades, the window's polarity changes, ensuring that it remains fully transparent. Chance watches the stars brightening. She says, "A flip is one of a very small class of join-related issues that give us a peek into a reality where we can't seem to distinguish the reflection from the observer."

·

Josette leans forward, one elbow on the table. "What happens?" she asks.

"I'm going to tell you what happens," says Oceanic. "This isn't what might happen or what would happen if you didn't get treatment. If you flip, this is what happens. The theory is that your psyche is oscillating very quickly, in very small fractions of a second, between a joined and not-joined state. At first, the oscillations are rare, and you might feel a little more tired than usual, maybe more irritable. In most cases, it seems to people as if the join has succeeded. But the integration is still partial.

"Slowly, the effect of the oscillations increases, bringing on any number of side effects. It usually becomes noticeable with an increase in memory loss, slight nausea, fatigue—which joins may be able to get around for a while through improved cycle management. So it can go on for a while during this period. But then you progress to tics, like simultaneous sneezing by all of the joined drives, and then to minor convulsions and seizures, bloody noses, uncontrollable bowels, blackouts. Pulmonary fibrillation is very common. Mood swings. Paranoia. Really, anything unpleasant you can think of that happens to a body could eventually happen. Each case is slightly different. Some happen very quickly; some take a few years. But every case is progressive.

"In the final stage, you see symptoms that look like paranoid schizophrenia, psychosis, and then ruptured internal organs. It can get very painful. I don't like to talk about it too much. It can be very gruesome. It almost always happens to all of the join's drives, but there have been two documented cases in which a single drive survived. And, of course, distress this severe has additional victims. Family members and other caretakers can have a very hard time. The join may become violent."

"Well, aren't you an hour of sunshine," Josette says, her face reddening.

"There's no treatment?" asks Leap One.

"Nothing worth discussing," says Oceanic.

"What are the odds?" asks Josette.

"Of a flip?" says Oceanic. "With proper vetting, and with someone who understands herself well, is clear about her motivations, and is honest with the process, the odds are very low. But it's still one reason why there aren't many joins with people above seventy. About one percent of joins with people over seventy results in any kind of flip, but most of them are minor. And I can tell you right now, if I approve the join, a flip will not happen. That's my job, the job of a CJA, to make sure we don't get in that situation."

·

On the airplane, Chance yawns for a long time, fans her open mouth. When she's done, she chuckles. "Sorry. That was a surprise. I need my second cuppa." She smiles at Leap, then continues, "Our only useful strategy, really, to reduce flips, has been subject profiling and screening. Without pre-screening, we think some kind of flip would happen in about ten percent of joins with elderly solos. These days, though, we can screen out most people who are likely to flip. With the most at-risk group, people older than eighty, say, and the most careful screening—using modern multidimensional testing and integrative techniques in the very best labs—we probably can't get the odds of a destructive flip below one in one hundred thousand, or one one-thousandth of one percent."

Leap doesn't look tired at all. She looks very alert. Very interested.

·

After describing a variety of ailments, and then claiming that none of them was quite what he has, Gnosis Two has finally turned and begun ambling out of the hospital. He also offered Leap Three many different opportunities to have his fortune told for free. Now, as Gnosis leaves, he calls enthusiastically over his shoulder, "You know, you're one in a million! No, one in a billion!"

·

Josette turns almost pointedly away from Oceanic and toward Leap One. She says, "I'm scared. What do you think?"

Leap can hear the fear in her voice. He knows how painful even the smallest things have been for her as the arthritis has worsened. He knows it will get much worse. "I think those aren't bad odds," he says.

Josette hesitates for only a moment, then her fear blows away. "I'm ready," she says. "I'll do it."

.

On the plane, Chance Two squints at Leap Two. "Why are you asking all these questions? What got you interested in all this? Anything?"

"No. Well, maybe the lovely scenery we're always flying through inspired musings on the nature of existence."

"It's almost like you're reffing me."

"Reffing" means surreptitiously using a casual social encounter to extract reference information while simultaneously using that information elsewhere. It's an old term, not heard much anymore because the practice has become so common.

"Ha!" says Leap.

FINDING A JOIN FOR JOSETTE becomes an urgent priority. Leap and Josette begin to make inquiries. They run ads. They meet people for short interviews, for long interviews, for meals. They talk with solos; they talk with large and small joins.

Oceanic is mindful and efficient. With her help, they quickly finish Josette's prejoin clearances. Leap has the impression that

Oceanic has done everything by the book, hasn't spent any time in gray areas, hasn't fudged anything. Despite that, Leap is left with the uncomfortable suspicion that they've only gotten through the clearances because of Oceanic. That any other CJA would have rejected Josette.

Josette's condition is a serious problem. When her body becomes a drive, it won't be very useful. Her mind, however, is healthy and sharp. Still, many of those willing to consider a join seem motivated by money. Josette rejects all of those candidates.

One candidate named Elevation, a join of three, sends over a contract that includes an agreement to euthanize Elevation Four, as Josette's body would be known, the day after the official integration period ends. Leap is astounded—after a join, Josette would be Elevation, so a prejoin contract is meaningless. Josette rejects Elevation on principle. (She calls it the bozo principle and says it's been very helpful over the years.) Several other candidates bring up the topic of euthanizing Josette's body. Josette isn't ready to confront that possibility, so those discussions create another category of rejection.

And Josette flares up at any hint of pity. Sometimes the heat of her anger is just barely perceptible. Sometimes she produces withering death rays of scorn in the midst of what had seemed like civil conversation. The end result is always the same: no join. Her condition worsens. She is spending more time in bed.

After the final vidcon with Elevation (Josette to Elevation, "I hope that's not too much of a letdown"), Leap One goes to fetch Josette's medication. As he's leaving the room, he hears Josette ask Oceanic in a hushed voice, "So, tell me quickly, how does sex work?"

"Mutual consent is an explicit requirement of the join procedure," Oceanic says. "After the procedure, all of an individual's needs for intimacy, both emotional and physical, can be addressed by the join directly . . ."

It's clear that both Oceanic and Josette would prefer a private chat. Leap One moves beyond earshot, then waits a few extra moments before returning.

⋅●⋅

LEAP FOUR IS DREAMING. LEAP is both in the dream and outside of it. Leap One is also sleeping, but not dreaming. Leap Two is in a cafeteria. Leap Three is talking with an orderly. The drives are like the hands of a pianist. They accomplish incredibly difficult tasks without conscious intervention. Leap experiences everything simultaneously. The experience of dreaming while awake is akin to feeling an emotion. Leap pays attention to the world each drive experiences. Leap says things. Leap makes decisions. Leap deliberates on responses, or weights the inclinations that shift a drive one way or another. Leap can do many things at the same time. Leap is not a core, not a trunk. Leap is an idea, a coherence, an overlap.

In Leap's dream, the Vitalcorp logo, four birds in flight, becomes a flock of thousands of starlings streaming across the bright afternoon sky. The dark ribbon of their bodies encloses space and the stars. Deep within that darkness, beyond what is possible, at the end of space and in the last few feet of time, is a decision that Leap must approach.

⋅●⋅

LEAP FOUR AND JOSETTE ARE walking a trail that passes by the distantly spaced neighbors' spreads and across the cold autumn slopes at their steading's edge. They've walked for forty minutes to the Benthic Bench, one of nine benches installed by the steading. This one is covered with colorful paintings of the old sea life of Puget Sound—crabs, anemones, clusters of mussels, oysters, purple curving millipedal worms, corals, the long-necked geoducks. Josette sits; her face is pale. She's wincing with pain, and her breathing is ragged.

"I need one of the large blue ones. I need it now."

Leap fumbles in the knit bag to find one of the large blue ampoules.

"Here," says Josette. Her crabbed hands scrabble at the black lining of her coat as she pulls its edges and the tear-away fleece beneath to expose the soft, loose skin of her neck above her clavicle. "Just quickly, please."

Leap Four touches the cold metal contacts of the ampoule's dispensing end to activate it. She carefully rubs it against Josette's skin for a moment, and then holds it still. It vibrates subtly with the faint ticking of a tiny pump as its nanowires fire thousands of microscopic doses into capillaries beneath Josette's skin. When Leap lifts the ampoule, Josette's skin is moist and reddened. Leap drops the ampoule back into the knit bag and watches Josette.

Josette's breathing becomes more regular, shallower. She sits back against the bench.

"I can't walk back," she says.

Leap says, "I'm sending for a pod."

Josette closes her eyes for a moment, then opens them and breathes deliberately, slowly.

"How is it?" Leap asks.

"Not too good," she says.

AFTER THAT, JOSETTE SPENDS MORE time in bed. Oceanic continues to come by daily to talk with her. Leap sits in on most of their conversations. Oceanic almost seems to be visiting a friend, but she asks specific kinds of questions, and her questions aren't always guided by the flow of conversation. Her questions both invite reminiscence and request factual responses. "What did the back of that church look like?" "Did you have a favorite neighborhood store?"

Leap has always known Josette as a private person, or at least a person who shares the morsels of her life sparingly and deliberately. The type of conversation Josette's having with Oceanic is something she would typically resist. Instead, she plays along.

Josette tires quickly, but each day when she leaves, Oceanic looks satisfied. Until one day when Oceanic draws Leap One aside after her conversation.

"You know, the sea isn't full of fish anymore. The two of you have rejected a lot of options. I don't know how many more will come along."

"She's not doing well," Leap says.

"No, she's not," says Oceanic.

Leap One says, "I try to keep her walking, at least for a while each day, but she's in pain, even with the medication."

"She's also depressed."

Leap would never have said that about Josette, never have thought of her in that light. He says, "She doesn't think we're going to find someone for the join."

"No."

"How close . . . should I be thinking about hospice?"

"I don't think so," says Oceanic, "but that's not really my

area. Her health is getting worse, but I think she's still okay, and her mind is fine. Even where things stand now she could have years left."

"We'll keep looking then," Leap says.

Oceanic doesn't respond. She's just watching Leap calmly. Not hinting at a response.

Leap is thrown for a minute but is not sure why or what to say. "We'll keep looking," he says again.

"Okay," says Oceanic.

.◉.

LEAP ONE SAYS, "I CAN'T do it for you. You have to say yes to someone."

Leap One and Josette are stepping out of the house on a cold autumn afternoon. Leap One has been reading a history of popular a cappella music and is a bit logy. Josette started the walk by telling him he was not doing enough to find her a join.

"Mark should help me," she growls. She's dressed in a shiny black down coat that falls to her calves and makes low rustling and squeaking sounds as she moves. "Without me, he wouldn't have had a goddamn practice. Sanctimonious bastard. I probably sent him a third of his business over the years. Said he appreciated it. Sends me champagne at Christmas. Of course, it hasn't been real champagne since the first bottle. Oh, God, what have we done to our world."

From Civ News this morning, they know that a superhurricane has split off one of the southern storms and ripped through the Cordial spire community in the El Coahuilón Mountains in Mexico. Over forty thousand bodies are dead or missing. Rescue operations are impossible as the hurricane is "squatting," with its eye just half a mile from the community. Once again, weather is the story, as it has been since the drowning of Dhaka.

And, of course, the Champagne region is completely arid—one more place on a long list of places—and no longer produces grapes. For years, a synthetic champagne—the pressed juice of closely engineered bacterial sediment formulated to produce the effects of terroir—has been the nearest thing to the traditional drink that's available.

They walk slowly and in silence for a while.

"It's all going to hell." Josette scowls. After a little while, she looks over at Leap One and says, with genuine curiosity, "You're happy, aren't you?"

Leap is surprised, and it takes a moment to find a thought that might lead to a response. "If you mean am I satisfied with what I have, then yes."

"I'm not," Josette says. "I'm fucking not." She's quiet for a few more moments, then she stops walking and turns to face him. "And I don't understand how you can be! Forty thousand bodies died. You can bet there were a lot of joins down there who aren't feeling very immortal anymore. And a lot of—" She stops, as if she's heard herself and is disappointed.

"You know," she says, calming herself, the discoloration on her face starker, the tendons of her neck taut, "when I was a girl, before you were born, we didn't have megastorms."

Leap remembers Josette's voice reading from a children's story, ". . . before them was a lovely, sunny country that seemed to beckon them on . . ."

Josette snorts, "Yes, you know. Of course, you know. You spend all day reading. You and the cute one, Himiko."

"Mom, she's me."

Josette waves a hand dismissively and winces in pain.

"Yeah," she says. Then she stops walking. "I love you, you know. I just can't see past this pain. I can't walk today."

Leap tries to change her mind, but she turns around and slowly walks back toward the house and then inside. He follows.

She hasn't taken her coat off. Her back is to him.

"You want me to ask?" she says stiffly.

"Mom—"

"You need me to ask?"

"Mom, I—"

Her voice is dry, stressed, reedy.

"You can't bring it up, so I will. I've fought enough battles. I'm not going to stop at this one. You can't bring it up, so fine! I want to join with you. You should let me join with you."

Leap One's throat and chest constrict. "I can't believe you want that," he says quietly.

She turns around. She's shaking, staring at him. He's afraid that she'll fall.

"I do. That's what I want," she says.

"I don't think it would work," he says.

"Why not? You're not a stranger. I've known everyone who's joined with you. I love you all."

Leap takes his jacket off as she watches. He's trying to think of a response that will make sense.

She says, "Ah, to hell with you."

⚬

THE NEXT TWO WEEKS ARE difficult. The arthritis is in retreat. For another person, dissatisfaction with Leap might be an excuse to exaggerate her discomfort, to emphasize her anguish and his guilt at not being able to relieve it. At not being willing to. Instead, what follows are many good days for Josette. She's more active. She's in a good mood. She's more of her old self, the self Leap remembers from when she was fighting with the corporate board and growing the company. She's gracious around all of his drives, but not excessively so. She's gracious to her normal degree.

She even spends a week back at her own home. She brings in help to pack it, and she works hard at getting things straightened up, stored, cleaned, arranged. She says that no matter what happens, her home should look good.

They interview a few more candidates. She seems ready to accept one, a join of nine who has achieved a minor international reputation, first as a logistics expert and now as a philanthropist. The join, Accord, is enthusiastic about her, believes she will strengthen it. But she can't bring herself to agree. She says the join is just too attentive. She can't see herself joined with a psyche that's so nice.

During this time, Leap tries to forget that she asked about joining and attempts to return to a more typical routine, with Leap One studying, Two and Three working, and Four spending some time doing both.

·●·

IT'S NOT THAT FAMILY JOINS are more or less risky than any other kind. It's just that something about joining with family members trips a boundary wire that sets off dull thudding explosions of disgust in most people. Leap can't imagine joining with a parent. Leap mentally inventories each drive's parents, all of the people who raised someone who joined Leap, in search of one who won't provoke the reaction, but all of them do.

Though Leap tries to behave as though the question weren't asked, it's not quite possible. Leap takes breaks from other readings to peruse articles and discussions about intrafamily joins. Most people avoid them, but they are done occasionally. There are many otherwise unremarkable joins who have added parents or children as drives. There are even some joins who raise children specifically to join with them. They're sometimes associated with evolutionist sects—fringe groups who aggressively proclaim that joins are the next step in human evolution. Who believe society should be designed around that central tenet. But there are others as well.

Leap notes an insistent internal hum of queasiness. There are plenty of published intellectual justifications for avoiding it, but none of them is fully satisfying. It just strikes Leap as wrong.

JOSETTE IS STRUCK DOWN. THE weather has changed. It's a damp, cold, and windy November. Josette's arthritis is stopping her completely. She doesn't return Leap's calls, but her nurse, Jenny, tells Leap that she's in great pain, and she wants to come back to Leap's house. That night, she returns.

Leap is shocked by the sight of her. Her nurse wheels her in. Her lower jaw won't stop trembling. Her eyes are half open, and she wears an expression of deadening effort, as if just sitting requires all of her focus and attention. The nurse takes Leap Three aside and tells him that Josette has made arrangements to poison herself but will need help.

The next day, at around 4:00 P.M., Leap One goes into the room where she's lying on the bed. She has recovered a bit, as if the change of location is doing her good. She smiles when she sees him and says weakly, "You keep a good inn."

"It surprised me when you asked," he says. "It never felt right to imagine that. Jenny tells me you've made other arrangements, though."

"You don't have to be here," Josette says. "Jenny and I can manage it. I just hate the thought of it. I'm having trouble bringing myself to do it. I'm being weak, so it's taking longer." She tries to smile, but her lips are trembling and won't quite curl upward.

"Mom, what I want to say is, it's okay. If you want to do it, I do. I think Oceanic would help us join."

There's a long silence as Josette digests the news. "I'm ready to go, Leap. I don't need to stay or to join," she says. "I'm ready."

Leap is struck that she says his name without a modifier or sarcastic addition. Leap knows that despite what she has just said, the two of them will join. Leap is relieved.

·◉·

OCEANIC IS CALM AND SUPPORTIVE. As if she knew things would come to this. Josette is still in terrible pain, so they're very careful to work slowly, trying to ensure that she's making the decision she intends. She wavers at first, and then she says, "I'm curious," and from that point forward she's firm. Oceanic has an inventory of questions for both Josette and Leap that she patiently works through. Some are asked individually and privately, some jointly.

They've talked about the effect of Josette's body joining while it's in so much pain. Oceanic isn't concerned. "A join can be very healing for a drive. I'm sure you've heard that. Terrible, terrible conditions sometimes heal. I'm not aware of cases where the join wasn't a positive for someone who was ill. Now, it might not make a difference, or much of one, but it won't put you in further danger, or her."

There is one topic that Oceanic is adamant about. "A family join is a very sensitive thing. I have access to a privacy filter. I'm going to do the work required to mask this join. You will have the ability to hide the fact that you've done it. I think it's also important that it happen quickly, because Josette is so ill. So we're going to have to fudge the licenses a bit. We can fix them easily enough after. No one needs to know that you've joined. Your records won't show the join. Then, when you're completely comfortable, you can submit the form and officially become a five. But when you do, that will be your decision."

Later, Oceanic tells the two of them that after the join, Leap will need coaching in special cycle-management techniques to handle the burden of Josette's body. "Have you ever had a drive with a serious physical injury?" Oceanic asks Leap. Leap is certain that Oceanic already knows the answer. If a drive has had a serious injury, there is almost always a record of it available to a CJA. If she's at all decent at her job, and Leap believes she is, she'll have done the research.

"No," Leap One says, "I never have." Josette is listening carefully. Leap expects Oceanic to go into detail, more for Josette's sake than for his.

Oceanic says, "Well, a join can kind of leave a drive. When you're focused, when you feel rested, you can leave a drive to sort of be and trust it to not do something terribly stupid. It can be very surprising at times. Sometimes, you might find that a drive has been talking, and you're not quite sure of what it's been saying, or it's been saying things that surprise you, or maybe a drive has been reading, and you, you remember reading through the words, but you don't really remember any of the content."

Seeing that Josette is interested, Leap says, "Yes."

"That's the kind of state you'll take advantage of with Josette's body. It'll require attention, willpower, but you'll learn to separate the body Josette has now from the rest of what you're doing, like an injured arm that's in a sling. Pretty soon you stop trying to use it."

"It all sounds very unlikely," Josette says with satisfaction, happy to play the skeptic in the face of Oceanic's reassuring certainty.

"I know. Before joining, I didn't believe it either. None of me did. But I see that it's true now. I don't think a solo can really imagine it. The experience of join is the good part of what you think it will be like, without the bad part. You'll go under, with the anesthetic. Then you'll experience the powerful psychotropic drugs, and when you come to, you'll find that you can naturally manage the activities of multiple bodies. You'll feel yourself blessed with companionship, even though you're the only person around. You'll begin to get used to the idea that you don't have to die.

"Some things that you believe strongly, you will probably no longer believe. For example, many people either become more religious or less. People's habits change. Their tastes often change. The changes are different for everyone, of course, because each join is a unique individual. But I have never talked with a join who regretted the changes. In my personal experience, the difference of perspective is most often compared to the change in perspective that a solo can experience after having a child. It can be a complete change of view, of values."

Josette chews this over for a moment. She says casually,

"Well, that sounds like it won't be me then." She asks, "What about when I die? I mean, my body?"

"That's never easy," Oceanic says. "And it may be especially bad in this case because of your illness. While your body may last years, there is a small chance it might go quickly. If that were to happen, you won't have fully integrated with the body, but your mind, your psyche, will be completely integrated. So of your several bodies, Josette—this one—will still feel special to you. And because it feels special to you, it will feel special to the whole of you, to the join. Initially, it could be very painful, very traumatic, when it dies. But you learn soon enough how to function without it. You will be okay."

ONE OF LEAP'S EARLIEST MEMORIES after becoming a five is a conversation with Oceanic. It is also her final memory of the adviser. It happens near the end of the psychotropic phase, and the memory is a bit disjointed, but Leap remembers Oceanic's voice saying, "It's done. It took a while for the two of you to get there, but I knew you would when I first saw you. This is why people come to me."

CHANCE HAS DIFFICULTY SAYING THE words. "You joined with your mother."

"Yeah," Leap Two says quietly.

"And one of you changed your mind. One of you changed your mind, Leap!"

"Yeah."

"Shit! Who was your CJA?"

Leap doesn't answer.

"Who was your adviser, dammit! You flipped!"

Chance Two and Leap Two are staring at each other. Leap says, "Yeah, I flipped."

"Oh, shit. Fucking hell," says Chance.

She stretches out her arm, but there is nothing near to support her. She takes a few breaths, then searches for a chair, walks to one, and sits down. She looks at Leap Two, standing beside the bed, beside Leap Five.

Chance stands and walks to the bedside. She takes Leap Five's hand and asks, "Does the join feel complete?"

"Yes," says Leap Five.

Chance spends a few moments orienting to this new information. She recalls case histories. She thinks about how the pathology starts, how it develops, how it ends. She cannot find even a sliver of hope. She groans. Looking at Leap Five, she says, "There's never been a cure."

Leap Five closes her eyes. Chance turns to Leap Two, who appears calm.

"That drive is in so much pain," Leap Two says. "I just keep it down, sleeping all the time. There's some evidence that killing it could slow the disease."

"There's a lot of evidence of that. And the slowdown is significant."

"Yeah, but I can't do it. That's me. I mean, it's still weird to see that drive when I'm not looking in a mirror. I'm integrated, but that body isn't. You, of all people, should know how I feel."

Chance understands. Chance Five's potential death has the morbid sense of permanent oblivion. Chance has been walking around choking on the risk of losing Chance Five and the trauma of losing Chance Three. Chance has been wailing about those difficulties to Leap, who all the while has been faced with an even-more-gruesome reality: a relentless and horrifying physical degeneration ending in complete join failure and psychic death.

Leap says, "To me, killing that drive would almost be suicide."

"You joined during your vacation?" Chance whispers.

"Three and a half months ago," says Leap.

The words that need to be spoken are heavy and sharp. Chance says, "You've got to kill that drive now."

Leap nods, and then Chance understands what Leap is asking. "You want me to do it?"

Leap Two suddenly folds into herself. She collapses against the side of the bed, leaning on it near the sleeping drive that was one of her mothers and is now her. She cries as Chance stands silently by, shocked and immobile. Finally, Leap pushes herself up and sits on the side of the bed.

She says, softly, "I can't do it."

Chance doesn't want to do it, doesn't want to kill an old woman.

"No one—no one else?" she asks dully.

Leap doesn't answer. She reaches out to take a pink tissue that rises from a green box on her bedstead like a perfect artificial lily. She wipes her eyes, pulls on her nose. She's trying to catch her breath, then wiping again. Her voice muted, high. "I can't tell anyone else about it. But I was dying. I had to do the join. And the adviser who helped us, it turns out she'd had her certification revoked. The whole thing was gray. It had to be. I had asked for that adviser; I found her because I knew there could be complications, and I knew it had to go quickly."

Chance understands. Leap and Josette hadn't prepared to kill

Josette's body after the join. Why would they? It's only important now because of the flip.

"The licenses are legitimate," Leap continues, "but from the emergency pool. I had to pay out a fee to reverse a data trace and convince someone to hide the licenses for up to a year. I'll get real licenses in two months. They'll go into the emergency pool to replace what I used, and no one will know. But I can't officially be a five for another two months."

"You borrowed licenses from an admin at Vitalcorp. Now you owe them licenses for a five, to replace what came out of the emergency pool?"

"Yes."

"But if that drive," says Chance, "is dead, how will you certify yourself as a five? You won't get the licenses without showing five drives. You'll have a Vitalcorp admin after you—"

"I know it. I figured I'd find an adviser who's certified and willing to bend that rule just a little. I can record all the evidence, the video interview, the DNA samples, everything, now. The only issue will be date stamping. I've got two more months to find someone to help."

"I don't know how to help with that. They will—" Chance can't finish the thought. She starts again. "Do you have connections? Who can help you with this kind of thing?"

"I do. I have some, from when I was building the bank."

"This is crazy, Leap. Really, maybe worse than crazy. If I kill that drive, I'm a part of it."

"I can't kill myself. I'm not strong enough. I'll just keep delaying. I've known something was wrong with the join. But I . . . Chance, I can't see the spasm. I don't know when it happens. For me, nothing happens. I don't feel it. But I noticed that I had knocked over a cup. I had no memory of doing it, but I must have.

Then I was brushing my teeth, and my toothbrush was suddenly jammed into the back of my mouth, and my mouth was bleeding. And then I . . . I saw the spasm on a vid. I've known for weeks now. I've known what was going on, but I can't do it."

Chance is cold, her voice remote. She says, "Just drink a calming poison."

"It's not that easy. I can't do it. If I could, I would have."

"What about the adviser who helped you, the one who had her certification revoked?"

"Oceanic. She said I couldn't contact her after the join was complete. No matter what. She said we don't know each other. She won't respond to my messages. I think she blocked me."

"And you can't go to a hospital because the join was gray."

"Chance, I can work through the licenses," says Leap. "I know someone who can do that kind of thing, deal with the legal issues. But I can't kill my drive. I am Josette. That's me. I'm scared of dying."

Chance remembers Nana rubbing her thumb across a birthmark on Chance Five's left arm, a light stain on his copper skin in the shape of a quarter moon. Her thumb was gentle, and she rubbed it and then regarded his arm closely, holding it until he started to squirm a bit. Then she kissed him lightly on top of his head and said, "Javier, you have the moon on your arm. You know the moon is the mother of dreams."

⠂⠠⠄

WITHIN TWENTY-FOUR HOURS OF HIS death, Chance Three's remains are properly identified. Chance, who is still enforcing a com block on personal contact, is informed about the correction through the office where Chance One works.

Then Chance One has a preliminary video interview about the incident. The poison Rope used has been conclusively identified, but as a result of some legal complications in Rope's status, Directorate staff have raised jurisdictional concerns with local authorities. Those questions will need to be resolved, and once they are, Chance will be re-interviewed.

.•.

CHANCE ONE SPREADS CHANCE THREE'S ashes into New Denver's River of Reflection. A feature of most spire communities, the river is designed to receive the ashes of the dead. It is still and reflective at its sides, with a current just beneath the surface that draws water from the edges toward its center. At the center, ripples stretch and break the glassy stillness as the watercourse flows downstream.

Chance is still scared of attracting any kind of attention and scared of gathering all of the drives in a single place, even along the banks of the river. Rope is an unknown, both in motive and capability, so Chance has decided not to complete the full Ritual of Retirement.

Chance has also chosen not to shave the heads of the four remaining drives and does not commit the undivided attention of every drive to the process of saying goodbye, as is the custom. Instead, Chance One and Chance Four complete a shortened version of the ritual alone, in New Denver. The day is overcast and though Chance is spreading ashes an hour before sunset— the proper time for the ritual—the light is muted, the river dull and dark.

Chance doesn't remember seeing Chance Three's ashes falling from the vessel into the river, or the water carrying them toward the center and then downriver. Chance is thinking about security protocols and is talking with Leap.

After spreading Chance Three's remains, Chance One goes home. He will complete various forms to register a change of status and to officially remove Chance Three's network-access privileges.

Chance Four sits on one of the benches near the banks of the river. She is bundled up against the winter cold and watches the meeting place of the still water and the ripple in the center until long past sunset. To do as Leap asks, all that's needed is a hypodermic needle. Chance already knows what to put in it, and how to use it.

·●·

ALL OF LEAP'S DRIVES SHAVE their heads. They each clip their nails and lay the hair they've shaved and their nail clippings in the casket with the body of Leap Five. Then they prepare for the Ritual of Retirement by cremating the drive that had been Josette.

Two days later, Leap's four remaining drives stand along the banks of the River of Reflection. The river in the Olympic Archipelago's spire community is a mile long, between forty and sixty feet wide, and languorously undulant at its center. It travels slowly from a slightly raised artificial wetlands in the east to a slightly lowered artificial wetlands to the west. Like every River of Reflection, it isn't allowed to freeze over. Snow is removed from within twenty feet of the banks, which are rush lined and gently sloped but cut with paths to walk upon. No bridges cross the river, and no boats travel on it.

Leap's drives, male and female, wear the identical, simple

cotton shifts of mourners, modified with a heat-generating and -reflecting inner layer. Their shaven heads reinforce the image of unity among them. Each holds a bowl with a measure of ash from Leap Five's body. Chance Two stands on the right side of the line of Leap's drives, beside Leap Four. Leap's drives step into the river in unison. They walk four paces in unison, into knee-deep or thigh-deep water. They bend toward the water at the same time. Each lifts the cover off their vessel and leans forward to tip the cremated drive's ashes into the river.

Watching all of Leap's drives acting in the river in unison, Chance knows that Leap is experiencing the sensation of the cold water underneath the still surface moving against four pairs of legs, each pair feeling the same river differently. She knows Leap is watching the four streams of ash fall simultaneously, each drive placing a similar but unique signature on the moment and the memory. Leap is memorializing the drive in a way that will recall not just Leap Five but also this period of Leap's life. As Chance Two watches, she feels the loss of her own ritual, the proper ritual she neglected.

When the ashes are gone, the drives stand still in the river, cold water rolling slowly about them. Leap is very much in a "between" period. Josette's psyche has joined but has not yet fully separated from her body. Unlike a healthy retirement ceremony, in which a fully integrated join says goodbye to a beloved drive, Leap's trauma will have a surreal touch: the dream of attending one's own funeral.

A tremendous shudder passes suddenly through all of Leap's drives. Their muscles tense. Their backs arch. Leap One drops his bowl, which had held one-fourth of the ashes. It splashes softly into the water, tips, then rights itself and begins to float toward the center of the river, as it was designed to do. Leap's drives straighten from the spasm. Chance is surprised that none of them has fallen into the river.

A moment later, Leap's other drives purposefully release their bowls, gently setting them on the surface of the river and letting them go. As Leap and Chance watch, the bowls dissolve, drifting toward the central ripples where they roll, weakening, folding in on themselves, collapsing, and then thinning to nothing.

PART

THREE

There is nothing special about humanity.

—Beal Fung,
Nobel Laureate in Economics

You have internal conversations and external conversations, and while the conditions are different in each, you are the common factor. Your awareness becomes the lens through which light passes between the two worlds.

—Advocate

CHANCE THREE ATTENDED ADVOCATE'S FAMOUS lens lecture
when he was sixteen. Advocate's clarity and passion for Join
spoke directly to him. Excited by Advocate's vision, his father,
a corporate lawyer and poet, worked to integrate Advocate's
ideas into an ethical framework that emphasized the struggle
of individual life and the constant renewal fundamental to
living systems. Chance appreciated his father's efforts but also
saw that, as Advocate said, both of his parents and all solos
were tied to the wheel of suffering. No previous technology
offered a fundamentally alternative vision of what it meant to
be alive.

Advocate said that, in centuries to come, humanity would
create additional alternatives. Each join was a reimagining of
life's basic assumptions. Each join had the potential to create a
new universe, an internal dimension in which life meant something entirely different. The challenge of Join was to have the
courage to try it, to cross the threshold. Everyone who crossed
the threshold was a pioneer. The promise was infinite potential.

Since that time, Chance has come to believe that Advocate's
metaphor fudges a crucial point. Joins live in the same physical
world as solos, and depend on it. Chance's awareness has not

become a lens between equivalent worlds. In fact, as Chance experiences it, the beefed-up, hyper-resourced awareness of a join just continues to do the same old job—help the mind order information and address priorities.

.●.

IT'S SUDDENLY POURING RAIN. QUAME and Lisa are laughing. A freak downpour, out of nowhere. Torrential, drenching. As if they live in the tropics, and this is the rainy season. They run the last block to the pod. By the time they get there, there's an inch of rushing water on the street. On top of that, no matter how he presses, the gate pad isn't picking up Quame's hand-print. The pod won't wake. Lisa shouts, "What's going on?" over the roar of the falling water. Lisa has no idea what Quame is doing, but whatever it is, it's funny. It's all funny—the rain, the inert pod, Quame's look of confusion as he swipes his palm over and over on the pad. The water's too thick for them to use their retinal projectors, and neither of them even has a hat. They're completely soaked through.

They squint at each other, both of them standing in the torrent—the falling, flashing water—and laugh. And they struggle with it and then see that they shouldn't laugh too hard because—well, Lisa laughs too hard and chokes on the heavy rain. With her sputtering and laughing, torn between enjoyment and coughing, Quame completely loses it and is bent over with uncontrollable laughter. He's pointing at her weakly. When she stops her choking and laughing, she bats his hand away, and they look at each other and start another uncontrollable fit of laughter.

Rope remembers spreading the cremated remains of both of

those drives into the River of Reflection in New Denver. New Yorkers, both of them. Both possessed of the hardened realism of the remaining denizens of that now-ramshackle lagoon of drowned personal ambition. Getting past all of that and into hilarity is no mean feat. Rope relishes those memories. Rope has so many memories like that, from so many lives.

Rope remembers the sudden downpour clearly from the perspective of each of them, and within their memories, the storm is suffused with wistful, earnest longing; a slightly fearful anticipation that at that moment they may be on the verge of actually doing something that will be meaningful to them, that will make a difference in the struggles they care about, that will make things better in the world. That sudden, unexpected storm was a symbol for both of them that they may have finally broken open the floodgates of hope. That's what they wanted it to mean. That's what Rope wanted it to mean. Every time.

The difference they were making—that was their decision to join Rope. So now, Rope is each of them. Just as Rope is each of the other souls who have joined to create it. And each one of those souls has grown older with Rope. And at this remove, with the intervention of time and events, Rope can clearly see the truth they willfully and uncharacteristically turned away from at those moments. The truth they knew, but chose to avoid. It was really just another freak storm. Another savage, inarticulate spasm of the rapidly changing world.

.●.

LEAP TWO IS TAKING A long vacation from work. The death of Leap Five and her cremation, combined with the irregular licensing, has created some potential issues for Leap's civilization

ID. Leap will talk her supervisor at the airline through what happened after she sorts out what happened.

Chance Two is on leave and has time to accompany Leap One to a meeting with Mark Pearsun about Leap's ID. When the door to Pearsun's office opens, he stands impassively behind it, waiting for something from them.

Chance says, "Hello, I'm Chance." She extends her hand, but he ignores it.

"You're the murderer," he says.

"No, Mark," Leap One says. "No one's dead. I'm right here."

"Oh, I didn't mean you, Ian. I was referring to Josette, your dead mother. And by the way"—Mark motions toward Leap One's shaved head—"the skinned look suits you. There's less of your natural weirdness."

Leap is calm. "No, Mark. This is me. Though in a way, you're right. I'm not only Josette. Not anymore. I've changed my name. My name is Leap. And I am Ian, as I am Josette. And I am Aurora. And I am Brian. And I am also Himiko. So yes, today, right now, this is actually me. And in, what, a month? With your help, this will be me legally."

Mark turns his back on them. He waves them into the office as he walks around his desk and sits down.

They sit in guest chairs in front of his desk, Mark slouched in his chair, watching them both.

"You know what I want," Leap says.

"Sure," Mark says. He sits forward, puts his elbows on the desk. "We have all the technical means we need to require perfect adherence to sensible and ordered laws around Join licensing." He smiles sourly and leans back again in his chair. "So to avoid that enlightened, functional, and overly regulated state of affairs, we've had to use the law to generate a more appropriate situation, one with a more appropriate measure of confusion. Within that appropriate confusion resides the flexibility that is sometimes required by people of means. You, whoever you are at this point, are still a person of means."

"Thank you, Mark," says Leap.

"I think this can be managed. The whole thing," Mark says it as if the fact that he can manage it upsets him.

"The licensing?" Leap asks.

"Yes."

"The forward dating on the samples?"

"Yes, but we won't know for sure for a couple of months."

"Thank you."

Mark seems ready to say something but then appears to change his mind. He says, "So, you flipped."

Leap sighs. "Yes."

"It's unfortunate. I'm sorry for you. But I'm not surprised. Josette would never have wanted this."

"Mark, I am Josette."

"Well, okay. Shit! Okay. I'll talk with your son as if he's you, Josette!" Mark's face is red, but his voice softens again, and he continues, "You told me you didn't want to join."

"Yes," says Leap.

"So you changed your mind."

Leap can't look at Mark. "Yes, I . . . the arthritis, the pain. I never, never imagined it could be that difficult. That painful."

"You didn't talk to me again. You didn't ask me."

"I wasn't thinking. The pain was terrible. My body was going to die. I needed a join with more drives."

"And then you flipped."

"Yes."

"I wouldn't have had doubts."

"I don't think"—Leap glances over at Chance—"with you I don't think I would have either. And it may not have been Josette who flipped."

"What, you then? Ian? Or . . . Leap?"

Leap doesn't respond.

Mark turns away dismissively, looks out the window. "And killing her slowed it down," he says.

"I didn't kill her."

"No," Mark says. "She did."

"No, I am still here, Mark. *Goddammit*, you bloodsucking twit!"

Mark is surprised into silence. After a moment he laughs lightly. "I'm gonna miss you," he says.

"Mark, I am going to keep working with you," Leap says. "I'm right here. I haven't gone anywhere, and I'm going to keep working with you."

"It's not the same," Mark says.

Leap is tight-lipped. He nods.

"One of my contacts mentioned the flip as a possibility, early on," Mark says. "The potential for complications of any sort was one of the reasons we chose that particular adviser. She took some legal precautions. She did a few things that will help me."

"I'm glad to hear that," says Leap, her voice prickly. "I was beginning to think she was just incompetent."

"It was your choice," Mark says.

"Yes, it was."

The anger rekindles in Mark's eyes as he says slowly, "You're here telling me we're going to work together, as if this is something you can just get through. But you, one of you, flipped. And now you're going to be torn apart, very, very slowly, at a subatomic level. Your body tissues will disintegrate. Your mind will erode. You'll experience unimaginable pain, full-blown insanity, and then the whole join, all of Leap, will die."

"Yes," says Leap, coolly meeting his gaze. "I am almost literally going to melt. Like ice cream."

·◉.

THE POD PASSES SMOOTHLY AND quickly over the greensward, between spires. They've just lifted off from Pearsun's office and are flying back toward Leap's home.

A paid subscription covers the use of the whole, unified fleet of pods. Even at rest, the vehicles are impressive—ovoids whose gyroscopic stabilizers maintain their equilibrium despite minimal contact with the ground. The bottom half of the pod is typically a single color with a smooth metallic finish. The top half is most often transparent, but passengers can use controls inside the cabin to increase opacity on any portion of the dome, turning it a glassy, bluish color. When they're traveling, pods are pure, distilled technical wizardry—from the beauty of the shape in motion to the torturously abstruse theory that explains their flight.

As Chance understands it, a pod moves by creating a rip in space and then allowing space to pull it forward to fill the rip. That apparently requires absolute bilateral symmetry in the distribution of the vehicle's mass. As passengers move in the top half, a "shadow mass"—managed by a mass calculator that manipulates a spongy gelatin, compressed air, and force generators—compensates with shifts beneath, keeping the vehicle balanced. The bilateral symmetry also enables the vehicle's energy translators. No one has figured out how to scale the flying cars up beyond a device capable of carrying a few hundred kilograms.

Leap One gazes out of the transparent upper dome, idly running his hand over the stubble that's emerging on his recently shaved pate. Chance Two, settled into her sofa seat, watches the faint cirrostratus above them, unmoving as they float along beneath.

"You need to find Rope," Leap says at last.

Chance has been trying not to think about her own situation, focusing instead on what's happening with Leap. Chance's drives have woken in a cold sweat five or six times in the last week, and Chance has been fantasizing about bringing all the drives to the Olympic Archipelago to hide out in Leap's house, behind Leap's surveillance. She's surprised to hear Leap ask about the nightmare they would be living in if they weren't living in Leap's nightmare.

Chance says, "I think we should leave that to the Directorate."

"Maybe. But you said yourself that he has a way to elude them."

"After everything that's been happening," Chance says, "I don't think we should go looking for more trouble. I just scattered the ashes of my Three. We did the ritual for you. I want to get back to normal life."

"Chance, I know you don't believe this. But just hear me out. Please. The network—the quantum network—has properties, usable, important properties that Vitalcorp doesn't make public."

"No, not that again, Leap. Not here. Not now."

"Please, Chance. Consider it."

Chance closes her eyes. She sees a faint red afterimage of the bright sky above.

"Chance, I'm going to die."

They pass several minutes in silence.

"I know you've met a couple of the first five hundred," Leap says. "You've read papers by them, about them. Did any of that prepare you for Rope? You said Rope is one of them and that he knew Music. Rope is different. What if he knows something that could help me?"

They're approaching the steep, wooded shore of a small island. In a neat clearing, set back a hundred yards from the water, are the blue-and-slate-gray angles of Leap's home.

"It's a fantasy," Chance says. "Rope is a sick fuck who's incredibly dangerous. He doesn't know anything that can help you. There is no way to treat what you have. Finding Rope will just get me killed along with you."

Chance can hear that last sentence tailing away in the still air of the pod, along with its implications: *You're going to die. I am not going to die. I won't help you.*

⁕

DIRECTORATE STAFF EVENTUALLY GET IN touch again through the office where Chance One works. They want Chance to come in and answer some questions, but they don't seem to be in a hurry. A join named Interest, who identifies himself as Chance's contact at the Directorate, collects a statement by video. After that, he becomes very difficult to reach. He sends Chance a list of requests that need immediate attention but lets several days go by without answering clarifying questions. When Interest finally does respond to Chance, he says the investigation is proceeding, but there are legal issues. Chance asks what they are, and Interest says he can't go into them.

Frustrated, Chance demands to know what's being done

about Rope. Interest sympathizes, but he can't offer anything further at this time. Chance insists—Chance's drive was killed, and the Directorate doesn't seem to be taking the situation seriously. Interest understands that Chance is concerned and will see what he can do.

Chance wants to follow the news, which makes the self-imposed, protective isolation from the net difficult to maintain. Several people—colleagues and friends—have made an effort to reach out. Chance finally augments the auditing of personal activity, creating a more complete record of all online contacts in case Rope makes an appearance. Then Chance One logs in to Civ Net and gives up trying to hide. Maybe Leap is right and Rope is busy trying to survive.

Chance connects with people who worked on research projects with Chance Three, hoping one of them can help get information from the Directorate. They listen. A few try to help, but nothing comes of it.

Days later, Interest finally suggests a date for a follow-on interview. It's in three more weeks. The Directorate doesn't think it needs additional information until almost a month and a half after the killing.

* * *

LEAP FOUR AND LEAP TWO are running over a woodland trail, a six-mile loop. The air is crisp, with a very mild savor of coastal spray. The Doug firs are widely spaced, the underbrush thinner than in the ungroomed native rain forest. An occasional sun-lamp hovers above, brightening a limpid, mellow gloom.

Leap loves running through the forest, and today it's better than on any other day Leap can remember. Her bodies' arms are pumping, right arms forward together and left arms forward together. With Leap Four, who is a bit shorter, but healthy and young, Leap stretches her stride. With Leap Two, whose extraordinary proprioception makes her balance effortless, Leap runs at a relaxed pace. Their feet touch the uneven duff at the same moment and lift away together.

Leap fills her lungs, her two drives breathing deeply in near synchrony, and fills her awareness with details—the smell of moss, the seemingly crafted perfection of slices of sunlight falling between the shoulders of the forest giants, the pleasurable impact of landing without worrying about her footing, the freedom from pain as the joints of her two bodies flex and strain. Her physical confidence.

Since joining with Josette, Leap's appreciation of sensual experience has intensified. And the loss of Josette's body, devastating initially, has also been an unbelievable gift. Leap sometimes becomes aware of reveling in simple physical tasks like lifting a basket of clothes or running down a staircase, mundane moments filled with something close to a sense of flying.

But the join has given many of Leap's intimate memories an almost frightening quality. Memories as simple as Josette enjoying the touch of her own hand on her waist can waver with a queasy uncertainty, or Ian intently searching his damp teenage face in the mirror for blackheads.

And surrounding everything is a creeping fatigue, a pain whose borders advance day by day, so that even as the movement of drives takes on a shine of fresh interest and wonder, Leap aches with the trickling return of decay.

THE AIRLINER'S CABIN IS QUIET, the passengers either sleeping or immersed in stories, their fingers, wrists, and mouths twitching to control the interfaces on private systems. Leap Four is finding sleep elusive under a thin wool airline blanket. She shifts position and then is still again, her mouth slightly open. Leap has continued to dye her hair red, even now, when it's stubbly and only beginning to recover from being shaved for the Ritual of Retirement.

With her blond hair tied in a low ponytail, Chance Two's eyebrows arch as she elaborates energetically on techniques for cycle management that might help Leap with the effects of the flip. Leap One, on the other side of Chance from Leap Four, leans forward, listening carefully, occasionally pulling on his beard.

The practice and central tenets of cycle management were an early attempt to address unforeseen consequences of Join. Initial marketing described Join as an evolutionary step that would help the human race meet intractable challenges, like global warming and interstellar travel. The mind would no longer be limited by a resource design evolved to protect a grasslands animal. But as millions paid licensing fees and created the new race of enhanced beings, it became evident that when left to their own devices joins were happy and unambitious, given to noodling. Art and science blossomed, but in curiously unfocused ways. In the first few years, it seemed that every join was a conceptual artist working on an intimate scale. Many became collectors of whatever type of oddment struck their fancy.

The world thickened with a baroque density of minutely elaborated objects, mathematics and theoretical physics made great strides, but progress on large engineering projects actually slowed. This was bad for Earth's living creatures. Global water levels continued to rise, and the weather convulsed. To keep the developed world on its feet, to keep productivity from cratering when so much of civilization's attention was focused on the confusing opportunities of the new technology, environmental regulations were actually eased.

Joins also helped puzzle out new nanomaterials and a variety of printing processes designed to assemble everything from lattices formed of individual molecules to towering, purpose-built habitats. Heretofore undreamed of miracles were mass-produced and widely released, but a small percentage of those miracles were profoundly toxic. There were three worldwide plagues. New revelations in genetic science bent links in the food chain. The consequences of so much change multiplied, and the world began to witness massive die-offs. In coastal cities, millions of bodies drowned as hurricanes and tsunamis delivered the news of increasing change. Growing swaths of the planet became hostile to life.

Joins made two critical adjustments. First, they realized that they weren't prioritizing their activities well. They could think more clearly than most solos but weren't being good about managing their fascinations. They needed to improve their judgment.

Cycle management, as practiced by joins, is the science and discipline of remaining present. The nearest analog for solos might be stress management. Every drive has cognitive potential beyond what it needs for moment-to-moment operation. When a join is stressed, it can find a drive that isn't at capacity and "borrow cycles." Additional cycles clarify the join's awareness. A clearer awareness means a greater reserve of willpower with which to make and take considered choices. Some degree of cycle management happens naturally, but joins realized that they needed to improve it and developed a formal practice.

Chance has always been good at it. Both Chance Two and Three studied it before they joined.

The second adjustment was more difficult. As stories of drives dying from gross negligence began to pile up, a joke circulated. How do you know if two bodies are joined? Put one in mortal danger. If the other tries to save him, they're not joined.

The second adjustment was born from the realization that, on average, solos simply cared more about survival. Given a long-range plan to clean up the environment, solos would work harder to figure out how to implement it. For the time being at least, until the legacy problems of human evolution could be addressed, a portion of the population would remain solo, to actually do things the joins thought of. Of course, because solos are naturally xenophobic, many of them resented being directed by joins. Tension developed.

·◦·

AN OLDER MAN IN AN aisle seat across from Leap Four leans toward her.

"You're all joined, aren't you?" the man says, meaning her, Chance Two on her left, and Leap One. The three of them fill the row's three center seats. He's about sixty-five, medium build, wearing a dark blue tank top, with a broad, bristly jaw and a walrus mustache. His gray hair shows remnants of an auburn color.

Leap Four, sitting closest to him, says, "Video-ID us."

"Ah, nah, I wouldn't be much if I couldn't tell," says the man. "The three of you are joined. Two women and a man. 'You are not a gendered entity.'" He puts the last sentence in air quotes.

During the trial of one thousand, Hamish Lyons had tried

to popularize the phrase "It is not a gendered entity" as a way to counter the sloppy use of gender pronouns when referring to a join. But people didn't stop using gender pronouns, and the saying lost currency. Now, pronouns are chosen to emphasize the action of a particular drive or to highlight an idea. There's still wide variation in their use, influenced by fashion and regional differences. The old phrase is considered something between cutely and clumsily ironic.

Leap can't quite smile at the man's joke and instead says, "Have you ever guessed wrong?"

To Chance's left, Leap One sits back and closes his eyes. Chance smells sour alcohol from the man whom Leap is talking with.

"Not that I know of," the man says, with a smile that's actually charming.

"Well, I guess your intuition is pretty good," Leap Four says, and turns to face forward, hoping to end the conversation.

"I like your music," the man says.

Surprised, Leap says, "What?" And immediately regrets reengaging the man in conversation.

"You know," he says, "the music that joins make, I like it. I think it's sexy."

Leap Four turns to him again. "You're solo?"

"Like the good Lord made me."

Leap thinks it over, then says, "Sounds like you think we've done something wrong."

"Oh, no, no. Not at all. I'm all for it, Join. But not for me. I don't swing that way, but, you know, whatever floats your boat."

Leap nods and turns to face forward again.

"I think it's kind of sexy," the man says. "The three of you. The one of me."

Leap Four is ignoring him.

"Anyway," the man continues, "I like your music. Your a cappella music. Harmonies are unbelievable. Unbelievable. Yeah. And jazz. Don't get me started. I wanted to play jazz, but nobody listens to jazz from solos anymore. How about that? We invented it. We invented jazz."

Leap Four pointedly closes her eyes, her broad face tense. Chance faces forward as well.

"Even people who want more than one perspective in their music still think having a lot of different joins is better than solos," the man says. "Can you believe that?"

In the face of silence from Leap and Chance, the man's voice softens, becomes reflective. "I am a musical genius," he says. "I think. *I* think I am. Alto sax. I am a damn alto sax musical genius, and I can't get a job."

Leap Four opens her eyes; something that the man has said has gotten to Leap. She turns toward him. "I'm sorry," she says.

After observing her for a moment, he says, "You're a musician, aren't you?"

"Yes."

"I knew it. I just knew it. You three are all joined, and you're probably an all-alto-sax musical trio! Aren't you? Aren't you?"

Leap laughs. "No, no," she says. "That's me," she indicates Leap One on the other side of Chance. Then points to Chance. "She's a friend."

"Ah," says the man. "Two alto saxes and percussion."

Leap laughs again, "No. I play guitar. I was a fanatic for it, in one of my childhoods. With that drive I'm pretty good. With the rest, well, I can plunk around."

"One of your childhoods," the man says. "Huh. That's such a strange phrase, 'one of my childhoods,' you know? I mean,

I only had those years once. I spent them learning alto sax. Because I loved it. It was everything to me, you know?"

"Yes," says Leap.

"No, you don't," says the man. "Nothing has ever meant that much to you. You know, I've thought about moving to a feral community. Really. To fight for solos. But, nah, I'm just too old. I'm not serious enough about things, you know? But I sure do hate what the world has become. And I mean it. Your kind. Everything."

⟡

LEAP TURNS AWAY FROM THE man, stares forward again, and closes her eyes. The drive's pulse was quickened by the bitterness in the man's last few words. With many solos, there are topics that are understandably painful, often around decisions they've made or regrets they have about what might have happened if they had chosen some other path in life.

Leap believes they're often thinking, If I were a join, I could have tried both options. But you can't rerun time, no matter how many drives you have. They don't understand that. Even if they're sensitive and listening closely. And if they do experience insight that's similar to real understanding, it's only temporary. And the truth is, joins do experience choice differently. After a join, each choice is still final, but no choice is as critical. There's a difference; it's just not the difference that solos imagine.

Within that distinction lies a gap that separates joins and solos utterly. Joins have lived on both sides of the gap. For solos who resist joining—because they can't afford it, because they're proud, they're afraid, or they just don't want to—the gap can become a cipher, encoding what they desire, what they've lost, what they want to destroy.

· ◉ ·

APPLE TWO IS TENDING BAR at Whatever You Want with someone Chance doesn't recognize backing him. Leap One—a bit worn, his beard scruffier than usual, his hair darkening the top of his head again—has accompanied Chance One to the bar. Of Chance's drives, Chance One has the most natural charisma. It might help cover for Leap One's intensity.

It's late afternoon, the beginnings of a happy-hour crowd. These are people who worked at the hospital with Chance Three. Some may know Chance One. Chance has set a privacy flag on his status, if anyone bothers to check.

A woman named Relief, in one of the booths in back, catches his eye. Her mouth half opens, and she turns away quickly to say something to her two companions. She starts to rise from her seat. Then she hesitates—she probably viewed his profile. She stops, looks over toward him, and nods her sympathy. He acknowledges her. She smiles sadly and sits back down. So, some people do check profiles before saying hello. He's always liked her.

Chance and Leap have agreed that a search for Rope is likely to be fruitless, but what choice does Leap have? Leap has also mentioned reaching out to some of the better-known names in alternate quantum research for leads on either flips or on Rope. Chance thinks Leap is probably doing that, but Leap hasn't shared any results.

Chance believes that the likelihood of Leap finding a treatment is nil, whether they locate Rope or not. For Chance, this search is about spending time with a friend who is dying.

APPLE GESTURES AT CHANCE TO wait for a moment. At first, Chance is surprised that Apple recognizes Chance One. Then he realizes that after what happened, Apple would have looked up Chance and his drives.

Apple hands off a drink, then moves toward Chance One and Leap One. He peers at them both closely and then turns away and says, "I'm glad you came back." He doesn't look at Chance as he continues, "Look, I thought he—Rope—was all talk. I don't know what else to say. I'm just really sorry."

For a moment, Chance can't respond. The memory of the violent disconnection from Chance Three in this same building blinds him. Each of his drives pauses.

"He wasn't all talk," he says, and anger settles on him.

It's a crueler response than he'd like. Apple had warned him about Rope; Apple certainly isn't to blame. But that reply is the best Chance is capable of at the moment. He realizes two things: that he does blame Apple, though he can't understand why, and that he should have prepared for this conversation, left a couple of drives sleeping so he'd have more cycles available to manage his emotional response. But he didn't. It will be more of a struggle to say things the way he'd like to.

"Yeah," Apple says, then waits for Chance to regain his composure. He asks whether Chance wants a drink.

"No," Chance says. Apple points at Leap One, who also declines.

"Okay," says Apple, and waits to find out why Chance has come.

"I'd like to find him," Chance says.

"You want to find who?"

"Rope," Chance says. "I'd like to find him."

Apple shakes his head slowly. "Doesn't seem like a good idea."

"Maybe not," says Chance.

"He's been picked up," Apple says.

"Reports are that two of his drives are unaccounted for," Chance says. "No one knows where they are."

"Fuck!" Apple says. Then he holds up a hand in the face of surprise at his outburst. "I'm sorry. I'm sorry," he says. "Look, I'm scared he's gonna come back, you know. I told you he threatened me. Threatened to kill my drives. I thought he was just an asshole, but then, when he did that to you—" Apple's face flushes. He looks down at the bar as he keeps talking. Chance has the stray thought that looking away might be a habit Apple picked up while working in bars, to help endure the reckless confidences of strangers.

"I wouldn't want my path, or yours, to cross that guy's again," Apple continues. "Anyway, you were a join doctor. I've heard it's not that hard to find drives and maybe even kill them without getting close. Is that true?"

"It's complicated, but there's a lot of truth to it, yeah," says Chance. "And that's the thing. They can't find his drives. My friend"—Chance indicates Leap—"thinks maybe Rope has found a way to mask his drives."

"Is that possible?" asks Apple. "Do you think it would work?"

"I don't know. I've seen things in the last few weeks . . . maybe I don't know as much about it as I thought."

Apple is still looking away. "Why do you think Rope would know anything unusual?" he asks. "He's just a regular guy."

"That's not what you said before." Chance is a bit taken aback. "You said he was one of the first five hundred. That he knew Music. I think you said he was connected. It sounded like he knew some of the original researchers or people high up at Vitalcorp."

"Maybe," Apple says. "He said a lot of things. I don't know. I mean, he was a big talker."

Leap says, "You look scared."

Apple glances at Leap. "Yeah, I am. I'm—I can't lose a drive."

"Look, I understand," says Chance, surprised that he's suddenly trying to make Apple feel better. "I just have a problem. I need to talk with someone . . . For my friend. If there are things that aren't commonly known about the quantum network. My friend is sick. You know, I helped invent a technique for finding drives. It should work. But Rope might be out there still. At least, according to Civ News. So maybe he knows something. We're grasping at straws."

Leap is watching Apple closely. Chance wishes Leap would sit back and acknowledge that this is a blind alley. But Leap is nowhere close to giving up.

"You've talked with Rope," Chance One says. "He flirted with you. He told you about himself. Can you help me find him?"

"I really don't think so," Apple says. "I told the Directorate what I know. He talked about fooling around with my One. Mentioned a hotel, but he never said which one. I don't even have that. Why do you think you could find him if the Directorate can't?"

"I keep remembering him, watching me," Chance says. "He said something. He said he was playing a game. I was paying an ante."

"A game?"

"Yeah."

"Like, poker?"

"That's what I was thinking of. But I don't know. Was he a gambler? Did he talk about games, or do you have any idea what else that could mean?"

"I really don't know," Apple says. "That guy said a lot of things."

Leap leans forward on the bar, then has one of his seizures. He spasms backward but stays on the barstool as his arms go up and back. He doesn't hit anything, and it's over quickly.

"Ah," he says, a hand to his mouth. "I bit my tongue."

"Is it bleeding?" Chance asks.

"No, I don't think so. Was . . . that one of my . . . things?"

"Yeah," says Chance.

"Shit."

"What was that?" Apple asks, surprised.

"It's a thing I do," Leap says. "I don't know when it's happening."

"Well, can I get you anything? Are you okay?"

"I'm okay. Just need to sit. My tongue hurts."

"You didn't break anything," Apple says.

Leap, clearly not finding the assurance too comforting, says, "I'm going to the restroom."

As he rises and gingerly makes his way through the crowd, Leap looks defeated. They just don't have much of a plan.

When Leap has gone, Apple says, "That looked like a flip."

Interactive vids, soaps, all the morbid narratives of the day go directly to worst-case scenarios. Incurable, deadly, mysterious—even though they're rare enough to make people doubt their reality—flips still make appearances in popular media.

"I don't think he'd like me to talk about it," Chance says.

"You sure you don't want a drink?"

"Yeah, I'm sure."

"Look, I gotta get back to the bar."

"Apple, there's nothing else? You can't think of anything else?"

"No."

"You asked why I think I might find him, even though the Directorate couldn't. I guess I don't think I'll find him if he doesn't want to be found. But I think he might want to find me."

Apple hesitates, considering something. He shakes his head violently as if trying to clear it. Chance says, "Are you okay?"

"Yeah, I'm fine!" Apple snaps back, then says, "Sorry."

Apple moves closer and lowers his voice. "There is something you don't know. I told the Directorate, but they didn't listen. I don't think it will help, but . . . He did come back. In here, with a drive I didn't recognize. After the Directorate had been in and everyone had cleared off. He says, 'Hey, Apple, it's me, Rope.' I couldn't believe it. I thought it was someone, maybe, making a joke. But a credit token popped up in his name, with a picture of the drive. I didn't know why he would come here. I was scared of him. You know—"

"What happened?"

Apple leans in even closer. "Nothing," he says. "He ordered my twenty-one-year-old Hibiki. Absolutely topflight whiskey. Rare. I have one bottle that I bought from another customer. I'd told him about it, I guess. He had three shots, fast. That's just wrong. Shouldn't drink that whiskey fast. Then he left."

"You told the Directorate?"

Apple nods.

"So?"

"Well, I don't know whether they cared," says Apple.

"Then I don't see how that could help," Chance says.

"No, but wait. The thing is, he likes his whiskey. Rope. And I don't mean that in a good way. The guy's a drunk, you know what I mean? A real one, I saw it. I mean, I'm a bartender and even I've never met a join who's a real drunk before. Even if both my drives are drinking, I don't get drunk. But there's a reason he started drinking drives to death, instead of going another way. Something about *him*, must be. What I'm saying is, he's not going to stop."

Common wisdom considers joining a treatment for many addictions. There was a short period in the early days when people with virulent drug addictions joined with other drug addicts in a mistaken belief in a kind of dependency cancellation. But that effort is now considered a disaster and an object lesson in the theory of join variety. Stated without nuance or qualification, the theory of join variety says it's better to join people with unlike characteristics. In his years of practice, Chance never treated a join for alcoholism.

Chance notices that Leap One is standing beside him. He's not sure when Leap returned.

"I told the Directorate," Apple is saying, "but they didn't pay any attention. How could he be an alcoholic? So here's the thing I didn't say to them. If I wanted to find him, I'd look in the bars where the real drinkers are. Solo quarter, the short spires. That's where I'd look for him."

Chance and Leap take in what Apple is saying. They have no other leads. "Thank you," Chance says.

"But if he does have drives left," Apple says, "why would they be in New Denver? They might not even be on this continent."

"Yeah," says Chance. Nonetheless, he and Leap can check out the solo bars in New Denver. It'll keep them busy while they're waiting for Mark Pearsun to work out the licensing problems.

EVEN THOUGH CHANCE FIVE'S PERCEPTIONS are muffled by painkillers, he's available to accompany Leap Four as she explores the short spires. They've both toured the area through interactive documentaries, and each has visited a handful of times.

The two of them land their pod on the rooftop of a seven-story faux-brick building. They find the roof-access staircase, press their palms to the security plate, and, when the electronics of the steel door slide its thick bolts back with a high-pitched hiss, they step into a stairwell lit by only a faltering, pallid LED. The stairwell absorbs sound in a way that drains vitality from the space.

When joins started building spires, they often found new locations where there had been no earlier city. Because access by pod made differences in altitude less important, and the evolving megastorms were devastating large open regions, many spire communities grew in mountainous areas.

Cities began to lobby for spires to help them maintain relevance and energize renewal efforts. New architecture slowly replaced the old, and cities changed from the inside. Solos, who remained more comfortable in earlier styles of architecture or who didn't have the money to move, stayed concentrated in the older parts of cities. The term "short spires" began to be synonymous with neighborhoods inhabited mostly by solos.

New Denver's short spires cluster around the west side of Lake Everwild, a massive artificial reservoir. Even though these short spires are only a couple of decades old, they already have the hard-used look of neglected urban areas, built on a grid to accommodate the automobiles that solos are only now giving up and the big twenty-four-wheeled articulated container trucks that so many solos are employed in piloting across the continent.

The stairwell smells of urine. Its walls are stained by slashes and blossoms of graffiti. The first door they reach is sealed off, boards nailed to the walls. The decay and disarray are otherworldly. Things improve slowly as they descend the stairs. On the ground floor, they enter a small, crowded, indoor shopping area.

On each side of them, tiny, packed storefronts belly up to a long, narrow corridor. A coin shop, colorful trinkets of indeterminate purpose, handcrafted ceramics. A couple of the shops display crosses prominently, their entrances draped with brown cloth in lieu of a door.

Apple named six places they could visit and warned them about each. They pass a small, narrow, and dimly lit pub, the Single Stamen. Chance steps in, but it's deserted. Just past that is the larger bar they're looking for, One Eye. Its long window is covered over with heavy gray paper. A large eye has been clumsily painted on the paper above two small yellow *X*'s.

In his brown slacks and gray artificial silk sweater, Chance Five is dressed like a join. His dark hair is short, with a shallow strip shaved clean from one side of his forehead to the other, a style that never took hold among solos. Leap Four is in worn blue jeans and a light green T-shirt that complements her tan skin. She's dressed more like a solo but still moves and somehow looks like a join.

There are solos who are good at spotting joins. In addition to obvious differences, like a collapse of personal boundaries, there are subtler signs. In some solo parodies, joined drives never let their field of vision overlap. Joins called impersonators make a special effort to pass as solo, but neither Chance nor Leap has ever practiced the art.

One Eye is a dark place with an open floor plan, a pool table, and a few bright pinball machines in a game area that makes up roughly half of the pub's space. In the other half are two booths, a couple of tables, and a bar lined with seven barstools.

As Chance Five and Leap Four enter, they get suspicious looks from the handful of sagging patrons and an open glare from the bartender, a thin, fiftyish solo of medium height. He interrupts his conversation at the bar with a heavier man to call out to them.

"Drinks?"

"A couple of pilsners, please. Something local," answers Chance.

"Middle Finger okay?" asks the bartender. "They make that just down the street."

"Yeah," says Chance. He walks toward a back booth. Leap is using a button camera to take a quick vid of each patron, to index them on Civ Net. Once she has them all, she and Chance will walk through their network profiles as they finish the beers.

Leap's notes pop up on Chance's retinal display with three profiles marked for him to focus on. The bartender brings them drinks.

"We don't get a lot of joins in here," says the bartender in a tone that's only slightly unfriendly.

"We were just visiting an aunt," Leap lies. "We wanted to get some work done."

The bartender grunts. "Joins usually want to work in brighter places."

"This is just fine," says Leap Four, smiling.

Retinal displays can get awkard for in-depth work. Leap and Chance unroll their personal displays, which then light up with the profile information. To discourage unwelcome interest, personal displays can make fine adjustments to their viewing angles, blurring content for people other than their owners. Chance has added the bartender's profile to the five Leap collected. It only takes a few minutes for them both to review all six sheets without finding anything interesting.

They ask the bartender about Rope. Nothing. They leave, dropping by the Single Stamen briefly on their way out. When they get back to the stairs, Leap Four is tired and has a headache that painkillers won't help. She tells Chance Five that it's just the light that was getting to her. She hides a minor tremor in her right arm and hand from him as best she can. They have five more bars on their list, then they might just explore a bit.

IF ROPE IS IN NEW Denver, he could be anywhere in the city. Apple said the bars he listed were guesses. Even if Rope patronized one of them, they have no idea when he'd be there, they don't know what he'd look like, and asking about him might just alert him. They visit four bars the first day and stop by the final two the next.

Then they decide to map out all of the bars in the solo areas and create a time line for regularly visiting them. While they're doing that, Chance gets a vidcall from Apple Two. Apple would like to meet at One Eye that evening. He looks nervous and unhappy.

The workday is over, so Chance decides to go with his One, as well as his Five, to watch Apple from different angles. If Apple is hiding something, Chance wants to know. Chance, uneasy after their other visits to solo neighborhoods, considers bringing Four, as the drive best equipped to handle herself in trouble, but decides the two male drives should be enough. Leap Four goes with them.

The same bartender watches them as they enter. Three of the patrons who were in the bar when they first visited are still rooted to the same locations. Three new people are gathered around the pool table. Two patrons have one of the booths, and Apple Two is sitting in the other, a beer and four full shots of whiskey on the table in front of him.

Apple doesn't greet them as Leap Four and Chance Five sit across from him. Chance One gently touches his shoulder to alert him to the need to make room on his side of the booth. Apple Two says softly, nervously, "This has all gone to shit." Apple's face is reddened. His eyes are bloodshot. His breath is heavy and sour. He's clearly been here for a while.

"What?" asks Chance. "What's happening?"

Apple glances up at Chance One. "You don't have to read through me. I'm not going to lie to you," he says. "Just the opposite. You didn't have to bring two."

"What's happening?" Chance One says again.

Apple downs one shot, then shifts over to make room for Chance One. Apple pulls the other three shots and his beer down the table, one hand protectively cupping the beer mug. "They're gonna find me," he says morosely.

"Who is?" asks Chance.

"The Directorate. You don't know the half of it."

Chance is watching him closely with both of his drives. He quickly realizes that there's no reason to. It's not just the drive, Apple Two, who is drunk. Apple is drunk.

Chance remembers Apple Two saying that he could drink without getting drunk. He seems to be proving himself wrong about that, and he's obviously not thinking clearly. A pall of misery hovers around the drive. He's not able to take his eyes off the drinks in front of him.

"I thought you would enjoy it," Apple says. "I've been doing it for years. People who come and talk with me, they want it."

"What are you talking about?" Chance says, annoyed at what sounds like rambling.

Apple scoffs at the three of them, then looks back at his drink. "I thought it would just be a temporary problem. But they're cleaning me up. Reason isn't talking to me anymore. He's blocked the encrypted line."

Apple eyes one of his shots. He picks it up and tosses it back, turns the glass upside down and sets it on the table. He smiles sadly at Leap and Chance.

"Chance," Leap says calmly, "it's him. This is Rope."

The drive they'd thought was Apple says, "Yeah, it's me. Still giving your life meaning."

Chance's sight blurs. It's as though he sat down next to a scorpion. Both of Chance's drives flinch away from the drunk in the booth. Rope regards Chance One, who is closest to him.

"This one's okay," he says. "The data modeler. And that's the sick one, isn't it? The one with cancer, that's gonna die?"

"Yes," says Leap.

Rope's face has gotten redder; his eyes more bloodshot. He nods toward Leap Four. "And you've flipped," he says.

"Yes," she replies.

"Ahhh, this is all such a joke," Rope says, shaking his head at the drinks on the table. "It just makes no difference at all."

He turns to Leap. "I am Rope. I am Apple. Apple is a fiction. You guessed it. You're a smart cookie. Apple doesn't exist, except as a hiding place for two of my drives. My emergency escape route, if you will. But in fact, this"—he motions at his body—"is my eight-hundred-twenty-eighth drive. I think. I've probably lost count." He motions vaguely with one hand. "Things . . . shift."

Leap is stunned. "Eight hundred . . . How?"

"Just by doing it. By joining. Though that makes it sound easy, and it's been a lot of work. I've joined with a lot of small joins, threes, fives, sevens, you know. That's helped."

Chance finally regains his voice. Bile is burning in the throat of his One as he says, "Why did you kill my drive?"

Rope looks slightly sideways at Chance One, as if he's been reminded of something annoying. "You got over it," he says. "I knew you would. Back in the bar I warned you, but then you came over to talk to me. I know what kind of person you are. If things had gone according to plan, this would be a very different kind of conversation."

Leap says, "I don't believe it. What about the risk of running more than twenty drives?"

"Yes," Rope says. "I've only ever run more than twenty drives for a very brief time. I always keep the number of drives down."

Leap's eyes are wide. She says slowly, "Then, you've killed—"

"Yes, I have. No one else would."

As Chance and Leap sit, stunned into silence, Rope adds, "And we had to know what it means."

Chance One says, "I don't understand."

Rope looks at Chance Five, who is watching him in horror. "Would either of you like a drink? No? Well."

He hoists his beer, nods at Chance One and at Leap Four, then drains the glass. It takes him several gulps to do it. When he's done, Rope studies the empty mug. He sets it down carefully and pushes it toward the end of the table. He wipes his lower lip with the back of his hand, takes a deep breath, and widens his eyes briefly. "Now we'll see how long I can do without another."

Leap says, "You're looking for the vanishing point?"

Rope laughs, lifts an empty shot glass off the table, and watches it as he turns it in a circle. "The vanishing point. Stupid. That was my original goal. I was working to answer the question, at what point is joining just the same as dying? The answer? I don't know. I think I've passed the vanishing point. I think that these days, when I join, the part of me that comes from the new join essentially disappears, but I just don't really fucking know. I mean, I think I'm still here, all of my selves. But I don't know. If I were to join with you, I don't think it would change me much. You would just become me, though you would still think you were you. That's what I think, but it's hard for me to know. I'm inside the picture so I can't"—he sets down the shot and then moves both his hands in circles as if against an invisible wall—"see the whole picture."

He turns back to Chance Five. "What I told you before is true, but it leaves a little out. Way back when, I was two of the original team, a psychologist and the only philosopher. We, the two of us, never believed in the immortality that everyone else was squawking about. We're all gonna live forever, blah, blah, blah. I mean, people have always imagined immortality, but the world, the real world, never worked that way. So, physically, something like it is clearly possible, as long as the Earth survives. But we didn't think a personality could persist through endless joins." He smiles. "Personality. Who cares? No one really bothered to disagree with us. They just didn't think it was an interesting question."

Chance Five says, "Perspective coheres through time."

Rope turns a look of utter disdain on him. "So what? What does that mean? Your perspective coheres through time. Softheaded commercial-marketing crap. So you remember yesterday, and the day before. And then you're part of me, and you experience today. And to you, it seems like it's all the same, except now you remember eight hundred childhoods, and you like things you didn't like and dislike things you used to like. And to you it all just feels like you've grown, you're different. And then you see all of the days as they arrive out of the future and you remember each one as it passes, each one"—he snorts out a sudden laugh—"to the last syllable of recorded time. But who are you? The things that you did, the things you believed, the people you loved? You"—and Rope leans over the table to drunkenly poke Chance Five in the chest—"are one tiny perspective among my more than eight hundred. That 'perspective coheres' crap just means you don't notice that you're already dead."

"That's been said," Chance One says coldly, "mostly by solos, who haven't experienced join and don't know what they're talking about."

"But that's where I'm different, isn't it? Aren't I different?" Rope takes a moment to carefully steady himself. He says, "I'm going to be serious now." He downs the third of his shots. His face becomes still. In a moment he appears temperate, tranquil.

"You see," he continues, "I am, literally, over eight hundred dead people. And I know they're all dead. Despite the fact that none of them experienced death, I know it beyond a shadow of doubt. Despite the fact that each of them is me, and I am alive. Despite their experience of living through me."

"I don't know what you are," says Chance Five. "There are no real records of who you are on the network. We could just be speaking to a three, or to a developing meme virus."

"Of course," Rope agrees. "You could be. But you know you're not, don't you. I know more about life than any living thing before me ever has known." Rope puts a finger to his temple and presses, hard. His voice has risen, and he spits as he speaks. "I remember living over eight hundred lives. I know everything worth knowing. And that makes me, what?"—with a flourish that the table prevents from becoming a drunken bow or a forward tumble—"A gateway to the underworld."

"Why?" Chance Five says. "Why are you doing it?"

At the question, Rope stretches his neck and makes a visible effort to relax again. "I might be insane. I might be. I started just trying to find the vanishing point. For every one of who I am, the vanishing point was an important question. I watched what people did online and found people who had the same questions, the same needs, as I have. I would join, then kill drives, then join. Everyone I join with knows what I'm doing and agrees to do it. The network requires agreement. And we join, and I kill a drive. And so we become an experiment."

"I don't see how you ran an experiment at all," Chance Five says. "Your perspective should shift with each join. You add the new life experiences, you add the new ideas. How could you maintain a plan through hundreds of joins? This just isn't believable. You either used a fixative, or you've got some kind of virus."

"Either way," Leap says, "you're not whatever it is you say you are. You're something else. You're a bogeyman, someone who just enjoys killing bodies."

As Leap says this, it suddenly strikes Chance as unlikely that Rope would have come to meet them with only a single drive. He quickly gets Chance One out of the booth and looks around the bar. But none of the other patrons is paying attention to them.

The bartender has seen him jump up and is clearly annoyed. Chance ignores the unspoken question of whether they want a round.

Rope, watching Chance One, says, "Don't worry, I really only have this drive left. And one more that's down. You know her.

The waitress. I'm borrowing cycles from her. So this is it. This is all I have. If I *had* other drives, you'd be in trouble. I've killed a few others, like yours. I might be starting to like it. But the Directorate took my supplies, my things." Rope's eyes widen with a parody of scary intensity that actually is scary. "They found me in my *lab-o-ra-tory*," he says. "They're not interested in my experiment anymore."

"Why now?" asks Chance Five. "Why not before?"

"They don't tell me. Changes to the network? I don't know."

He drinks the fourth shot, then turns to Leap. "As to what you said before, I don't have a virus. I'm not using a fixative. I autopsy drives, or did. No prions. I'm careful because the work is important, the search for a join's natural life span. If a join lives thousands of years, tens of thousands, it's the sum of many, many people. As I am. I'm a simulation, as close as science can come to immortality, but without the wait. And I found the vanishing point, or maybe it found me. But I don't know where it is, or what it means."

"You're saying that you're what we're heading for?" Leap asks.

"Yes. That is what I'm saying." He glances at Chance Five and Chance One, then looks back at his empty shot glasses and continues, "At first, ferals joined me because they understood. They believe join is murder. Wanted to prove it. For a while, they were enough. But everyone I am shares one particular thing. A two-sided coin, hope on one side, hate on the other. Hope for a better world. Hatred for this one. That is what I am now. It's all that's left. So I have become a drunk."

Leap asks, "How did killing Chance's drive help the experiment?"

Rope is becoming even more bleary eyed. He speaks slowly

and carefully. "Look, nothing personal. I killed you because you wanted me to. And because it's what I do. Maybe. Or no, I killed you because killing is . . . killing is a funny thing. It has meaning. It's real change."

Chance Five shouts, "Killing my drive didn't change anything!"

"Well, it changed my legal standing, for one thing. You'd think we'd have sorted that out by now."

The last few words are nearly inaudible, spoken through a yawn. Rope looks very tired, and his head is slumping toward the table. Leap Four rises quickly off the bench, leans across the table, puts a hand on both of Rope's shoulders, and pushes him savagely up against the back of the booth.

"You know I've flipped," she says. "Can anything be done?"

"Hey, hey!" shouts the bartender.

Rope regards Leap, blinks, but it's clear that he's still fading. Leap slaps him, hard, snapping his head to the right.

"What do you know?" she demands. Rope doesn't respond. Leap grabs the back of his head, gripping what she can of his hair, and shakes him.

"Hey!" yells the bartender.

"What do you know?" Leap shouts again, and now she's just hitting him, his shoulders, face, and head, leaning as far as she can across the table. At first, her blows slide off, then, just as Rope appears to be shaking himself awake, she lands a bruising punch to his chin and one to his cheek. Chance Five throws himself against her, knocking her into the back of the booth.

Chance One turns toward the open room just as the bartender is coming around the bar with a sawed-off shotgun.

Leap has managed to knee Chance Five, knocking him far enough back to give her another shot at Rope. She's stretching across the table when the bartender, who has reached the end of their booth, starts yelling.

"Get out! All of you! I don't need fights. I don't need your kind."

He racks a round in the shotgun, and the room becomes very still.

Rope has been slowly lifting himself in the booth. His head lolls, and then he raises it up. He smiles.

"Flipped," he says.

"Get out!" snarls the bartender.

"I do know someone," says Rope, slurring, barely audible, "to meet you. Ask Hamish Lyons. He's with . . . ferals . . . in Arcadia."

His eyes close. Leap Four stretches across the table and shakes him, but he doesn't respond. Leap lowers him slowly to lie on the table.

"Get out and take that trash with you!" growls the bartender. The three of them slowly slide out of the booth. The bartender steps back and watches as they start toward the exit.

Rope shudders and sits up. "I'm gonna stay," he says. "Need a drink."

Leap asks loudly, "Where is Arcadia?"

Rope can't remain upright. He begins to slump toward the back of the booth.

"Don' know," he says, "but I tell 'em yer comin'." His eyes close again.

⋅●⋅

TEAM TEENAGER IS BACK ON the planes of Uyuni: Chance One—Ashton. Chance Two—Renee. Chance Three—Jake. Chance Four—Shami-8. And Chance Five—Javier. Which, Chance realizes, means all of the drives must be asleep. Chance tries to ignore that, tries to avoid waking up by focusing too much on the fact of the dream.

"Hamish Lyons was joined with Music." Jake, Chance Three, is speaking.

They're standing shoulder to shoulder in a circle, their backs to one another, facing the endlessly receding white salt plains. Each of them throws a long, distinct shadow that extends outward, as if the sun were in the center of their circle. But there is no heat from behind them. Their bodies are cool.

Jake's voice is felt as much as heard. It is audible like the sound of wind hissing across the plain. Then with each syllable, his voice takes a firmer shape, until at last it detaches from the sounds of the wind and becomes more fully the sound of breath shaping words.

"There's no record of him among ferals."

"Before he joined Music, what did he do?" Shami's voice is sweet and comforting, high and strong. The five of them are clothed in loose denim and fleece. There is no concern about misunderstanding, no worry about perception, no work to say things well. They can each feel the bodies of two others touching the sides of their own, and the whole shifts gently as each of them breathes.

"He's the neurophysicist whose work is most closely identified with the quantum network," Jake answers. His words sound like an article Chance once read, but Chance's mouth is speaking them. "He created experiments to demonstrate the effect of consciousness on the physical world. He was twenty-nine when he joined Music."

"Should we tell Leap?" It's Renee who asks, her curly hair shifting slightly in the breeze.

"Tell Leap what?" asks Javier.

"That he can't help her," says Ashton thoughtfully, considering the most likely shape of events. "That Hamish Lyons is gone. That whatever he was disappeared a long time ago into the meme virus that claimed Music. That I don't think our conversation with Rope provided anything useful."

"Why say that?" insists Javier. "How do we know that?"

At the far edges of Uyuni, miles across the salt plain, in a distant gray dimness, each of them sees very slight movement. They each notice it at the same moment and strain to see it better. Javier realizes that he really should be seeing mountains rising up at that distance, at least in that direction, but the mountains aren't there. Instead there is a shifting, as if a storm were shuffling dark clouds very slowly toward and then away from a vanishing point on the horizon. With a chill they each have the same realization at the same moment: that movement is of bodies pressed together, people perhaps, so distant that they are indistinguishable from one another and indistinguishable from the weather that is moving them.

The five teenagers know that the faraway bodies are both familiar and alien. They are sure that they understand what the people who move those bodies long for, what they want, what the people see, and how they decide, why they shift so slowly on the far horizon. But they also know that the distant cloud of bodies is not them, is different from them, and that the clouds of people on the horizon are moved not by weather but by hunger, an essential hunger that each of the five of them standing in the circle shares.

Shami says, "It's getting cold." And her voice sounds distant.

"Rope knows more than we do," says Javier. "We think Hamish Lyons was part of Music, but how can that be if he's living with ferals now?"

"Arcadia isn't a real place." Ashton speaking.

A cold breeze carrying the strong, sharp taste of salt brushes over each of them, blowing in from every direction.

"Why did we leave Rope?" asks Renee.

"He was in pain. He couldn't help us." Shami.

"The bartender forced us out." Ashton, remembering a sting of fear as the bartender pumped the shotgun.

"Hamish Lyons knows more about the network than anyone else alive." Jake.

"We should find him." Javier.

Their shadows are fading on the white plains. The gray shifting clouds in the distance are closer and the distance is smaller. In the whistle of the high wind on the plain they begin to hear voices.

"Rope can't help us," says Ashton forcefully. "He's gone. He's mad."

Now they hear snatches of voices, each asking a piece of a question, and the questions themselves are indecipherable, the questions are the sound of the wind and the scraping of wind-borne salt crystals against the flat plain.

"We have to help Leap," says Shami.

"I practiced for years. There is an enormous amount of research. There's nothing to be done." Jake's voice is restrained, sad.

ALL OF CHANCE'S DRIVES AWAKEN at the same moment. The world floods in through four sets of senses. Chance One, Two, and Five are lying across one another in a tangle of limbs that includes Leap Four. Chance is aware of many pulses beating, the warmth off the skin of limbs, chests, and stomachs, the shifting and sounds of many bodies breathing. It takes a few moments to sort through which of them doesn't belong to Chance; which belongs to Leap.

Chance's drives are each experiencing a pulse of adrenaline as the dream, which felt preternaturally real and sharp, recedes from experience into softer memory. Chance carefully stretches and flexes limbs, moving out from under and moving off of Leap, trying not to wake her while finding spots on drives that have gone numb—feet, hands, and arms—and working them slowly to reduce the tingling. Return them to normal feeling.

.●.

CHANCE FOUR SITS UPRIGHT ON the couch in the living room where she'd fallen asleep. It's still dark out, and the room smells of soft leather. She stands slowly and stretches. She arrives in the kitchen at the same time as Leap One.

Chance One and Five roll out of bed, and they and Leap Four form a line for the bathroom.

In the kitchen, Chance Four says, "I didn't want to wake you up." From the way she rocks slightly forward as she walks, to the constant movement of her hair, Chance Four always conveys the impression of being about to do something.

"My Four's going back to sleep," Leap One says. "She's beat."

"Ah, I'm so sorry about that," says Chance Four. "I didn't mean to tackle her that hard. Is anything hurt?"

"No. And I was out of control, so you had to. Good thing your Five knows enough karate to stop me. Guess I'm lucky he doesn't know more."

"This drive would have restrained you more effectively," says Chance Four.

"Without beating me up?"

"I can't guarantee you wouldn't have been hurt." Chance smiles.

"I'm gonna join with a professional wrestler," says Leap.

"So," Chance says, "have you been able to hide the flip?"

"Up until yesterday, yes. But that was bad, what happened while we were shopping. Autonomy marked the video for review. I'm surprised it took this long. I thought Autonomy was stricter. Made me wonder how much we might have gotten away with."

"Who were you flying with?"

"Regal. I don't think he even noticed."

Chance Four laughs.

"He's such a piece of work," says Leap One. "He invited me for a mixer and suggested I not bring One or Four. He said, 'It would work against the aesthetic vision.' I thought, God, if I could have just shown up with my Five."

Leap and Chance share a further laugh. Then Leap suddenly stops. At first he holds his breath, then he exhales cautiously, his eyes closing in pain as he leans back against a counter. After a moment, he breathes in slowly. He opens his eyes and says, "I can actually feel it now, all the time. Before, I didn't notice the spasms. I just felt a pain if my hand banged against something. The last couple, though, I've experienced them. It's like having razors in my mind, separating me. Like being cut by numbness. The worst thing is, it almost feels like the same thing I had as Josette."

"Leap, I don't know if this lead, this Hamish Lyons thing, is going to work out."

"Yeah, I know. He was part of Music, right? So, he's gone."

Chance Five has entered the kitchen and is getting orange juice. He sets a glass on the counter in front of Leap One and one near Chance Four.

"How is your treatment going?" Leap One says, directing the question to Chance Five.

"As expected, I guess," says Chance Five. "Not good."

Chance Five drains his juice and shuffles slowly out, Leap One watching him go.

"I'm sorry about that," says Leap One.

"I just had a nightmare inspired by that talk with Rope," says Chance Four.

They had returned to the house in a state of shock, eaten dinner with minimal conversation, sat about the house for an hour or so, and then all went to bed. Chance was surprised but pleased when Leap Four decided to spend the night with Chance's three drives. While leafing through Civ News reports, Chance Four fell asleep on the couch.

"I'm going to turn him in," Chance Four says. "Turn Apple in."

"That's probably the right thing to do," Leap says, "and I know it might be dangerous not to. But he said himself, he would have hurt us if he could have. He doesn't have the resources anymore, to hurt people. Can we wait, just a day or two? What if he does . . . help?"

Chance Four drinks a bit of the orange juice. She says, "I don't understand how he's doing it. If he's telling the truth, about the eight hundred, then he's got to be cycle starved—"

"To maintain awareness with only two drives, after that many joins." Leap finishes the thought.

"He's a miracle and a horror," Chance says.

"Yeah," Leap One says, "like we are."

"What do you mean?" Chance asks. Leap doesn't answer.

"Isn't Arcadia meant to be a kind of ideal place?" Chance says. "Where everything's simple and good? That sounds like the right place to find a cure."

"That sounds like a place that doesn't exist."

.•.

LEAP'S HOUSE IN THE OLYMPIC Archipelago is quiet. It's late afternoon, but Leap Three has just finished a shift at the ER and is sleeping. Most of his long body is underneath light covers, but one leg is kicked out to cool. While gathering her coat from the coatrack by the door, Leap Two pauses to gaze out of the living room's big picture window.

In this house, Leap remembers raising Ian and also remembers being raised by Josette. The memories from both sides of the relationship braid together into a single time line, filled with inconsistencies, doubt, bright moments, conflicting emotions. Sometimes Leap can untangle the different points of view and examine events fully, learning how each perspective saw things differently or how they agreed about what was happening. Sometimes the perspectives blur and can't be teased apart. Secrets and intimacies are threaded like bright baubles through the dark places. The secrets can inspire revulsion, fascination, dread; but over time they dull. As they're examined, their volatility fades.

From Ian's perspective, this big picture window has the solidity and permanence of landscape, a reliable thing that never changed its basic character—its height and width, its dusty transparency, the thick molding of the casement that holds the frame in place. The house and window were constants in a childhood shaken endlessly by the temblors of family strife.

In other memories, the window is a thing Josette planned and then had built. A thing painted four times over the years; twice, this same periwinkle blue. And then there are the incidental memories of it, contributed by Leap Three and Leap Four. In the union of those perceptions is yet another experience. As Leap Two gathers her scarf, each perspective fades and shifts into the others. Each is fully realized, independent, and also a part of a comprehending whole.

When choosing action in the face of conflicting desires, the push of desires informs a center, and the center chooses. Leap has become stronger after the join with Josette. The clarity of Josette's thought has buttressed Leap's courage, allowed Leap to handle and examine possibilities once perceived as limits. Choices that at one time might have remained unimagined are now within reach. The conversation with Rope left Leap asking herself—is there anything she can do, on her own, to treat the flip?

Josette and Mark Pearsun had talked about joining. Mark loved her mind. She was flattered but found the prospect of shaving the edges from even one of her sharply held beliefs, of subduing any bit of her individuality, distasteful.

Still, Mark had an uncanny knack for winning, and he worked on her in a simple, effective way that had her wondering whether staying in the world for a few more centuries might not be the more interesting of her options. Then, one late December evening, during the period when she was formulating an agreeable response to him, he called her. He was miserable, lonely. He sounded like a stranger, a shadow of himself. He refused to open video.

"There's no place for me anymore." He started off sounding whiny and just got worse. "Joins are smart. There's nothing I can do. Nothing I can do. It's as if they see me coming. They've gotten so much better at it. They're designing themselves now to include different kinds of personalities."

Josette tried to interrupt. "Mark, this is word soup. I don't understand. Start at the beginning."

Undeterred, he talked over her. "And it's like they can antici-pate all of my moves. I can't do what I used to be able to do. They understand me. Pieces of themselves, one from here, one from there, they put them together to figure out what I'm thinking. And the real-time communication. It's complete. It's uncanny. I can be talking with a join in New Denver, and one of his drives in Detroit will be trading on what I'm saying, *as I'm saying it*. And I don't know it. It's not like a *conference call*. It's not a *transfer of information*. It's really what they say, shared under-standing. At first I thought there'd be a critical flaw. I just didn't believe it. But it's been so many years. And the things I've done.

"Josette, it's real. I can't fight it. I'm going to end up beaten. And it's unfair. They're better than I am. I'm good, but I'm losing. In the last few years, it's gotten worse. I think, really, it's like I'm a scrub in this world. That I almost don't even count. Before Join, I would have been a rainmaker until I retired. I would have been the best. A kingmaker. Today, I'm . . . I'm an endangered species, a dead end."

Josette was repulsed. This was about him. "Are you telling me you want to return my retainer?"

There was a long silence. When he finally spoke they both knew that a join was no longer a possibility. "No, Josette. I'm not."

"Good, Mark. Then we don't have anything else to talk about tonight."

Now Leap Two is wrapping a belt around her long, green tweed overcoat. Beneath the coat, under her left shoulder, is the comfort of the handgun that she has strapped against her ribs. When the pod arrives, she directs it to Mark Pearsun's office.

.●.

CHANCE AND LEAP FIND THAT Apple has disappeared. Of course, Civ Net has records of many joins named Apple, but none is the Apple they know. The bar where both of Apple's drives worked is closed. Building management won't acknowledge that it knows who he is.

Of Hamish Lyons, however, there are plentiful records. None of them appears to be useful. Endless hagiographies, reminiscences, explorations of the irony of his death as one of the first casualties of the new world that was made possible by his discoveries.

So Leap and Chance focus their effort on finding the place Rope mentioned—Arcadia. The name is from a region in Greece, but it's also used in Northern California and in other places. They search Civ Net and the areas of the darknet they are able to access. They discover no connection between a place named Arcadia and a feral community.

Which leads them to feral communities. Most trace their beginnings to a specific belief or concern that they felt was either ignored by civilization or was incompatible with Join. Many have religious roots. The response to Join from organized religions was fragmented and provoked several highly publicized schisms. There were Christians who felt joins were predicted by biblical passages or holy mysteries such as the Trinity; but others saw them as the work of the devil or an attempt to usurp the prerogatives of the Almighty or simply as unethical. Alternatively, some Hindus associated the technology with avatars of divinity. Some believed this was a good thing; some believed it was bad.

Most of the swiftly marshaled decisions about the meaning of Join left no room for revision. Forty years after the trial of one thousand, several groups of objectors have left the embrace of civilization and formed their own feral communities.

Feral communities are generally governed and inhabited only by solos. Some are violently opposed to Join; some are more tolerant. While their size and technological levels vary, they are typically isolated and poor. Most joins see them as eking out a near-subsistence existence without the hallmarks of modern life, such as pods, spires, and Civ Net. As long as they don't become too big or act out their hostility, civilization more or less lets them be.

But there is no scent of information that leads Chance and Leap toward any particular feral group. They all seem equally unlikely to be sheltering a founding developer of the very technology that defines their opposition to modern culture, assuming he still lives.

Chance suggests recruiting Mark Pearsun to help. Leap is evasive but clearly doesn't want to. Then Civ News reports on Pearsun's apparent suicide, by carbon monoxide poisoning. The death had gone undetected, the body sealed in Pearsun's garage for a few days. Leap says something like "I guess that settles it," with a tone of voice that doesn't invite further inquiry.

TWO WEEKS AFTER THEIR MEETING with Rope, as Leap's

health continues to deteriorate, Chance and Leap admit to each other that they're not going to find Arcadia. At which point they receive a recorded audio greeting. When the message arrives, it announces itself through a very slight pulse on their retinal displays. They open and examine it at about the same moment. It's addressed to both of them.

They play it over their cochlear implants, so each of them is playing it privately. At first, it's difficult to hear the words being spoken through distortion and static; but it becomes easier after a few listens, and after they've found the thread of the voice, which is male.

"Hello. This is Shimah Snoyl. I understand you're looking for me. You'll have one opportunity to find me. To the join that's ill, bring all of your drives. You won't need to bring food, changes of clothes, or anything else. Your affairs should be okay without your attention for at least three weeks. Be ready in three days. Don't discuss this message over the net, or we will never meet."

Chance One and Four and Leap One are sitting in Leap's kitchen. Chance One closes the audio message, which immediately disappears. "Don't close it!" he says, and Leap One hesitates.

"Why not?"

"Mine is gone. I think it self-destructed."

"Ah," says Leap One, "mine just disappeared too."

Chance Four is finishing lunch. All three drives are silent as Chance One and Leap One open personal displays and begin to search their histories. The Civilization Network service automatically archives messages. Things don't get lost. But the audio file is not there.

Chance Four says, "Where is it?"

"I don't know. I had it."

They keep looking. After a few moments, Leap says, "It was real. I saw that you had it too. We both heard it. Was it real?"

"Yes," says Chance One.

"Then it should be here, shouldn't it? If it was real, it should be here." Leap One stops looking and turns to Chance One. "What did you hear, verbatim?"

Chance One recites the message.

"That's exactly what I heard," Leap says.

"We both heard it," says Chance.

"So it's real."

"But . . . ," Chance One says, "but I don't have the message. It's not in my history."

"You must have destroyed it," says Leap.

"I didn't, but I checked the routing path too, and it appears to be gone from the servers."

"You did a full delete, accidentally, maybe?"

"No, I didn't. I don't even think that's possible. Do you have it?"

"No."

"Did you do a full delete?"

"No."

They look at each other in disbelief. Leap One says, "It's as if the table disappeared."

"This is all fucking crazy."

"It can't really be that simple to bypass the audio filters," says Leap. "Just lowering the resolution of the recording, adding in some garble, and saying your name backward?"

"Oh," Chance One says slowly, "yeah, Shimah Snoyl, Hamish Lyons. And the name Hamish Lyons is probably a flag for net sensors. No, I don't think it's that simple. I bet that audio distortion wasn't random at all. A lot of work went into that message."

"How would he know we're looking for him?" Leap asks.

"Our research?"

"Okay," says Leap, unconvinced.

"Or Rope told him."

"Maybe," says Leap, "in which case, how do we know this message was from Hamish Lyons?"

"We don't."

After a few moments, Chance says, "He can't authenticate it because use of his authentication would trip the net sensors."

"I'm supposed to pack up my drives without any assurances?"

"Who else would it be?"

"Rope."

"Yeah, it could be Rope."

Leap One throws up his hands and says, "Okay. Can you put my Two and my Three up here for a day?"

"Yes," Chance says.

Chance One and Four are both watching Leap One. Chance One says, "We never really talked about Mark Pearsun's suicide."

Leap One looks at Chance One, on his right, then across the table at Chance Four. Leap's jaw clenches. Then he relaxes and says, "I think it's terrible. I don't want to talk about it."

Chance realizes with surprise that Leap is hiding something.

THREE DAYS LATER, AT 4:30 P.M., Leap One, Two, Three, and Four and Chance Four are waiting in Chance's spire apartment. Chance receives a delivery notice. They've been there all day.

They have agreed that Chance Four will try to accompany Leap but that Chance's other drives should be elsewhere. For protection, Chance has spread them out, putting distance between them. Chance Five is at a hotel, Chance One has gone to Leap's house in the Olympic Archipelago, and Chance Two is now en route to Barcelona.

They've been keeping the exterior walls of Chance's apartment opaque. A pod-approach video opens on a wall display. It shows a short middle-aged man with a slight potbelly exiting a pod that's just come to rest on Chance's balcony. Recognition routines identify him as Don Kim, a code-green truck driver. He has dark, thinning hair, is wearing a T-shirt and jeans. He stuffs his hands in his front pockets. He's rocking back and forth on his heels with the habitual impatience of a solo delivery driver. He does not appear to have brought anything to deliver.

Chance motions for the door to open.

"Hi," the man says. His voice is gravelly, worn. His face is pale and unhealthy looking. "I'm here for a pickup."

At his hotel, Chance Five is searching the man's profile information on Civ Net, but there's nothing unusual. He's self-employed, with a leased rig. Based out of Detroit. Married. One eight-year-old boy.

"I don't have anything," Chance Four says. Leap Two is now standing behind Chance.

"Yes, you do," Don Kim says. "You have at least part of what I'm looking for. I just need her and the other three."

Leap Two says quietly to Chance, though Don Kim can certainly hear it, "A truck driver. Really?"

"You're Leap, right?" the truck driver says. "I'm Don, but you should already know that. Look, this isn't a joke. I'm going to send you coordinates for my truck. Send over one pod with two of your drives. Land it behind the truck. I'll open the doors. Those drives'll come into the truck. The pod comes back here. Fifteen minutes later—and you have to wait at least fifteen minutes—the pod picks up your other two drives. Then, same thing. Don't worry about clothes, food, whatnot. You're covered. Don't bring anything."

"I'm coming," Chance Four says.

"This is the drive that fights, right?" Don says. "Jai Kido? There won't be any need for that. I really wish you'd chosen a different drive . . . All right. Okay. Then you're gonna come fifteen minutes after the second group. We'll be waiting for you."

Don's upper lip and forehead are both shiny with perspiration. He says, "Now I'm going back. Give me fifteen minutes, then send two of Leap's drives. Got it?"

"Yes," says Chance.

"Okay, look. This is probably scary, but the reality is that both of you are safe. Please don't vid or in any way record anything. Please set your location to mask. And two things. First, the precautions are about avoiding notice. If they want to find us, they will. We want to avoid looking interesting. Second, I'm the only one who's really putting his neck on the line here. If one of you screws up, my rig'll get confiscated, and they'll fish around in my brain. Leap has money. You'll both be fine. I'll be SOL. So please, do as I say for my sake. Okay?"

Chance and Leap both nod.

Don Kim returns to his pod.

As Chance closes the door, Leap says, "Fish around in his brain?"

"I don't think anyone does that," Chance says. "That would be a prime violation. Unconstitutional."

PART FOUR

We used to say that stories had a primary theme: either person versus nature, person versus person, or person versus him or herself. That was before. For stories of our time, I believe those themes have become one.

———Jalisa Romero,
interview on *Fresh Air*

*if you like puddin' and pie
one simple question will tell you why
where's that sugar you wanted to try?
it all got baked into puddin' and pie*
—Lulu's Rhymes 'n' Things

CHANCE WATCHES AS LEAP THREE folds his lanky frame into the pod, settling in beside the smaller Leap One. The pod carrying Leap's two male drives rises quickly to transit height and then speeds away. Even though Leap is connected to Civ Net and would presumably let Chance know if anything went wrong, a few minutes from now this solo whom they've only just met, this Don Kim, will have all four of Leap's drives in his delivery truck. What if the truck is shielded from net access? In fact, that seems likely. And what if the truck is no longer there when Chance arrives? Why had Don Kim insisted that they wait fifteen minutes? A delivery truck could get miles away and be lost on one of the new intercontinental thruways within fifteen minutes. And why wouldn't Don Kim just drive away? After all, someone wants Leap badly enough to mount this whole farcical cloak-and-dagger exercise.

As a point of professional interest, the sheer improbability of the situation both repels and fascinates Chance. What's irresistibly compelling, though, is the potential involvement of Hamish Lyons, a founding pioneer of join science, a man whom Chance has both studied and idolized. Hamish Lyons helped to provoke events so important that they were immediately obscured by a welter of conflicting interpretations and torrents of questions about key information. And Hamish Lyons himself—a man generally believed to be dead, or *gone*—may have sent Leap and Chance a message. Could a simple truck ride actually lead to a meeting with him?

Chance One is searching for networked cameras that might show the truck. Chance is pretty sure that Hamish Lyons, or whoever has sent Don Kim, would consider a search for cameras problematic. Don Kim is concerned about observation by the Directorate. This is just the kind of unusual activity that might trip a network sensor; but the fear of making a catastrophic mistake by trusting the truck driver overshadows everything else.

Chance One lucks into a camera feed that shows an empty pod rising from behind a truck of the class Don Kim drives. There are two other trucks parked nearby. In the background, pods are arriving and leaving from an adjacent shopping district's parking lot. During the ten minutes or so that Chance waits, nothing looks suspicious, nothing seems untoward. Shortly after, the pod returns to Chance's apartment. Chance Four steps nimbly into it. The pod door closes, and the pod flies quickly to the truck.

From Leap's house, Chance One continues watching it through net cams. The pod, blue-gray—almost the color of the cloudy sky—cuts a perfect line through an otherwise immobile world and tucks itself into the truck's looming shadow.

．●．

IT'S LATE AFTERNOON, COLD, THE gloaming already stealing through the sharpened light. Don Kim is standing behind the truck. As Chance Four steps out of the pod, Don motions toward the open doors at the back.

The truck is massive, one of the new class of freight haulers designed to move goods through the stormy continental interior. Its trailer is two and a half stories high and eighteen feet wide, built for recently upgraded thruways. The trailer's bottom is four and a half feet off the ground. Inside are eight standard shipping containers, two on the bottom, two on top, and then four stacked in the same way behind those. Don says, "Just stand on the lift," meaning the large platform beneath the open doors. Chance does.

The lift rises. When it's level with the inside floor of the truck bed, it starts to tilt upward, forcing Chance to hop into the truck's interior. The lift settles in an upright position, and Chance watches enormous metal doors swing shut behind it. The network cameras that Chance One is watching lag slightly, so the doors close first on Chance Four, and then Chance One watches them clamp together.

Just before the doors clank shut, as the afternoon light is blocked, lights come on inside the truck. Chance Four hears gears moving and parts clanging and assumes the doors are locking.

The back end of one of the interior containers slides aside, and more light spills from it. Leap Two leans out of the container, a note of grace in the drab enclosure. Relieved, Chance says, "We're locked in."

"Yeah," says Leap, "but you can karate chop your way through that, can't you?"

Chance Four laughs.

Leap says, "C'mon in. Meet my new friends."

"YES, WE DO LIVE HERE. We call it an armadillo." A tall, broad-boned woman named Jackson is speaking. At her side is Terry, a dark, curly-haired man, maybe thirty, two or three years older than Jackson. The two of them are Leap's "new friends."

From inside, the shipping crates that appeared to be separate are united into a single two-story apartment. Other than the bathroom, the first floor is open, with furniture and paint dividing the space into a kitchenette, a compact living room with two couches facing each other, a couple of chairs, and a dining area with a large welded table and several other chairs. Leap Two tells Chance that there are bunks on the second floor.

The apartment is brightly lit and clean, and the furniture is comfortable. Leap Four and One are already sleeping upstairs. Three is reading, his long body bent awkwardly into a low-slung chair.

"The truck is the hardened shell of the armadillo, protecting us," Jackson says, "and we're the soft body inside."

"I see," Chance says. Chance Four's shoulders feel stiff. Chance rolls them, stretching slowly as she scans the truck's interior.

"So you need protection?" Leap Two asks.

"Yeah," Jackson agrees, "you could say that."

"You want a beer?" Terry asks.

Leap and Chance both decline. Terry says, "Suit yourself," and heads to the kitchenette.

"What do you need protection from?" asks Chance.

"Well, you, for one," says Jackson. "I don't know if you've noticed but the human population isn't exactly thriving."

"By 'human' you mean people who haven't joined," says Leap Two.

"Yeah, humans," says Jackson. "As opposed to, you know, you. No offense, but you know what a Hydra is? That's kind of how I see joins. That's my thing. I don't have anything against you. But you creep me out a little."

"And you don't seem to want to let us be," Terry calls from the kitchenette.

Chance and Leap exchange a glance. Neither likes the turn the conversation has taken, especially not while they're in Jackson and Terry's custody. Leap, attempting a reset, says, "So, you call it an armadillo?"

"Yeah," Jackson picks up the thread again. "It's heavily shielded. That is, there's a lot of obfu-tech inside the first foot of the interior container walls. Throws off their sensors, you know, and paints a picture of a cargo ship. So the idea is that the Directorate doesn't know we're living inside here."

Terry is back with an opened can of beer. "But of course they do know we live inside trucks," he says. "At least, they know that there are trucks like this out there. But they probably don't know how many, and they don't know which ones. There aren't a whole lot of setups this nice. We swap containers between trucks every once in a while to keep them guessing. A shell game." He smiles and takes a swig of his beer.

"We're pretty good at disabling sensors," says Jackson, "but they know we're here. Out here. I mean, I guess the point is we're not in any kind of war. We're just trying to figure out how to be in a peaceful kind of coexistence."

"And just who are *you*?" Leap asks.

"We're us," says Jackson, slightly affronted. "Like I said, the humans."

"I think Leap's asking," Chance says, "if there were to be a war, who would the war be between?"

"Between the humans and the joins," says Jackson, with a spark of belligerence.

"Wait, wait. Look, we're maybe getting off on the wrong foot," Terry says. "There's not going to be a war. That . . . that's all just a figure of speech."

"Okay," Leap Two says.

"To be clear," Chance says, "we consider ourselves human."

Jackson shrugs. Her face is turning red, and she's staring at Chance Four, who appears relaxed but has shifted her weight slightly and opened her stance.

Terry says, "Okay. Okay, Jackson and I, we're not like a lot of the others. We're both open-minded, and we have nothing against you, and especially not you personally. And you joins have all the advantages. We wouldn't have anything to gain by violence. So we're not going down that road. And because of our teachings, we understand that one day you'll all just"—he makes a wavy gesture with his hands—"go to the stars, *peacefully*, and leave the Earth behind for us."

"After you've poisoned it," Jackson mutters.

Terry looks quickly from Chance to Leap and then takes a swig of his beer. He's obviously embarrassed by Jackson. "Yeah," he says, "that's what our teachings say."

Jackson continues, "Our teachings *show* that the world will be poisoned and visited by plagues and by the destruction of fire and storm. This has already begun, and the evidence is before your eyes. We know you have good intentions, all of you, but you have too much power. Joins are apart from the world. And like Adam, you're bad custodians for the Earth. There will be for three hundred days a storm of ash and destruction. It will rise up, and it will rain down. You'll leave to the stars while we stay behind to complete our task and our purpose: to heal the

Earth and redeem what is unredeemable. To recover original paradise."

As Terry is listening, his face tenses, his mouth pinches shut and finally he closes his eyes briefly. When Jackson is done, he opens his mouth and takes a short breath. Then he says, "Yeah, like she said, we know you have good intentions."

.●.

FOR THE NEXT FORTY MINUTES or so, Leap Two talks with Jackson and Terry, mostly asking questions, while Chance Four listens from one of the couches. From inside the armadillo, access to Civ Net is closely managed. Leap and Chance can get to a few mass-media outlets but not much else.

From Leap's house in the archipelago, Chance One scours Civ Net for information about Jackson and Terry. The only mildly interesting tidbit concerns their church, the Apostolic Brotherhood. The church is small and its adherents almost universally peaceful. They tend to avoid people who don't share their beliefs. They also teach of the corrupting influence of many technological innovations, though they embrace some current technology, and Chance finds he can't predict what they will or won't condemn.

The Brotherhood's teachings start with the twelve apostles and incorporate the basic tenet that if God had included Join in his design for the human race, the apostles would have been joined. They were not joined, though, as Judas shows by acting against the others. The Brotherhood concludes that God's messages aren't meant for joins, and we have to look elsewhere to understand his plan for them.

The Brotherhood has only been provoked into organized

violence once, during a clash decades ago with the Church of the Apostolic Union. Records concerning the Church of the Apostolic Union end roughly four years ago. There is some discussion implying the members disbanded it. The Church of the Apostolic Union taught that the closeness of the twelve apostles to one another and to the Messiah symbolizes divine approval of Join. They believed a join of twelve would be particularly blessed.

The violence between the two churches had something to do with a condominium on the Derrick—a big orbital station that serves as a base for some space-mining operations—and a disagreement over divine intention as expressed through the Mars colonies. But Chance is tired and just not interested enough to parse through the complex details.

While Chance One is in the archipelago reading about the Apostolic Brotherhood, Leap Three stands up inside the truck. He crosses to the couch, and drops down beside Chance Four, his long legs stretching out in front of him. He shifts his body to peer surreptitiously at the others, then leans toward her, his blue eyes intent, and says under his breath, "Find out what you can about Jackson and Terry."

Conscious that Jackson and Terry, although deep in conversation with Leap Two, may be close enough to hear her response, Chance Four whispers back, "Is something they're saying worrying you?"

"Other than the talk of possible war?" Leap whispers.

"Yeah, I guess." Chance chuckles. "That, and the fact that they don't consider us human?"

"Well, those are the two main things," agrees Leap with a quick grin. "But I just don't like them. They do seem friendly, kind of, but . . . Anyway, I can't do any real research. All my drives are here, in the truck, so they're cut off from anything worthwhile."

At that moment, Chance hears Leap Two asking a little more loudly than she had been speaking, "Why have you crippled the network?"

"It's just to reduce network noise," Terry says, "that could help them profile our cargo. All the armadillos have limited net access from their apartments. Standard stuff."

Chance Four says softly to Leap Three, "I've been looking. They're just who they appear to be. At least on the net, there's nothing contradictory about them."

.●.

THE JOURNEY GOES SMOOTHLY. AFTER the initial friction, Terry and Jackson turn out to be accommodating, if somewhat clumsy, hosts. They tell Leap and Chance that they're going to be driving for three days, without stops.

The armadillo's control center is in a pilot's cabin separated from the cargo area by a mantrap, a sort of foyer with security doors on both sides. Terry, Don, and Jackson take shifts driving. When they're not driving, they have a regular safety routine to check the truck's systems. It reminds Leap and Chance of their flight checks. There's also a lot of gin rummy, meal preparation, and sleep. The truck moves nonstop.

Leap and Chance aren't allowed in the pilot's cabin and aren't allowed to know where they're going. After about thirty hours, a huge storm passes outside. The armadillo stops moving and lowers its massive trailer over its tires until the trailer sides are resting on the road. They all wait out the storm for a couple of hours while the armadillo hugs the ground. They hear rain and thunder crashing like the fists of mountains against their armor-plated sides.

From the storm's start, Jackson is agitated, irritable. Terry is drowsing in one of the chairs, glancing around blearily in response to the storm's most vicious sallies. Jackson is glowering in the direction of Leap Two. Leap Two is listening to the storm but notices Jackson's look and offers an interested smile.

"You know, the Directorate could stop this," Jackson says.

"Stop what?" asks Leap.

"The storms. The poisons all over the planet. I've read things. I've seen reports. This could all be fixed. The Earth made whole again."

Leap Two's light brown eyes narrow with friendly skepticism.

"There are ways to fix it," Jackson persists, "but the Directorate doesn't want to figure them out."

The armadillo reverberates from a blow, and the howling of the storm is momentarily deafening. Leap Two looks away. Jackson glares at the container's roof, above Leap Two's head, and mutters, just loudly enough to carry, "They want to kill the solos first."

At that moment, Don Kim drops down the stairs from the sleeping quarters. "Our schedule is now officially toast," he says loudly, to be heard over the noise. "This storm is killing us. Let's play cards."

* * *

CHANCE ONE, TWO, AND FIVE have each spent time looking for the armadillo on information feeds from the road systems. With both Two and Five unemployed, at least temporarily, Chance has decided to return One to the data farm soon. The office might get access to additional feeds.

Several rigs of the right class left New Denver at approximately the right time, but they were all moving cargo that was accounted for. And it's not clear that the truck carrying Chance Four and Leap actually left New Denver on the same day that they got into it. It might have just driven around for a day and then left.

The storm could have been a clue, but four large storms occurred within the required combination of time and range, and there were more than two hundred twelve trucks of the same class held up during those four storms. Chance can't find anything that sets the truck they're in apart from the others.

⁕

LATE ON THEIR THIRD NIGHT in the truck, Chance thinks they've been driving downhill for a long time. Chance guesses that they're going to one of the underground transfer cities— vast subterranean facilities that allow cargo transfers to happen without too much concern for storms. There are four such facilities that the truck might be visiting. Chance One starts scanning video feeds from them, but there's a lot of activity, and Chance is not sure what to search for.

In the early hours of that morning, Jackson announces that the container apartment is going to be moved to a different truck bed. Don and Terry will be outside supervising. Chance and Leap will stay inside with Jackson.

Jackson has taken Leap Four under her wing and told her things about the church while asking her not to tell "the other Leaps." When Leap Four confessed that she actually was the other Leaps and that Jackson had, in fact, just revealed those confidences to all of Leap's drives, Jackson winked at her and responded, "If you have to tell them, I guess it's okay. I wouldn't want you to lie."

There is a loud cracking and banging as the jaws of a crane close on the outside walls of the armadillo's apartment, the metal frame shivering. Immediately after, an earsplitting creaking and winching begin, and the gravelly churn of immense gears vibrates raggedly through the apartment's floor and walls.

Leap Three and Chance Four have been reading on the couches set across from each other. Everything is trembling, though not enough to knock things down, as the apartment gathers a slight upward momentum. Then with a very subtle shift and a dramatic lowering in the timbre of the grinding and ragged buzzing, they start to descend. After several more minutes the entire apartment is bathed again in welcome quiet.

The engine starts, a bass thrumming that breaks into long phrases bracketed by whines and thumps. The living quarters begin to vibrate lightly, as they have for the past few days. The new truck sounds louder than the old one.

About an hour later, and after two five-to-ten-minute stops, the new armadillo's engines cut off, and the noise ends.

Leap Three answers a call. He walks shakily to the bathroom, feeling internal reverberations from the last hours of uncertainty and racket. He briefly snags the top of his head on a rope slung just below what appears to be a rectangular beam but is actually a long table that can be lowered and unfolded into the center of the living space. As the tallest person in the transport, Leap has to keep an eye out to avoid smacking into high shelves or other ceiling-mounted, space-saving contraptions.

The quiet doesn't last long. The pneumatic lock on the door

to the pilot's cabin hisses loudly, then pops as its seal is broken. The door swings smoothly and silently open, and Don appears beside it. "We're going to step outside for a little bit while some folks sweep the apartment. Then we'll come back and see what's what."

Chance asks, "Sweep?"

"Just to make sure there're no trackers. The Directorate would be pretty interested in what happens next. C'mon, everyone. And that means all the drives upstairs too."

Jackson waits behind for Leap Three, whom Leap expects will need to stay in the bathroom for a couple more minutes. Chance and the rest of Leap's drives file out. They exit through a side door in the mantrap, then down a few stairs to the ground of the facility.

They're in a subterranean warehouse filled with a very fine mist, almost a light fog. The ceiling is barely visible, maybe fifty feet above them, and there are no walls visible in any direction. The ground is a uniform, coarse gravel.

Other trucks of the same class are parked within twenty or thirty yards. On one of them, two bodies blurred by the mist are climbing about like a symbiotic species grooming a host. The air is slightly chill. A steady glow from the ceiling supplements broadly spaced poles that support more powerful arc lamps.

Terry is humming absentmindedly as he offers a hand to help Leap Two step down from the cabin. While it's become clear that among Jackson, Terry, and Don, Don is the only one who's really on the ball, Jackson and Terry have been making awkward efforts keep Leap and Chance comfortable throughout the trip.

Leap Two smiles at Terry but doesn't take the extended hand. "Thanks," she says, as she steps down from the cab. She recognizes the tune he's humming and says, "I used to play that. Scott

Joplin, 'The Entertainer.' I played it for a while in college. We had a 1920s theme party."

As Leap Two is saying this, inside the apartment Leap Three has just finished washing his hands and has opened the bathroom door. As he ducks to exit the bathroom, Jackson is leaning against the back of a couch. She's singing, "Da da da, da, da da, da da . . ." The same tune. Leap Three stops just outside the bathroom door. Jackson's singing is precisely synchronized with Terry's. Jackson glances over at Leap Three, sees the question on his face, and the singing stops. Jackson's face slackens and pales.

Outside the truck, Leap Two says to Terry in astonishment, "You're a join."

Don is standing a few feet away, waiting for Jackson and Leap Three. "What?" he demands. "What did you say?"

Leap Two says, "Terry and Jackson are joined."

The same look—mouth widening slightly, skin tightening with alarm—passes like a quick shadow over both Terry's and Jackson's faces, simultaneously.

Then Terry says, in a friendly voice, "What? What are you talking about?"

Leap Two takes a step away from Terry and turns to Don. "They're joined," she says. "That's the only way to explain it."

Three unfamiliar men had been waiting on the ground as Leap, Chance, and the others exited the armadillo. Don motions to one of them, who quickly climbs into the control cabin and heads toward the apartment. Inside the apartment, Jackson has regained her composure. She says to Leap Three, "C'mon, let's go outside." Leap Three takes a step back from her, into the open bathroom.

Jackson says, "What's wrong? We should go to the others."

But the color hasn't fully returned to Jackson's face. To Leap, her calm seems forced. They hear the man climbing through the control cabin toward the apartment.

Don has a handgun pointed at Terry's forehead. He says, "Keep your hands where I can see them, Terry."

Terry is loose, relaxed. "Don, what are you doing?" he asks.

In a quick motion, Terry's left hand lifts his jacket and his right hand dives inside it, toward the place where a sidearm would be holstered. Don shoots him in the forehead. The report of the handgun sounds for moment. It doesn't echo. It doesn't reverberate. It happens quickly enough almost not to have happened. Terry's body drops.

Inside the apartment, Jackson staggers backward as she's turning toward the man coming through the apartment entrance. She falls against the back of the couch, her eyes wide, gasping for breath. The man shouts something at her. With visible effort she straightens up. Then she turns toward Leap Three, her lips pulled back, teeth clenched. Very slowly, she draws a hunting knife from its sheath at her hip. She sways, straightens, and then takes an unsteady step toward Leap, the knife held just before her.

A shot booms through the metal apartment, deafening Leap Three. Jackson's head jerks sideways, pulling her body off-balance. She drops against the couch and slumps to the floor. From the clean hole in the side of her head, above her ear, Leap sees a wisp of smoke rise. Then thick blood bubbles for just a moment.

The man who shot Jackson is at Leap Three's side. "C'mon," he says. He's got a firm hold on Leap's arm and is pulling him toward the truck's exit.

DON IS BENT OVER TERRY'S body. He moves Terry's right hand and opens the jacket. He grunts, "No gun." Then he turns and says clearly to Leap and Chance, "You're going to have to trust me for now. Don't ask questions yet. We're going to move quickly, and I'll explain everything in a bit." He turns to one of the men who met the truck. "What do you think?"

"I don't know," says the other man. "Maybe Alan saw something inside."

Don straightens as he's looking at Terry's body. "Dammit! He made like he was going for a gun."

"That's what a join would do," the other man says. "You did what you had to, Don."

Don says, "Whatever this was, we're gonna have to melt the inside, then get the hell out of here. They can't be more than a few minutes away."

"Yeah," says the other man. He and the third person who met the truck run around toward its back.

Leap Three is at the door of the truck. He jumps awkwardly down from the control cabin, ears still ringing, followed by the man who shot Jackson, a tall thick-limbed man with dark hair. He's wearing jeans and a worn denim jacket and might be in his midforties.

"Alan," Don says, "tell me you saw something."

"That was a join," Alan says. "When you shot this one out here, that one took a hit. She was staggering. She could barely move."

Don looks at Leap Three.

Leap Three, pale, blue eyes squinting, says, "I think they were a join. They were humming a tune, the same tune, an old one. But they were humming it at exactly the same time, I mean, exactly. When she saw that I knew she . . . I know it was a join."

"Okay, then," Don says. "Alan, you're gonna have to help Raj and Deepak melt this thing. Sorry, man."

"No, never mind," Alan says. "We'll get outta here okay. You guys get going." Then he nods to Don and runs toward the back of the truck.

Don turns to Chance and the four Leaps. "We're gonna have to run," he says. "I'm going to be figuring out where we're running to as we're going. Stay close, and just follow me. I'll get us out of here."

Chance Four nods, but none of Leap's drives acknowledges the instructions. Something is not right with Leap. Chance glances toward Leap Two and Four, who are standing on her left. The two bodies could hardly be more different physically, but right now both of their faces are frozen and tense. Chance shouts, "Leap!"

All of Leap's drives stiffen and begin to drop to the ground. Chance is jostled by Leap Three, who has fallen on her other side. Then all four Leaps are on the ground, thrashing violently, mouths open, making choking sounds. Chance takes a few steps to avoid hitting the writhing bodies. Don moves forward and bends, struggles to hold Leap Four.

Chance watches Leap's drives shiver and twitch in the gravel, with Don pressing down on Leap Four. It doesn't look real. Chance bends so that she's nearer the shoulders of Leap One, Leap's closest drive, who is thrashing about, cutting himself on the stones, but she can't think of any way to help. A moment later, the seizure has passed, and Leap's drives are stretched out and panting on the ground. All of them have a glazed look in their eyes.

Leap One looks up at Chance. Between clenched teeth and rasping breaths, he says, "Aw, shit." There's gravel in his hair. His face is cut, abraded, and his chin and right cheek are bleeding. Chance Four's right hand is on his chest. She moves her left hand to the side of his head. "Are you okay?" she asks.

"I don't know," Leap One says, and then begins to sit up. Leap's other drives are also trying to rise. Leap Two is clutching her knee and rolling. Leap One, staring at the gravel, says. "I think I twisted Two's knee."

Alan is back, standing next to them; his voice is urgent. "C'mon, c'mon! You guys gotta go!"

Don says, "Get these drives water. Quick, Alan."

Alan climbs into the control cabin. Leap Two is sucking in each breath. Chance helps Leap One rise unsteadily. Leap One says to Don, "I can't walk on that knee."

Don says, "She's gotta come with us. We have to move fast."

"I can't use that knee." Leap One is shaking his head. "I think the joint might be separated."

Don says, "Shit." All of Leap's drives look drained, shaken. In a moment, Alan jumps down from the control cabin and starts handing out water.

Leap Two is raggedly gulping breath. She's pale, lying on her back with her injured leg outstretched, her other leg bent, her face squeezed in pain. Leap One takes a bottle of water and pours some on Leap Two's face, then puts the tip of the bottle to Leap Two's mouth and trickles in water while Leap Two struggles to drink.

Don says harshly, "Alan, help Deepak and Raj." Alan leaves them reluctantly, jogging toward the back of the truck.

Don says, "Okay, listen. Whoever that was, whose drives we shot, they work for the Directorate. The Directorate is trying to find Hamish. This is it. You have to make a decision. I can leave you here. The Directorate will pick you up. They'll probably question you, but you don't really know anything. You'll be fine. Back to the world you came from. Leap here will die from this flip. Or you can come with me. You've seen it. This isn't a game. I'll get you to Hamish, but we're gonna lose bodies. There is a possibility that Hamish can help with the flip. Maybe, maybe not. But you've gotta decide now."

Chance doesn't think, but says through Chance Four, "We're going with you."

Leap Four, sitting with her arms around her knees says weakly, "I know all of my drives may not survive." She swallows, props herself with one arm, pushing her hand into the sharp gravel. "I want to see Hamish."

"All right," Don says. "Leap, I need all of your drives, except Two, to be sitting."

Leap's drives sit. Don moves close to Leap Two, pushing Leap One aside a bit to get closer to Leap Two's head.

"Wait a minute," Chance Four says, suddenly, panic rushing through her. "Why did you tell them to sit?"

Leap Four looks up at her. Leap Four's eyes are pained, aware.

Then Don, very quickly, puts his gun to Leap Two's forehead and shoots her. Again, the report of the weapon is flat and quick. The air after is clear as if nothing has happened. Leap Four drops backward from her sitting position to the ground. All of Leap's drives have collapsed again, are unconscious.

Chance Four steps forward and pulls Don up from where he's squatting by Leap Two's corpse. Don comes up quickly, smoothly. The hot barrel of the gun is suddenly under Chance Four's chin, pressing into the skin. Chance's eyes are smarting, tearing, and she can smell the burnt cordite from the shot. "Don't make me shoot you," Don says evenly.

Neither of them moves. Chance is aware of Chance Four's

speeding pulse. With great effort, Chance focuses, clears as much noise as possible, as much fear and grief as possible, out of the situation, works to borrow cycles from other drives. And then Chance Four's arms relax slightly. Her voice is choked. She makes two attempts but can't speak. Adrenaline surges through the drive. Finally, she asks, "Why?"

"You know why," Don asserts calmly. "That drive couldn't keep up. The Directorate would have gotten it, and then they'd use it to find us. To find Hamish. You helped make that kind of tracking possible, remember?"

Chance reels, tightening her grip on Don, the world leaving and then returning. Chance Four tenses.

"Don't." Leap Three's voice. "Don't, Chance." There's a pause, and then Leap Three continues, his controlled, deep voice inflecting his language the way Leap Two would have. "I knew. I knew that's what he meant. When he asked if we wanted to keep going, I knew I was going to lose her."

Don lowers the gun. Then he growls, "We've gotta go, fast. Or it won't matter."

Chance lets go of Don. She turns away from him and bends over, her hands on her knees, eyes pressed closed. She's gasping. "I didn't know," she rasps. "You knew, but I didn't. I didn't know." And then she can't speak.

.●.

IN THE NEXT FEW MINUTES, Leap's remaining drives rise haltingly. Leap and Chance follow as Don leads them from the truck. They move slowly at first but gather speed until very soon they're running.

They run between a handful trucks separated from each other

by twenty or thirty yards and then through a building. The few people they pass are weather-worn, dirty, hardened. Some stare at them; some point in one direction or another. Don seems to recognize some of them, and some respond to an unspoken question from him.

Once, he stops running to talk with a tall, thin man, entirely gray except for his sun-reddened face, and then they're running again. They run for a long time, turning and winding through areas with walls that close in claustrophobically, then suddenly open outward. They run between vehicles and around a massive machine with belts that roll and shriek and gouts of steam venting upward; they pass huge metal limbs hammering slowly and shifting panels that slide and turn in front of other panels. They rush forward for what must be close to an hour.

Then they round a final corner, stagger a short distance, and Don stops in front of a tough and battered-looking gray van. He slides open a side door to load them in.

They sit on fraying black vinyl cushions. Don fires up the van, and it speeds away, swaying and bumping. He's driving fast, the van jerking when he turns. They hear gravel rattling around its wheels and off its underside.

He drives the van into a tunnel, and then they're barreling through a close, dimly lit space, Don jerking the wheel occasionally to take a sharp turn. On one turn, the van ricochets violently off something to its left, smashes into something on its right, flinging everyone back and forth as it jostles, but they keep driving.

They come into a broad open area, mist clogged like the place where they left the armadillo, and Don barrels through it, swerving sharply to brush by shapes that suddenly loom out of the dimness, stopping twice to let people clear vehicles and machinery out of the way. Both times, the disassembly and removal happen with efficiency and precision. Chance has the impression that what was cleared was only there in the first place as a distraction.

After several minutes in the new open area, the van stops near a massive wall. Don tells them to get out quickly. They slide the door open and tumble out.

As time allowed, Chance has been using One, Two and Five to search vid feeds from the underground facilities. Despite all the desperate movement of the group accompanying Don Kim, there hasn't been a sign of them.

Now Don hurries them through a heavily reinforced door into a ten-by-ten room. He slides a separate, interior door closed and punches a button on the wall. The room, an elevator, begins to accelerate upward.

⚬

AFTER FIVE FULL MINUTES, MAYBE longer, the elevator stops. Don opens a compartment in one of the walls. He distributes masks of a kind that Leap recognizes from working as an EMT. "Rated for gas," Leap says. Don tugs each mask in turn to check its fit. He jabs a button, and the thick elevator doors slide open, and then they all step into a damp, bare cement anteroom that's lit by only a low-power glow lamp. When the doors have shut again, Don hits a red button on the wall. The opposite wall slides upward.

Bright sunlight floods underneath the door. It blinds them when the door reaches waist height. They hear the steady high-pitched whistling of wind rushing. As their eyes focus they see an endless landscape of twisted metal over jagged edges, ground carpeted with heaped and tangled metal strips in all directions, a silver-gray coating that rises and falls across a hillocky terrain that blocks their view of the distance. Fast winds whistle loudly through.

They step into early morning light and the long vista of wreckage. "Careful," Don says, "some of this stuff is sharp."

They follow a flattened path around a short mound of shattered junk. On the far side of that, a man is standing between a junk buggy and a hovercraft. The man is about Don's height. He's wearing a thick black jacket cinched up to the bulky mask that covers his face. Don steps up to him, and they hug.

"I am glad to see you," Don says, shouting to be heard over the wind.

"Glad to see you too," the other man says, his voice muffled by his mask. He hands Don a thumbnail-sized token. "Here's the starter. You guys better get a move on. This place is throwing rads."

"What about Deepak, Alan, and Raj?" Don asks.

"They got out," shouts the other man, "just. We think the armadillo's melted. They did a good job. If you guys get clear, we might be okay."

"Any sign they've got us, that they're tracking us?"

"No, but you've gotta keep going."

Don steps toward Leap and Chance and yells, "Into the hover." He waves them toward it.

"Leap," shouts the other man above the wind. "You're Leap?"

Leap One, Leap Three, and Leap Four turn toward him. "I'm sorry about your drive," he yells.

Leap Three nods acknowledgment, then Leap's drives turn from him. Leap and Chance pull open the door of the hovercraft. When they're all in and the doors are sealed again, Don turns on the air cyclers and pulls off his mask.

The others remove their masks as they watch the man who'd met them maneuver the junk buggy over the jagged piles of refuse, his driver's cage rocking as the five-foot-high, inflatable tires spin a bit and then bounce him up a hill of garbage and away from them.

Don says, "I wish these things weren't so expensive to run." He flips a switch, and the hover fans roar to life. The hovercraft rises a foot and a half above the carpet of junk, sending a spray of shrapnel out from beneath its deafening fans.

"It's pretty loud while we're flying," Don shouts. "But we'll drive when we get outside the junkyard."

Chance is exhausted. Chance Four needs to sleep, the muscles of her arms and legs twitching with fatigue. Don seems wholly alert. Chance closes her eyes and manages a light doze, despite the noise of the hovercraft.

At Leap's house, Chance puts Chance One down for a long nap, thinking that spare cycles will be useful. Chance Five has been sleeping and needs exercise. Chance gets him out of bed and into the shower. Chance Two is sitting in a coffee shop near the fountain in the Plaça Reial in Barcelona, hair mussed from the knit cap she's just removed. She smooths her fingers through her hair, orders an espresso, and watches the late-morning crowds pass by in the clear and cool winter sunlight.

.•.

CHANCE FOUR REGAINS CONSCIOUSNESS AS the hovercraft's fans are winding down, their roar quieting slowly. Outside, the vistas of twisted metal have been replaced by dirt that is torn, clumped, and piled as far as the eye can see. Here and there, bits of thin ground cover show a hint of green. The hovercraft jerks forward on its wheels as its fans stop turning.

In front of her, Don bangs on the steering column and says fiercely, "That's right, she works!"

Chance Four says, "You weren't sure it would drive?"

Don doesn't respond immediately. He reaches out and hits a switch next to the steering column. A green light pops on in the center of the wheel. He says, loudly to be heard over the road noise, "We don't use this thing much. Too expensive. It was ghosting the truck in case something happened, though, and Raj left a note that it was sounding rough. Well, he actually said he didn't think the drivetrain would engage again. So."

Chance Four leans forward. Leap Three is bent into the seat beside her; Leap One and Leap Four are sitting on the bench behind. All of Leap's drives are sleeping. Chance stands, steadies herself against the jerky motion of what is now essentially a small bus. She pushes her dark hair behind her ears and then pulls herself forward into the passenger's seat.

Don nods to her.

"Your rig, you . . . melted it?" Chance asks.

"Something like that," says Don.

"What will that mean for you?"

"I don't know. My family's in Arcadia right now. I guess it could mean we can't go home to Detroit."

They drive for a while over the unvarying, churned terrain before she says, "Why did you kill them?"

"Leap Two? I told you."

"No, the others, the two of them, Terry and Jackson."

Don turns away from her, toward the driver-side window and the sunlight. Then he looks back at the terrain in front of them. "I wish I hadn't," he says. "It would have been better to hold them, but they do that on purpose. They're trying to find Hamish, and whatever else they can about us." He shakes his head. "We're usually pretty good at spotting joins, but those two were professionals. Imps. There aren't a lot of joins who can do it that well, pass as solos. If we'd caught one of them alive, we might have traced him to other drives from the same join. That's a lot of training wasted, so they can't be caught. They try to force us to kill them. Bad for our morale. If we don't do it, they'll try to kill themselves. They wear bulletproof mesh so we'll take a head shot. Terry made like he was going for a gun."

"And Jackson pulled her knife on me."

"Yeah."

They bump along for a while without speaking. Don says, "I don't really have anything against joins, per se. They just came around at the wrong time."

"Jackson and Terry?"

"No, joins."

"The wrong time?"

"For the planet."

Chance gazes at the chewed-up plains they're driving over. "You're a planetist."

"I guess you could call me that. Though I don't agree with most other planetists. But I do agree that the planet comes first. And right now we're navel-gazing while our house burns down around our ears. Join was just bad, bad timing. We're in the middle of it—oceans, the weather, the die-offs—and then this damn tech. Almost, almost helpful. But we stopped paying attention to what was happening.

"What does it mean to be human?" he asks. "Who the fuck cares. That's a question for another time. But Join split us, some for it, some against, right when we needed to be working together. And you joins? Really, most of you are nearly useless. Trying to build mimetic material to coat your spires. Working on ways to get around the twenty-drive limit, or whatever other ridiculous project captures your fancy while the planet's dying. No time for the list of things that would actually make a difference. A bunch of genius retards. Look, I'm sorry. Nothing against you, personally. I don't know you. But look around. You should be helping to fix this."

.•.

THEY'RE DRIVING NEAR THE RIM of one of the megastorms. As they push forward, gales of wind explode against the front or right side of the vehicle, sometimes rocking it violently so that Leap's exhausted drives wake bleary-eyed, turn fitfully, watch the unvarying terrain as they try to sleep again.

Don is using the danger of proximity to the storm as cover. Within the megastorms, even the most powerful radio signals degrade or fail completely, and the Directorate isn't interested enough to make the large investment required in personnel and equipment to keep eyes on an area that's regularly savaged by smaller storms that spin off from the larger system. Chance and Leap both know how quickly those smaller storms can spawn; how utterly destructive they are when they first split from the megastorm. Driving through this area is like running through a house on fire. At any moment, they might all be killed. They know Don is also aware of the risk. There's little conversation as they jolt as quickly as possible toward their destination.

They reach a very gently sloping hillock, and they drive to the leeward side of it, where a cluster of other piles of bunched dirt extends for thirty yards or so. At the end of the cluster, they see the very edge of what might be a metal shaft. A camouflaged, sloped entrance grinds open slowly, revealing unlit tunnel access that plunges into darkness.

Don says, "No lights in here. The burn can be detected by flybys. We'll be driving in the dark for a few minutes." He turns to Chance. "Okay, you've been trying to track us. We've been watching your activity on the net. Now I have to ask you to stop. We can't risk you seeing something or hearing something, and then looking it up on the net. I guarantee the Directorate's watching you too. You just can't do any more research, okay?"

"You knew I've been looking for us?"

"Of course."

"And who are you communicating with?"

"I can't answer any of your questions. You've just got to stop looking, okay?" Don's voice is matter-of-fact. His cool brown eyes are gazing levelly, directly, at Chance Four. Chance has seen how quickly and remorselessly he moves to address emergencies. What if Chance doesn't stop quickly enough?

Chance One and Chance Five both switch their displays off.

"Yeah," says Chance Four. "Okay, I'll stop looking."

"Thanks," Don says, but he doesn't even blink.

He turns back to face the tunnel. "All right, in we go."

Complete darkness envelopes the hovercraft. Don drives slowly, seeming to feel his way between the gently upturned edges of the tunnel by occasionally driving on them. After a minute in the darkness, Chance says. "Why doesn't the Directorate pick up one of my other drives and use it to find us?"

Don's voice is dry, calm. "You'd tell me if that happened, right?"

Chance says, "Yes."

In the dark, above the rumble of the vehicle's engine, Don's voice sounds deeper.

"Good," he says. "I'd need you to do that. You're here because Leap wants you here. Your presence helped Leap make the decision to come with, and we might need you later. But we're taking a big risk, of exactly the kind you just described, by bringing you with us. You don't know where on the continent we are. And everything you do know, they already know. When we're done, you won't be of any use to them. But right now, you could be. And right now, they know that if they grab you, you'll tell us about it. And then we'd kill this drive, so that they can't use one of your other drives to find us."

As Don says it, Chance hears the logic of it. When Don asked for a decision earlier, this was what it meant for Chance. If the Directorate moves on Chance, Chance will tell Don, and Don will kill Chance Four. After the link to Chance Four is severed, Chance would have nothing to offer the Directorate. This new clarity almost carries a sense of relief.

·◉·

A LIGHT IN THE DISTANCE quickly becomes a chamber whose ceiling is only a few inches higher than the top of the hovercraft. Two other craft are parked within. Don pulls up beside one of them, sits back in the driver's seat, and sighs deeply.

"So this is Arcadia?" Chance Four asks.

"Every place has a name," Don says.

"I thought it would be . . . it sounds . . . prettier," Chance Four says.

"Different strokes," Don says. Then he presses a button, and the side door slides open.

A tall black woman, a frail-looking olive-skinned woman, and a medium-height black man meet the hovercraft. All of them are wearing heavy faded-yellow parkas over loose gray trousers. The tall woman takes a step toward the open door and says, "I'm Elicia. Welcome."

"I'm sorry. I'm feeling very ill," Leap Four says.

She gasps, and Chance Four turns toward her. Leap Four is looking down at the worn floor of the hovercraft, her face reddening. Leap Three, just behind Chance, and Leap One both look drained; their eyes are closed, their breathing shallow.

Leap Four looks up and then turns her head jerkily, like a startled animal. Her broad face is damp, and she is squinting with nausea, pain, or both. Leap is beginning to panic, and then her gaze finds Chance Four and holds.

Leap doesn't blink. She keeps her eyes on Chance while striving to regain her composure. She says, "All of my drives are sick. I need to eat and sleep. Is that possible?"

It's Elicia who responds. "Yes. Of course. We'll find you some food," she says, "and then take you to a place where you can sleep."

Don jumps down from the driver's seat. He steps up beside Elicia, who is reaching into the hovercraft to help steady Leap Four. Leap Four seems to have recovered.

Elicia leans toward Don, and he gently kisses her cheek. "My wife," he says to Chance, by way of explanation.

The eight of them walk through well-lit narrow tunnels to a large mess area where Chance and Leap sit. The other two people who met the hovercraft, Marco and Emily, work with Elicia to quickly prepare a meal of mushrooms, potatoes, and leeks.

As they work, they talk to Chance Four, sensitive to and

attempting to provide distraction from Leap's obvious misery. They describe their underground garden under full spectrum light and talk about smuggling in an occasional pallet of canned food. They're obviously proud of their underground haven, Arcadia.

Fresh water is filtered out of an aquifer, whose flow also provides some electric generation, supplemented by high-quality fuel cells. There's a constant, very low hum of an air-rejuvenation system that Elicia says is their largest power drain. After the meal, Marco shows Leap and Chance to a room with eight empty bunks, and they quickly fall asleep.

Chance is happy to focus Chance Four on food and sleep while using other drives to address an inflow of questions from friends and colleagues. They want to know where Chance's drives are, why they're missing appointments, why they're taking sick days, whether Chance needs any help.

After the conversation with Don, Chance is especially vague in response, carefully crafting messages meant to allay concern without informing. Chance says drives are sick or had a planned vacation or are working on special projects or whatever helps end the conversation as quickly as possible. Chance streams a few vids of Barcelona and the Olympic Archipelago, giving credence to the stories of vacations. People are satisfied enough to stop asking questions.

.●.

TWELVE HOURS LATER, AFTER THEY'VE had another meal, Chance Four is in the mess area with Leap One. Leap is keeping Leap Three and Four asleep to borrow cycles, but Leap One is still groggy, scattered. He tries to smile but his lower lip puckers out a bit and the smile goes awry, becoming a grimace before he gives up.

"I was glad to sleep," he says, pressing his beard, massaging the tension in his jaw, "but I'm too old for this."

Chance is a little surprised. She says, "Yeah." Then "I guess, I don't know how old you are anymore."

Leap gives a half laugh, says, "That's right, you don't. Anymore. I was born seventy-three years ago. Josette was."

"You remember the world before Join."

"Yes, I do. And it wasn't what you think it was. It was quiet. It's a good thing to have those memories." Leap One steeples his fingers in front of his face and says in mock seriousness, "You are but a child, Chance. But don't worry, I know you. I know the kind of creature you really are, and the promises you will fulfill."

Chance laughs drily. "Yeah, okay."

Then Leap One notices something behind Chance, and Chance turns around. Elicia and Don have arrived. They're followed by a tall white-haired black man in a loose red shirt and black jeans. The three of them cross to Chance and Leap.

"Oh, my God," whispers Chance, under her breath.

The tall man smiles as he's introduced to them. His voice is low and soft. He gives the impression that each word he uses has been carefully chosen. "I'm sorry about your Two drive," he says to Leap One.

Panic—the same look that Chance saw on Leap Four in the hovercraft—flashes briefly across Leap One's face. Leap One struggles to manage a somewhat-grim smile. He says, "I am too."

Hamish Lyons watches Leap One for a moment, then says, "I might not have made the same choice Don did. But then, left to myself, I probably wouldn't have maintained my independence this long."

Chance had recognized him instantly, the high forehead, the heavy chin, the mild look of his clear eyes. Among the developers of Join, Hamish Lyons is said to be one of the few who was truly essential and is widely praised for his specific contribution, a deep understanding of the fundamentals of quantum networking.

During the trek in the cargo truck, Chance and Leap had asked Don whether the apocryphal stories of Hamish joining Music were true. Don was evasive, answering with a shrug. So they asked how Hamish Lyons could still be able to do anything after the meltdown that Music became. Don simply told them to "ask him yourself." Leap asked again, a bit later, and Don said the same thing.

Hamish has a slightly disconcerting, open gaze. He turns it now on Chance. "I understand you have some technical knowledge of Join."

"It was the specialty of my Three drive."

"Yes, the one Rope killed."

"Yes," says Chance.

Hamish hesitates. "I'm very sorry about that as well," he says. "You know by now, I'm sure, that Rope is mad?"

Leap One scoffs softly, and Hamish turns back to him.

"I'm just not sure what difference that makes," Leap says.

"I don't know what Rope is," Chance says.

Hamish frowns. "Yes. Rope is one of many new types of consciousness, I suppose. We don't yet have a name for what it is. But I do think it's safe to say that, at least by the standards by which we judge each other, Rope is now insane. It has become a volatile, fragmented personality, the combination of many lost and courageous souls. You know, it told me about both of you."

"No, we didn't know," Leap One says. "Don didn't tell us. Rope said something, but we thought you might have contacted us because you saw we were looking for you."

"Yes, we did see that. But many people are looking for us, or for one of those among us in Arcadia. Rope was several of my colleagues. It has ways to contact us directly."

Leap says, "The last time we saw him, he seemed terrified, was drinking himself to death."

Hamish thinks for a moment, then says, "Yes. You know, of course, that it's incorrect to ascribe a gender to Rope. It is not a gendered entity."

Chance is surprised to hear the phrase actually used by Hamish, who acknowledges Chance's recognition with a rueful smile. "Indeed," Hamish says, "I coined the phrase. I think it's still useful, and accurate, so I haven't given up on it."

"Rope," Leap One says, "said that eventually all joins would be like him." Leap pauses for a moment to give the pronoun a very slight emphasis, then continues, "He said he was searching for the vanishing point."

"Yes," Hamish says. "I've heard it say things like that. It has an endless closet of reasons to wear to explain why it has done what it has done. But every one of them is transparent. The naked truth is Rope is a mercenary. Rope took a Directorate contract, promising to deliver a method of safely joining an unlimited number of drives, without a subnet."

Leap says, "I don't think Rope is interested in more money."

"I agree. Rope's appetite, Rope's ambition is not for money. Rope wants to teach us something, to be judged brilliant by history, and to create an irrefutable legacy."

"Which you think won't happen," Leap says, "because Rope is crazy."

"Rope has a secure place in the history of our species for other reasons. But, yes. That is basically how I see it." Hamish turns from Leap to Chance and continues, "Rope hypothesized that a meme virus results from competing personal preferences. What we in the trade would call ego codes. Rope believed that personal preferences could be diluted through the creation of a very large join, until they would no longer have a meaningful impact on the overall system. Rope's method was to create an enormous join while keeping the number of active drives low. It believed that at some point, it would contain so many ego codes that no individual would possess enough influence on the join to precipitate a meme virus. Then it could safely add as many active drives as it wished.

"It tried several times to increase its number of active drives above twenty. But it kept panicking. The science simply doesn't support Rope's hypothesis. In fact, it's actually ridiculous on the face of it because there is no reason to believe psychological phenomena alone can generate prion growth. And there are many other substantive complicating factors. Eventually, I think a desire to join and kill drives became Rope's only clear motivation."

Leap says, "Rope said it was the product of over eight hundred joins."

"Yes. I believe, as I suspect you do, that that may be an exaggeration. Though there are no records. It's been working on the project for four decades, however. It's not too difficult to find join candidates among terminally ill bodies or among the poor or the dispossessed if you promise them eternal life or an opportunity to help shape an important scientific breakthrough.

I'm sure Rope promised other things as well. Rope, without doubt, underwent several hundred joins."

"But if those promises weren't true," says Leap, "and Rope kept that fact a secret until the join procedure . . ." Leap leaves the thought unfinished.

Hamish is clearly surprised, his brows lowering briefly, and his eyes clouding with a look of hurt—all of which quickly dissolves back into the same equanimity he had been showing.

"If I understand what you're implying," he says, "then as far as I know, and this seems to be the fact of the matter, during all of those joins, Rope did not experience a flip. Flips are rare, even among elderly joins, and Rope chose candidates in low-risk demographics. Pressure adequate to create a flip would have been highly improbable."

Chance says, "The Directorate, did they recruit bodies—"

"The Directorate is not evil," Hamish says. "None of Rope's joins, of course, were coerced. They were all freely entered into, as the network requires. The Directorate simply made an exception to allowable size limits in order to make Rope's activities legal. In any case, Rope had a Directorate contract. But they do seem to have shut it down now, since Rope . . . branched out and has killed so many bodies that were not part of its join. There is simply no way to dress such acts as scientific progress."

.●.

FROM ACROSS THE ROOM, THEY hear someone loudly clear his throat. Don had left while they were talking and is now approaching them carrying a large double-layer flat cake.

"All right," he says loudly, "there are other things we need to do today!"

Hamish closes his eyes and smiles. "Don," he says, "right now?"

"Yes. You may not know it down here in paradise, but the days keep passing out there in the phenomenal world. And today is the day!"

"Please, forgive us," Hamish says to Chance and Leap. "I'm sure this will be more than you anticipated."

"Carrot cake!" Don says to Hamish. "Your favorite. It's not real cream-cheese frosting this year, but it's pretty good."

Chance and Leap are momentarily speechless. Then Chance says, "Cake?"

Don steps close to Hamish and stands, waiting for the older man to lean back so he can lower the cake to the table. "Yeah," Don says, "it's the birthday of the world's first join."

"Now?" Hamish asks. "Can we wait a little while? I think our guests still have questions."

"Well," Don says. "A couple of the little ones have to go to bed soon."

"Ah," Hamish turns to Chance and Leap. "You'll have to indulge us, I'm afraid."

Chance says, "But it's February, right? The first join happened in May."

"That's the story," says Don as he sets the cake down. "But this is the real anniversary."

Elicia is now standing beside Don. Around them are gathering Marco and Emily and many other people whom Leap and Chance haven't met yet, including several children. Only a moment before, their discussion with Hamish had felt intimate and close, but now they're surrounded by movement and noise. A young boy briefly tries to get Leap One's attention but then disappears, and other children are dodging one another while the voices of men and women rise and fall with a constant and comfortable regularity.

Elicia has begun placing candles in the cake. There's a burst of loud laughter, and a child's hand repeatedly creeps toward the cake while Elicia swats it back.

Don moves around the table toward Chance Four and Leap One. He raises his voice so they can hear him over the greetings and talk of the others. "Hamish says he joined Derek Okoro two years before the official date," Don says, "and that it happened in February, not in May."

Hamish, who is now fielding multiple congratulations, takes a moment to interject. "Yes, Derek and I joined in February, forty-two years ago. More than two years before the official date." Then he turns back to the others.

"You see?" Don says.

Elicia has lit the candles, five of them.

"Hamish is a join?" Chance asks. Don gives her a sidelong glance as Elicia works to get people's attention.

Chance wants to ask about Music again, but Elicia is calling out, "Quiet, quiet everyone." Then she says, "Ready?" She lifts her arms and brings them down, and the group begins to sing "Happy Birthday" to Hamish, who smiles broadly.

·•·

AFTER THE CAKE, THE TABLES are cleared, folded, and then stacked near the wall with most of the chairs. The gathered crowd makes quick work of the cleanup, and when they're done the room seems much larger than it had. Chance estimates close to a hundred people in the room, and there's still space for a quickly assembled platform and an open area in front of it. The flush, bright light fades to a softer glow. The group still seems to be growing.

Hamish produces a banjo, and a few other people—including Elicia, who plays guitar, and Marco, who summons an upright bass—spend a couple of minutes organizing themselves on the raised platform and then launch into a snappy folk tune. Chance and Leap have moved to seats near a wall and are feeling separate from the celebration but thankful for it. The band, led by a woman whom they haven't met, follows with an energetic set.

People are dancing, improvising steps. It's clear that this kind of thing isn't unusual. There's an occasional, disorganized line dance and a single, disorderly attempt at calling from the band that ultimately dissolves into laughter. Don joins Chance and Leap, but the room is noisy, and the two of them are hesitant to interrupt the festivities with their several remaining questions.

Though obviously tired, almost morose, Leap finally tells Don that the party is a welcome distraction. Don steps away from them for a few moments. Chance Four says, in a voice she hopes only Leap One can hear, "You're doing well."

Leap One relaxes. With his beard short and his hair not fully recovered from the Ritual of Retirement, his jaw looks heavier, and his eyes are sunken and shadowed.

"You looked pretty bad," Chance says, "when we got here in the hovercraft."

"I felt like hell," Leap says. He watches the band as he talks. "Still do. When I woke up in the hovercraft, I got confused. I thought, just for a minute, that I was sick again. That I was trapped in my old, sick body." He pauses, staring silently at the musicians, then says with a deadened voice, "Instead, I am—this. I have many bodies, and every one of them is just worn out." Leap stops speaking, as if following the thought further would be too taxing.

Chance Four doesn't say anything. She looks down at her hand—strong, reddish brown fingers tapering out from their broad bases. Chance wants to move closer to Leap and put her hand on his shoulder, but she can sense the work Leap is doing to hold emotions in check. She moves her chair closer to Leap One—an awkward, jerky motion as the chair scrapes across the floor of the mess hall.

THE BAND PLAYS A BLUES number, sung by a guitar player they don't recognize, who follows it with a danceable rock song. After that, Hamish steps forward to sing a sweet and shaky rendition of "It's Only a Paper Moon."

When the song ends, the crowd applauds loudly, and he takes a short bow.

Don has returned and is staying close to Chance and Leap, but not so close as to be intrusive. After Hamish's song, Chance Four stands and steps closer to Don to ask why there were five candles on Hamish's cake.

"Well, you do that too, don't you?" Don says.

"What?"

"Number of candles equals the number of people who joined."

"Hamish is a join of five?"

Don fidgets, rubbing the back of his ear and then scratching his temple lightly. "In a manner of speaking, I suppose, yes."

"What do you mean?"

Don runs a hand across his chin as he faces the band. Then he says, "This probably isn't the place for it, but"—he pulls a chair closer so he can sit facing Chance and Leap—"you two have made a pretty big effort to get here. I don't think we should be keeping secrets. It's really for Hamish to tell you, but, well, here's the thing. Hamish is Hamish Lyons, Derek Okoro, Qi Wei, Marina DelThomaso, and Duff Berjer."

Chance knows every one of those names. Anyone who has done join science knows them. She says slowly, "That doesn't make any sense. It's impossible. Every one of those people was a join with Music. The bodies of three of them were drives that were killed by the meme virus. Duff Berjer's autopsy was the first finding of reflective prion growth."

"Yeah," says Don. "Look, I'm not an expert. I don't know how this stuff works. Hamish was part of Music, but . . . he separated. He just, he wasn't part of Music anymore. He says he doesn't know how it happened. The network connection failed or something. He was the first join, and the protocol developed a lot after that. He says that might be significant. But he is a continuation of all those five. He thinks the five of them were replicated, in him, and in Music."

Chance Four says, "And in someone else."

Leap One turns to Chance. "What do you mean?"

Chance says, "Marina DelThomaso was a philosopher. The only one on the original team."

Chance can see the thought taking shape as Leap works through the implications. Leap One's face wrinkles into an expression that Chance hasn't seen before but that appears to be extreme disbelief. He says, "Rope?"

Chance turns to watch the elderly man playing banjo. The singer is delivering a lovely, quavery rendition of "Will the Circle Be Unbroken." The room's artificial light is very close to early evening light. It has a natural, cool quality, but it comes from light strips that line the walls and stripe the ceiling. The effect is that of limpid, golden sunlight, but without the clear contrast of early evening shadows. It comes from every direction at once, filling the closed room.

Chance Four says, "Rope and Hamish are the same person."

"No," Don says, "of course not. Not the same. But maybe they both separated from Music."

The band's tune bounces against the stone walls and reverberates softly, giving the sound an odd, additional solidity. The effect of the music and the sourceless light is of a strange, dreamlike world in which sound hangs almost palpably, a familiar presence in a world of denatured time.

Don looks over at the band.

After several moments, Chance Four says, "You're a feral community throwing a party for someone who invented Join. And if Hamish is a join, then why is he living here, with you?"

Don says, in a tone that remains conversational, friendly, "Some of us don't like being called ferals. To our faces, at least. As if we were animals."

"Sorry."

"Yeah," Don says. "He saw what was happening. How joins were—not paying attention. He saw the effect on those of us who hadn't joined. He says he's trying to influence the Directorate's priorities, and he thinks he'll be more effective from outside the Directorate. He's helped us. He's tireless. He built this." Don motions around the room. "Or planned it, showed us how to build it. Arcadia. He improves it all the time. It's actually pretty hard to live here. We wouldn't be able to do it without the things he does."

Chance feels as if a world she had thought was comprehensible has been revealed as a facade. She knows it's a temporary emotional state, but the effect is so strong that everything she's sure of, even probability itself, seems at that moment like irrelevant artifacts.

The man playing banjo may be Hamish Lyons, though Hamish Lyons should no longer exist. He may be a separated join, even though such a thing has never been recorded. He may be the same person as the psychopath who killed Chance Three. Whoever the man is, he does have the face of Hamish Lyons.

.●.

THE NEXT MORNING AS THEY walk back to the mess for breakfast, Chance is struck by how similarly Leap Three and Leap Four wear their weariness. Leap Three is a tall, lean, middle-aged man, and Leap Four is a short young woman with a healthy, heavy frame, but both are showing slightly hunched shoulders. There's a tentative quality to the way they walk—as if the soles of their feet hurt. And both squint at times, as if fending off a hangover.

Leap had another seizure shortly after the music and dancing ended. Leap One—who is still sleeping—was also up for several hours afterward, working with one of the solo medics to staunch a torrential nosebleed.

Leap Three says, without looking at Chance, "I'm planning to avoid the happy Arcadians today."

"That might be difficult if we're going to do what we came here to do."

"Ah," Leap Four responds, "I can see you're going to have answers today. That's very good. There'll be less for me to do."

They walk for a moment, and then Leap Three says, "Any answers for this headache?"

"Aspirin?"

"The miracle drug. I tried. That is, I tried . . . well, something quite a bit stronger."

The mess hall is busy. A small buffet of scrambled eggs, dried fruit, salad, tea, water, toast, and preserves has been arranged on one table. Fifteen or so people, including Hamish, are already working their way through breakfast.

Appearing energetic and refreshed, Hamish rises from his place at one of the tables and motions for them to sit with him. Leap Three and Four take small servings of eggs and a slice of toast each and then stand numbly near the food table until Chance Four has filled her plate.

"We're going to get things started today," Hamish says mildly. He has risen from where he was seated to guide them toward the table. Neither of Leap's drives appears to be listening.

After they sit, Leap Three says, "What is it that you said we're going to start?"

Don and Elicia arrive at the table, each sitting quietly at the end near Hamish. "Leap," says Hamish, "we're going to start going over what a treatment for the flip might consist of."

Leap Three hesitates, notices Don and Elicia, then peers at his untouched food and asks, "So you can treat the flip?"

"I don't want to suggest much in the way of confidence," says Hamish. "But we have developed a protocol that we believe has been successful."

"You believe? Have you cured a flip?" asks Leap Three.

"We believe we've successfully treated one," Hamish says. "One. It's difficult to know whether it's actually cured. It's been two years, and there have been no further symptoms. No seizures. The subject tells us that the fatigue and depression are gone. I believe the flip has been treated in a way that may ultimately result in a cure. But, of course, two years is really not a long time. The signs, however, are encouraging."

"Can I meet the join you treated?" asks Leap.

"No, that's not possible," Don says. "There's no official record of the join's treatment or of the flip. And the join isn't here anymore."

"So I have to accept this treatment on faith?"

"Of course," Hamish says. "As you would any treatment."

Both Leaps are watching Hamish closely. Leap Four says, "You have information that you won't share."

"Yes, I do. But I don't believe that that information, if you were apprised of it, would affect your decision. And I believe it should remain confidential."

The Leaps continue to stare at him, their faces reddening, their breathing slightly labored.

Hamish is quiet and then says in his mild way, "You're well beyond the realm of certainty. You've come this whole way on faith."

．●．

HAMISH SAYS THEY'RE GOING TO start the day with a video consultation with a group that isn't currently in the facility. After eating, he, Elicia, and Don direct them through a maze-like warren of identical corridors.

People they pass seem friendly and at ease. After walking for a little while, they climb seven flights of stairs and shortly after pass through a hall that's roughly three times wider than most of the others. The wider hall continues as far as they can see in both directions and has a subtle curve, as if it's part of a very large circle. Hamish explains that this is their running track and that they will need to walk on the outside of the curve. Immediately after he says this, a few joggers become visible in the distance behind them. The whole facility is larger than either Leap or Chance suspected, but there is very little automation, few signs of robotics, and they haven't seen any powered vehicles.

"We conserve energy," Don explains, "and keep our heat signature as low as possible. We have obfu-tech to baffle sensors, but we also do what we can to avoid relying on it."

"How did you build all of this without being found out?" Chance asks.

"Well," says Don, "of course, that's one of our secrets. I will say that there are parts of North America that had underground installations already. And there are geologic formations that present a lot of opportunity for places like this. We may have used some of those. Or we might not have."

They open a door into a wood-paneled room with two rows of four dark gray office chairs each, all facing a blank white wall. Don says, "We'll be projecting the video conference against that wall. Elicia and I will be standing against the walls on the sides. Please don't look at us or mention our presence. We're really here as security. We can't think of any reason we'd need it, but we're not going to take any risks."

Then Hamish, Chance, and Leap's two drives sit in the first row of chairs, Hamish flanked on his left by Leap Four, sturdy but sagging, and on his right by Chance Four, wiry and controlled. Shortly after they sit, the lights in the room go down except for a bright cone from the ceiling that falls around the two rows of chairs.

Hamish says quietly, "This is actually going to be a

conversation with the Directorate. They don't know where we are. This data stream will be run through several layers of obfuscation. Don't be worried about what you say. Despite appearances, we often cooperate with them."

Seeing the incredulity on Leap Four's face, Hamish continues, "And despite our cooperation, we cannot afford to have their agents in Arcadia. If they could find us, the Directorate would likely close Arcadia, and the people living here would lose their homes. And I choose what I share with them very deliberately. If I were in their custody, they would be in a position to influence and benefit from all of my research, my inquiries. The sacrifice of your drive allowed you to come here without compromising any of that."

Then the wall at the front of the room disappears, replaced by a black background. Four white birds soar onto the screen from its upper-right corner. When they reach the center of the screen, they become the four birds of the Vitalcorp logo. The logo centers over an official seal, a circle of embossed gold. Beneath the circle are the words OFFICE OF THE CEO, and beneath that is SECRETARY OF JOIN AFFAIRS. After a few seconds, the logo and background fade, and the wall dissolves, becoming an opening onto another office. In that office, they face a narrow desk with a shine so brilliant it prevents them from clearly seeing the color of the wood beneath. On one side of the desk are four small flags; on the other side is a small bronze globe.

Despite the logo that warned him, Chance is startled to recognize the CEO of Vitalcorp and secretary of Join Affairs himself. The man sitting in front of them in the immaculately tailored, slate-gray, subtly pinstriped suit is Excellence Four, the Voice of Excellence. His perfectly sculpted face, square jaw, relaxed smile, and leonine white hair are recognizable from countless online images and news stories.

"Hello, Hamish," he says amiably, his famous voice resonant and reassuring—confident, formal and intimate all at the same time.

"Hello, Excellence," says Hamish.

"And this must be Leap, whom you've told me about," says Excellence, "and Chance. Good to meet you both. I'm looking forward to working with you."

"It's a pleasure to have an opportunity to talk with you," Hamish says. "Might I suggest, I think it may be a good idea to start with an explanation for our guests. And then they may have questions."

"Of course. We'll do it that way, then," says Excellence. As Excellence continues, Leap and Chance each feel as though he is focused on them personally. "First, I want to thank you both," he says, "and you particularly, Leap, for taking on this difficult challenge. As I'm sure Hamish has told you, the treatment is not guaranteed, but initial results are very encouraging.

"You're probably wondering why you're talking with me. Despite some differences, Hamish's group and the Directorate have a history of cooperation. Hamish has pioneered this particular technique. He takes the initial steps and makes an adjustment to the caduceus. After that, a new join procedure will be required as part of the treatment.

"While Hamish's facility can complete a join, Vitalcorp, indeed the entire world, is very interested in this technique. So after Hamish has done his magic with the caduceus, we will be honored to have you complete the treatment with a join procedure in our facilities. The best join facilities on the planet. That will help us better understand what he's doing. For the two of you, our involvement in this project means that it will have the full authority of the Directorate behind it. As a consequence, when this is over, there will be no obstacles to reintegrating with your old lives. You'll be helping us. We will be in your debt."

Chance has a sensation of floating. When she says, "We're honored," she means it. She's been reading research from top Vitalcorp scientists and medical teams, and from Excellence itself, for years. The opportunity to work with them directly, or even directly observe their work, settles in with a delightful thrill. But then there's a question of money.

"Sir," she says, "this would be a very expensive effort."

"There will be no charges," says Hamish quickly.

"I am personally moved," says Excellence, "by the willing-ness of both of you to take the risks you have already taken to find a treatment for your illness. From where I sit, you are both heroes. The Directorate honors heroes."

Leap Four says, "If I may?"

"Of course," says Excellence.

"I'm dying. So I am going to have this treatment, I believe. I don't feel that I have a choice. This conversation can't be about whether or not I choose to have the treatment. So the question under discussion seems to be whether I consent to having a part of the treatment, the join procedure—"

"The final part of the treatment," Hamish says softly.

"Yes, the final part of the treatment," Leap Four continues, "here, with Hamish, or in Directorate facilities. From my per-spective, I would assume there are some benefits to being in a well-funded facility for the treatment. So I can benefit from working with the Directorate. But I'd like to understand why you're offering me this. What seems likely is that the Directorate would like me to use Directorate facilities so that you can learn more about how the treatment works. Is that correct?"

"Yes," Hamish confirms, "that's right."

"If I stay here," asks Leap Four, "what then?"

"Nothing," Excellence says with patient, reassuring authority. "If you stay with Hamish for the join, you can still return to your old life. Your experience will not be any different, except, perhaps, in the quality of the care."

Hamish says, "No matter what you choose, there will be no legal charges, nothing punitive."

Excellence nods his agreement.

At first, Leap Four seems prepared with a swift reply, but she checks herself and then visibly concedes a moment to her exhaustion. Finally, in a voice that is surprisingly calm, she says, "I am concerned, after what I've seen."

Excellence seems saddened. "Yes. I can see how you might feel that way. First, let me say that the stakes are very high here. It is probably not an exaggeration to say that the future of the human species is likely to be directly influenced by your actions. Flips are rare and have become increasingly so. We work to prevent them. It would be unethical for us to induce them artificially, and even if we tried, the nature of the network resists that kind of manipulation.

"You may not be aware of the experiments that were run around coercive joins? A distasteful and unfortunate episode for us. Also a complete failure. The quantum network is radically egalitarian. It does not respond to coercion or to our notions of power, status, or value. Within its embrace, each consciousness is equal, and it requires that a subject's conviction state be true. To join, one has to want to join. Who would choose to join if they believed the odds of a flip were high?

"As I'm sure you both know, we have done our best to find a treatment for this condition. Without success. But now, Hamish tells us he may have a protocol that works. To learn what Hamish has to teach us, we need you. We will gratefully accommodate and protect you."

"You say you work closely," Leap Four says. "Can't Hamish just tell you what he's discovered."

Excellence smiles. "Hamish?"

"Of course," Hamish says. "The first time I completed this treatment, I was essentially acting on a hunch. I am still trying to grasp the full implications of that success. My ideas would seem bizarre, would generate a great deal of confusion and disagreement, if I simply tried to communicate them. The evidence of a shared procedure, on the other hand, would be persuasive. And an active flip is valuable. In any other facility, I would not have absolute control over the process, as I require. Without a clear, common understanding of my ideas, any number of things could go wrong. No. I'll offer my work in the context of a treatment, and only in that context."

"As you've said," Excellence notes. "And we're grateful for it."

Excellence turns his attention to Leap Four. "We have tried to convince him to work directly with us. His understanding of the network is too valuable to leave his well-being to the quality of the jury-rigged air-filtration system that his band of rebels is protecting him with. Forgive me, Hamish. We want him to be safe, to carry on his work. But he has other ideas, so we work with him on his terms. We are comfortable compromising where it makes sense and partnering to reach common goals.

"Many have the mistaken impression that the Directorate is driven by a thirst for power, a desire to shape the fate of our species. They believe we are megalomaniacs who are trying to rule the world and to have everything for ourselves. I speak for the board and the executives of Vitalcorp when I assure you that is just not the case. The greatest gift of Join is perspective. We're at the very beginning of understanding this technology and its implications. Its potential wasn't dreamed up by clever MBAs. It's real. Advocate's dreams are real."

"Sir," says Leap Four, "respectfully, the people here, in this facility with Hamish . . ." Chance glances over at Hamish, who is listening intently, worried. In the darkness at the side of the room, Don Kim shifts, becomes more alert. "The people here," Leap continues, "are solos, for the most part. They're not worried about the network. They're worried about other things."

"Yes, so they are," says Excellence. "Well, I am going to say something that I hope you will not repeat. Something that will make a considerable difference and that I'm sure will be welcomed by all of those working with Hamish. We are going to launch a program shortly that will be very meaningful to them.

"It's been forty years since the first join. There are children being raised today by parents who have never known a world without Join. It's time to move to the next level, and we're prepared to do that. It's not public yet, but it will be soon. We're going to change the ground rules. We're going to make licensing very inexpensive, free in many cases. Everyone, and I mean everyone, will be able to afford it. There will no longer be any reason for anyone to remain solo."

Leap is unsure of how to respond. As she hesitates, Excellence recognizes his error. "Of course," he catches himself. "That's not what you meant."

"No," she agrees, and there is a silence.

"I see," he says. "Well, still. That's a secret." Chance chuckles. Excellence smiles.

Excellence then says. "You're talking about the planet. The storms?"

"Yes," says Leap.

"Solos are generally more concerned about that because they feel vulnerable. Joins are able to take a broader view. You understand the benefits of Join, so you know what I'm talking about. But we understand that there are issues to address. We will address them. You will start to see very significant changes very soon. You have my word on it. No one takes these threats more seriously than I do, and I speak for all of Vitalcorp when I say that."

Leap appears to be considering a reply, but Hamish says, "Thank you, Excellence. The offer of a premier join facility to complete the treatment is extremely generous. Of course, I can't speak for Leap, but I trust this opportunity to demonstrate some of the practical applications of my recent network advances will result in a fruitful collaboration."

Excellence appears satisfied. "As do I, Hamish. We need to be working together on these things. They are so important. Thank you for contacting me this morning."

"Not at all, Excellence, not at all."

"I look forward to our shared success."

The black screen with the logo on the embossed seal of Excellence's office replaces the live feed. Then lights come up, and the video display turns off.

.●.

CHANCE IS STUNNED, "I CAN'T believe I was just in a vid con with Hamish Lyons and Excellence."

Don is standing at the end of the row of chairs. "Starstruck?"

"I guess so."

Leap Four says, "He doesn't have a clue."

Hamish turns toward her quickly, "Of course it does. It is a very serious mistake to underestimate Excellence."

Leap Four says, "His attitude toward solos—"

"Is realistic." Hamish interrupts her. "And if it says it's working on environmental concerns, then it is working on environmental concerns."

Leap Three is leaning forward, with the elbows of his long arms on his thighs, stretching his lower back. He and Don exchange a look that Hamish misses.

Leap Four says, her voice taut with restraint, "I've worked with a lot of people who had neat answers to difficult questions. I had to come up with a few myself, when I was fighting for the bank. I don't trust him."

Hamish says, with a persuasive calm, "Integrity is among Excellence's defining characteristics."

"Integrity is often the problem," Leap Four says. Then, "What happens next?"

Hamish stands. "This is very important," he says. "You have to decide."

"Whether to do the join here, or in a Vitalcorp facility?"

"Yes."

"What do you recommend?"

"I think it would be an enormous mistake to do it here. In twelve years, we've done the procedure eight times and failed twice. Both of our failures killed both participants."

Chance says, "Can Leap trust Vitalcorp?"

Hamish is emphatic. "Leap can trust Excellence without reservation. Every single word Excellence said during that conference was true to the extent of its understanding and was spoken without artifice. What you may perceive as deceptive, or evasive, is simply its nature. It does not intend to manipulate you. It is as open and honest in its dealings as human nature allows. It is a very great human being."

Leap Four says, "I just don't understand. What do you get out of working with Vitalcorp?"

"I am working on a treatment for flips."

"And why are they so interested in this work?"

Hamish blinks and then slowly sits back down, the energy and force he had shown just a moment before abruptly gone. He says, "They hope"—he pauses, gathering his thoughts, then starts again—"they hope to learn how to create subnet joins."

"What?" Chance says. "You've been working on that *here*?"

"No, not me," says Hamish.

Chance Four says slowly, "But your work can help them do it?"

"It may," Hamish says.

Elicia, who has been standing near the wall, takes a step forward. She is watching Hamish and is clearly shaken by his sudden uncertainty. "Hamish, what's a subnet join?"

"It's a way around the twenty-drive limit," Chance Four answers. Hamish is turned inward. He's looking at nothing, completely lost in thought.

Chance continues, "If subnets are a viable way to deal with the physiological limits we're encountering, then they might safely get us around the twenty-drive limit. Developing subnets might allow an unlimited number of joins."

"The whole human race," says Leap Three.

Don smiles wryly and says, "Oh, what'd they call it? 'Assimilation'?"

CHANCE ONE AND LEAP TWO are playing chess, many years before. They're in a suite they rented in the Tzinquaw Aerie, a high, solitary spire in the Olympic Mountains, only accessible by pod. The suite has no interior walls, and the external walls are all transparent. It's winter and the landscape is buried in snow, but the sun is roaming near the horizon, and their suite is flooded with cool light.

The sky is clear, but a fast wind worries itself against every outcrop of the spire, creating a faint and high-pitched hum. Both drives are naked, sitting on the floor on top of thick, down comforters. They made love, then napped; had toast with sunflower butter, mimosas out of the central larder; stretched; gazed out from their perfectly climate-controlled perch over the high, windswept, and rocky spine that descends into the frozen lands surrounding them, the rolling miles of snow and wind below, the ragged peaks and serried ridges that cup the sky around them.

Leap's game is quick, surprising. She often opens critical vulnerabilities in her board position, but just as often creates unexpected threats. Chance is methodical, comprehensive, and can be beaten by unexpected tactics deployed with resolution and courage. They're a good match. Chance tries to play when he can borrow cycles from drives who are resting. From things Leap has said, he believes she takes similar precautions.

She lifts a knight but, instead of moving it, regards it speculatively. "You know, chess pieces should join," she says.

"Then they'd be Legos. Different game."

"No, I mean, if the king could see what the rook sees, or the knight, would that change his play?"

"Well, that's . . . the king does see, through you. You see the whole board position."

She sits back. Her body is lit brightly by the sunlight stretching through the curved glass on her right. Her center and her left side are lightly shadowed. The sunlight draws Chance's eye to the line running from beneath her arm to the side of her breast, the full curve from under the nipple back to her side, and then the answering curve of her body that starts beneath her breast and arcs to her hips as she bends forward, examining the knight pensively.

"I think that's what I actually mean," she says. "Not that the individual pieces of one color become joined but that pieces from both sides of the board should join. How would the game look to a single mind who was playing both the white and the black pieces?"

"You mean a practice game?"

"No, not at all. I mean if the stakes were real, and you actually saw all of the pieces in motion. You chose the moves for each one—"

"Would there be a point to it then? What would the stakes be, if there was no opposition?"

"Exactly. That's what I mean, I think."

.◦.

"FINDING THE RIGHT PARTNER FOR your join may not be the first question you have to answer." Hamish is speaking. "But you will need to put some thought into it."

"I don't know," Leap Four says. "This isn't usually how it works. You know, I think usually you either work with a certified join adviser, and agencies, or you tap the fertile ground of your rich social life. And the last time I went looking for a join partner, well, let's just say things didn't go well."

"This may not be how things usually work," Hamish responds, "but they work this way often enough. Yes, this a special case. Joins are often a special case. Correctly understood, they are always a special case. As for your last experience, why didn't you ask your friends?"

Chance is half listening to the conversation with Leap and Hamish while reading an academic paper in the Olympic Archipelago and sitting in an oncology waiting room in New Denver. Chance had wanted to rest Chance Four. Chance Five's recent treatments have been intensive. He has felt wrung out, exhausted, and even while sleeping has been a minor drain on Chance's attention. Chance Four is usually the last drive to tire. Now, with the stress of the cancer therapies and the excitement in Arcadia, she needs a break.

After the conference with Excellence, Hamish continued to argue in favor of the Directorate. The solos, Don, Elicia, Marco, Emily, and the others, seemed divided. They'd left civilization to live in relative isolation because they didn't see the Directorate working on their environmental concerns. Many had lost loved ones in storms or to unmessaged environmental poisoning. And they see an additional, growing threat: an increasing organization of society and privilege around joins. They have stories of bureaucratic blindness and the brutal inertia of misconceived policy.

As it turns out, several of them are terminally ill themselves. Those who are ill, however, refuse to join. There's a general acceptance of the proposition that joining separates them from the concerns of the planet. Chance hears their passion and the unspoken accusation leveled at her and at Leap, but Chance finds their attitude unconstructive. They're angry, so they won't accept an obvious solution? They won't live longer and preserve their hard-earned experience because they can't also save the Earth? They're passionate, convincing in their concern, but blinded by their anger into senseless, self-destructive action.

It's early evening now. Chance wants time away from all of the noisome conviction to think about what's been happening.

Hamish's question has quieted Leap. Leap Four sits back before she replies, clearly uncertain how to respond. Then she straightens up and leans forward on the table again.

"You assume that I had friends." She glances at Chance as she responds to Hamish. "Leap has friends, but I'm not sure Josette did."

Leap Four is exhausted, her red hair somehow appearing disheveled despite being barely longer than stubble. Leap One is exercising at the moment, a tired affair composed of Leap staggering about, jumping, stretching, walking a treadmill until his vitals spike and the solos attending hand him a cup of water and tell him to sit down.

Leap Three, the drive most affected by the encroaching flip, is sleeping. The sclera encircling his blue eyes has gone pink, shot with threads of bloody red. When he's awake, all of Leap's drives are affected.

The lights draw down in most of Arcadia to simulate an eight-hour night, but Chance and Leap have been in areas that aren't running the simulation. Having been in the truck and then the facility for so long has confused Leap's sense of time and, unlike Chance, she has no drives outside to help her calibrate.

Hamish says, "It may take a while for you to find someone willing. The important thing is that the entire situation, your condition, all relevant information, be disclosed to anyone with whom you think you may want to join. Not many people would risk a join with a flip. Even if they tell you they agree, their conviction state may be questionable, and the join could easily fail. I suspect that your best opportunity will lie with someone who already knows you.

"There's often a temptation in a situation like this, when all other options seem to have played out and you still don't have a solution, to find someone who is willing to join with you in order to join with your bank account, as it were. These people are often sympathetic. A student, for example, whom you might genuinely like. But in those situations, people are highly motivated to hide their own histories."

Leap just shakes her head.

"Yes," says Hamish. "Well, it may be difficult to find a partner. That's why you're better off considering your options sooner rather than later. I'll send out word to my contacts as well. We will find someone."

⁂

TEAM TEENAGER DOESN'T HAVE TO tell Chance what to do. Chance knows the nature of the thought that's been trying all night to gain a moment of undivided attention. Still, the team is there, pointing out the obvious.

"It has to be us," they each say with conviction, every one of them, one at a time, from a sort of moonlit tableau where they sit on folding chairs arranged in a circle on what appears as a dock floating on a rippling alpine lake.

Sure, Chance thinks. Sure. Of course, I know that.

The whole team is waiting expectantly. There will be no backing out. But Chance can't quite say it, not yet, not that easily.

Chance thinks, This could kill me, if the treatment doesn't work.

None of the teenagers says anything. Chance knows why they're not talking. Chance knows everything they're thinking. Chance is the teenagers, after all. They aren't responding because whether or not Chance survives after the procedure is, to some extent, beside the point. There is another, greater concern.

Suddenly, Chance is standing on the dock, which is actually a raft anchored and floating in a shallow alpine lake. The chairs are gone. The teenagers are gone. Chance is as alone as a join can be. It's a warm, comfortable evening with a full moon and a cool breeze. Standing at the edge of the raft, Chance looks into the water. The moon is floating there, and a reflection of the lip of the raft ripples gently. Above that should be Chance's reflection. But it's not there. There is only beautiful lake water in clear moonlight, reflecting everything else. No one is looking back.

"Coahuila" —From the Nahuatl,
"Place of the Trees"

So, these guys have their vision of the future, and they're trying to sell it, but all I can think of as I'm reading this shit is, "Oh, cute puppy!"

And then my seven thinks, "Fuck it! I'm gonna eat it!"

So, you know, I'm, you know, I get all backwoods, "I'll kill the puppy, cook it, candy its big puppy eyes for some night when I'm having a friend over for beers."

"Hey, dude, what's that?"

"Puppy eyes!"

And I'm, you know, frissoning like a motherfucker, and then I hear the voice of God!

And God's like, "Dumpy!"

And I'm like, shit, I forgot, a bunch of my parents are religious. So I'm like, "What, God?"

—Dumpy, join comic, from
Change Who You Are, Change What You Are, or Eat Candied Puppy Eyes

AS EXPECTED, CHANCE FIVE'S CANCER doesn't respond to initial treatments. Chance's oncologist has started Chance Five on an aggressive, experimental protocol that has knocked the drive completely out. Chance is groggy and sends Chance One—who is working remotely on projects for the data farm—off to sleep as soon as Chance Four wakes up in Arcadia. But it doesn't help much. Five's treatment is taxing the well-being of all the drives.

Chance Four stands on the cool, tile floor of the bunk room. Her sinuses ache. And maybe she has a touch of bursitis. It feels like it. Overall, she's healthy, though, and these are just visitations, shadows of illness cast by Chance Five's treatments.

Chance Four sits back on the bed and pulls on a pair of thick socks. She stands again and stretches, her long black hair sliding in front of her face, then pads over to a bureau, where she finds a clean blue sweatshirt and loose trousers. The light in the bunk room is kept low for every hour but four out of each twenty-four. She opens the hall door carefully, trying not to disturb the other sleepers.

It's a short walk to the mess area, where at least one of Leap's drives has been sitting continuously almost since they arrived. The hall lights are dampened in a simulation of dawn.

Leap Four is sitting by herself, reading from a screen. A half-eaten bowl of cereal is on the table in front of her. Seeing her raises Chance's spirits. She's one of four other bodies in the room. The other three are solos, talking quietly on the other side of the room.

Chance drops onto a bench across from Leap Four. Leap sets down the screen and smiles at her.

After joining with Leap Four, Leap changed, as a join will, but it has always seemed to Chance that Leap's mannerisms did not map well onto Leap Four's body and features. There were several adjustments, a new kind of pause between words, slight alterations in intonation. But many of the gestures and expressions that Chance thinks of as most directly characterizing Leap didn't change fundamentally. Instead, with Leap Four, those mannerisms seem less "translated" and more "mimed." It surprised Chance at first. As time passed, Chance realized that Leap Four was different than the other Leaps.

Leap Four has always seemed relatively independent, capable of functioning well with less conscious involvement from Leap. There are heated debates about what makes a drive more or less independent and about what drive independence even means, but to Chance, Leap Four embodies it in the best sense.

"I'm only barely able to read," she says. "I realize after a couple of paragraphs that although words pass through my mind and I feel like I've read them, I don't really know what's going on in the story. Then I go back and reread paragraphs, and it happens again. It's almost hypnotic. Just processing words without following the sense of them."

Chance laughs. "Are all of your other drives asleep?"

"Yes," says Leap.

"Well, my Five is in heavy treatment right now," says Chance.

"I've just drained another bag of poison into my central line. It feels to me like Five is melting, and my brains are working from underneath a large, damp rock."

"What are the odds for Five?"

"The oncologist said she would prefer not to tell me the probability of a full five-year remission. She said that every individual is different." Chance laughs. "But it's less than three percent. About ten percent that I'll make it two more months. It's gonna get hard to keep my other drives active. This treatment of Five could knock me out for a while."

"Huh. I can't believe I have someone to commiserate with. Did your oncologist talk about recovery for joins versus recovery for solos?"

"Yeah, that usually works in our favor, but this particular disease is much worse for joins, so she didn't give me those numbers either."

"But you know them?"

"Yes, I do. And she knows I do."

"And they're that bad?"

"Yes, they are."

"Are you hungry?" Leap asks.

"Not yet, I'll eat in a little bit. I was looking for you."

"Here I am."

"Despite my Five, I think I have good news."

Leap Four brightens, her eyes widening, her mouth falling slightly open, and then she carefully and willfully suppresses her excitement. She smiles self-consciously and says in an almost casual way, "Oh, and what kind of news would that be?"

Chance takes a deep breath. "I want to join."

Leap doesn't miss a beat, "You have cancer."

Chance Four erupts with laughter, it starts in her chest and nose, but in a moment it's full throated, belly shaking. She leans back to accommodate it. Leap Four is laughing too. Looking at each other laughing makes them both laugh harder. Chance manages to raise a hand toward Leap and choke out, "You're one to talk," which sets off another round of laughing. In Barcelona, Chance Two laughs out loud while she's walking toward a coffee shop. Chance One laughs into a pillow in the Olympic Archipelago.

After a few more moments, Chance says, "I know. It's asking a lot. But I'm just really hoping you'll consider it." She stops for a moment. As her composure starts to break, she focuses to regain it, to prevent another laughing fit. Though the light-headed feeling started in Chance Four, it's becoming an independent thing and is rolling through Chance One, who continues to chuckle and laugh in one of the bedrooms of Leap's house.

"You know, I'm having a hard time," Chance Four says, "first my Three with a paralytic poison"—and after almost choking on those final two words she closes her eyes and continues to laugh for couple of beats before resuming—"and now the slow, painful, and exhausting destruction of my Five. It's been really trying recently. I'm looking for someone who can, who can *buck me up*." And this breaks them both up again. Through laughter and watering eyes Chance finishes, "Someone I can rely on for the strength I really need to get through this bad patch."

Eventually, Leap manages to nod and say, "Yeah."

When they've calmed down, Chance says, while recovering her breath, "I don't know how to say it. How to really suggest it, really. It seems strange."

"I know," says Leap.

"But I'll join with you," says Chance. "You don't have to do a search again. You don't have to look for strangers you might or might not be comfortable around."

When Chance is done, Leap puts her head in her hands and stares at the table. Then she stands up. She says, haltingly, "Look I . . . thank you. I'm gonna go. I'm feeling overwhelmed right now. I've been up too long. I had a small seizure about an hour ago and banged my head against the wall, there." She touches the wall. "You know I appreciate what you're saying. You know I do. And I've hoped you would say that. I just don't . . . right now, I don't know whether it's the right thing. Hamish, he isn't sure the treatment will work. It could just be that after I join again, the flip doesn't end, and this . . . pain . . . just starts over."

"I know," Chance says. "And I've also known, since I realized it was a flip, that a join might be needed. It's been part of most of the unsuccessful treatments in the past. I've been thinking about this for a while."

"I don't want to take advantage of you while you're exhausted," says Leap softly.

"You aren't."

Leap Four walks around the table. She bends to kiss Chance Four on the cheek. Then she straightens and stands gazing at Chance before sitting to face her, with one leg on either side of the bench.

"There's something you don't know," Leap Four says, "about the flip. Something I would have to tell you, and I don't want to. I don't want to talk about. Don't want to tell anyone."

Chance nods.

Leap says, "Why do you think it happened?"

"Well," Chance says, "you were joining one of your mothers, who was only in her seventies, but very sick. That kind of thing would, during the coupling at the seventh layer, be a classic conviction state weakness. One of you basically changed your mind completely, after it was too late but before there was full integration."

"I did change my mind," Leap says, "but not because of the joining of a mother and son, and not because of the age of Josette's drive."

Chance says, "There was a secret?"

"Yes," says Leap.

"Was it Josette's?"

"Yes. Something that Josette, that I did, that I can't . . ." Leap is quiet for a moment, then says, "If we were to join, I'd have to tell you what it is."

Chance thinks for a moment. "Pearsun?" she asks.

"Yes, Mark was involved."

Chance waits. After another moment, Leap says, "Let's hear what Hamish says, about the rest of the treatment. Let's hear what it involves. Then you can think about what you want to do."

Leap Four is waiting for agreement from Chance. It's clear that Leap wants to leave, but Chance feels a need to revisit the topic that Leap has avoided.

"Mark Pearsun, your attorney, committed suicide," Chance says.

"Yes, he did," Leap Four says. "He . . . he gassed himself."

"You've said some things that have made me wonder whether you might know why he did that."

Leap Four looks at the half-empty bowl she had been using, pulls it toward her, and stares at it. She turns it with both hands as she says, "What if I told you that at one point Mark wanted to kill me? Kill Himiko."

Chance feels a dizzying shift, a current pulling toward deeper water. "Why would he want that? Why would he possibly want that?"

"There was something . . . between Mark and me that I haven't told you about. I'm not sure if I'm ready to tell you. But Mark had had problems for a while. I don't think he ever felt comfortable in a world with joins."

"But that's not everything, is it? It still feels as though you're being . . . evasive about Mark's suicide."

"Right now, I'm tired," Leap Four says. "I want to tell you. But it's hard to talk about right now."

"All right," says Chance. "But if we're talking about joining, we need to have this conversation."

"You just brought this all up," Leap says. "I'm going to need time to get used to the idea."

Chance says, "You hadn't thought about us joining before this?"

"Hamish will find someone to join with me," Leap says. "He sees me as an opportunity. So does the Directorate. I'm sure that they'll do everything they can to find a join I'm comfortable with. You don't need to do this."

"You once told me you didn't understand how anyone could join with a stranger."

"Now I do."

"Okay, yes," Chance says. "I agree that you don't *have* to tell me."

Leap Four shakes her head, as if trying to clear the conversation. She looks at the table while one of her hands rests on her lap, clenching and unclenching.

"I mean it," Chance says. "I'm ready to go into the join knowing that I'm going to learn something difficult about you. When I learn it, when we're joined, I won't flip because I won't be surprised."

"And what if it's more than you can handle?" Leap asks.

"It won't be."

Leap Four straightens and turns to face Chance. "Thank you," she says. "But you know I can't do that."

She glances about, noting the other people in the room. They're out of range of moderately raised voices and are intent on their own business.

"I've thought about telling you before," Leap says.

Chance waits patiently. Leap tries to start several times. Her mouth starts to move, but as she looks at Chance she stops. Finally, she says, "To tell you, I have to tell you something that I did. But *I* didn't do it. I *never* would do it."

Chance Four watches Leap Four while they both try to find a way through the impasse.

"Can you use your names from before the join?" Chance asks.

"Yes. But I've been trying that. Those names *are* me, and it doesn't work."

"You said," Chance begins, "that Mark might have wanted to kill Himiko. Did Josette?" The last two words are spoken quietly and float delicately into the space between them.

Leap closes her eyes and shakes her head no.

"Did Mark kill someone?"

Leap nods.

"Who?"

"Mark, he killed . . . he killed my uncle."

Chance's perspective shifts again. The two of them are both drifting, held by a current that's circling. She asks, "Did Josette—"

Leap speaks before Chance has finished. "*I* told Mark to *kill my uncle.*"

"Why, Leap?"

Leap Four is shaking her head no, but her head is also simply shaking, as if in a seizure.

"Leap, why did you do it?"

"I *didn't*. I *wouldn't*."

Chance stands and quickly walks around the table to put her arms around Leap Four. "It's okay," Chance says. "I'm sorry. I don't need to know anything more. We'll join. It's okay."

"I was alone," Leap Four is barely able to speak. "*I killed him*, and it left me alone."

.●.

HAMISH'S STEADY GAZE TAKES IN both Leap One and Chance Four. The three of them are sitting in one of the many chambers that the Arcadians have carved out of the Earth's mantle. Most of the rooms are meant as places for informal conversation. They're painted in bright colors and filled with soft, comfortable furniture. This is one of a small minority that's painted off-white everywhere, even on the cement floor. It's also filled with severe, welded furniture and is lit by glow strips, which cast light in every direction, canceling shadows. Chance prefers these areas, which incline toward clarity over comfort. Leap says it's a false choice, that comfort encourages clarity. Chance still prefers these areas.

As he speaks, Hamish is leaning forward from one of the angular metal chairs that forms their small triangle of chairs in one corner of the room.

"To create a flip," he says, "as you know, one of the individuals in a join changes their mind completely, decides they will not join—not just that they don't want to but that they will not, under any circumstances, join. And this happens at a critical moment.

"So why does this happen?" Hamish's voice takes on a slightly professorial tone, as if long explanations come naturally to him and he believes it's important that they not be hurried. "Well, we don't fully understand the quantum network that makes a join possible, but we think of the network connection as happening progressively over seven layers.

"The caduceus, the physical interface with the mind, is the first layer. The subject's conviction state, their commitment to the join, is the second. An interesting thing to note is that while we may consider convictions flexible, during a join, a participant's *conviction state* is binary and absolute. It may be worth noting that possessing the required conviction state appears to be a uniquely human attribute.

"Together, these first two layers create the possibility of a quantum gate. The word "gate" is only a metaphor, and in some respects is very deceptive. We might say instead that an identity is realized, but the gate metaphor will be of use later.

"The third layer is a required similarity in the physical structure of the connecting brains. Because only humans have joined, the third layer is largely hypothetical, although there is some evidence to suggest it exists. For example, there have been mental injuries that we believe prevented a join at this layer.

"The fourth layer is developmental similarity. Two brains may be physically compatible initially, but over time they may develop so differently that a join between them is no longer likely. The fifth layer is compatibility. This is where you see failure due to cultural or linguistic incompatibility. Compatibility at the fifth layer, in particular, is very difficult to predict. Differences that seem substantial to outward appearances may be negligible in practice. Or the reverse may be true. Failure at the fourth or fifth layer is rare and suggests that the individuals simply don't understand each other. Not that they can't, but that they don't right now. After integration at the fifth layer, a large amount of information is exchanged.

"Which establishes the possibility for integration at the sixth layer. The sixth layer of the join is values compatibility. Failure happens here when individuals have incompatible values. Human beings are generally compatible at the level of fundamental values, but there can be critical differences, and people often learn to hide their true values, even from themselves. If the sixth layer does integrate, however, then information flows freely.

"The seventh and final layer of integration happens in response to the free flow of information. Some consider the seventh layer simply an extension of the sixth, but whereas failure during the sixth layer is safe, failure during the seventh can be catastrophic. A symmetric failure, where both sides change conviction state, is typically harmless. It's also very rare. What's even more rare, though, is an asymmetric failure, what we call a flip. Only one individual's conviction state changes.

"The classic case is an elderly person joining to avoid dying. On confronting the reality of Join, they are repelled by the prospect of complete integration with another individual. But this is not the only type of case.

"Now, in a healthy join, we believe that two minds use the caduceus to create a reality in which a quantum gate is opened, and information passes through that gate, if you will. In a flip, many of us believe the gate oscillates—although there is vigorous debate around its relationship with time—between a reality in which it is open and one in which it literally does not exist, and the join has failed.

"One obstacle in treating a flip is that we cannot adequately model the full, observable effects of the caduceus at a quantum level. For example, a healthy join of four sustains four open quantum gates, one for each active drive. If a drive dies, a gate closes. But if three of the four drives die, a single gate remains open. This final gate, as I'm sure you're both aware, is one of the deepest mysteries of join science.

"Though our instrumentation says the final gate is open, that gate no longer spans minds. So what keeps the gate open? To what is it connecting? Some believe the caduceus connects to the *possibility* of a join." Hamish allows himself a rare moment of unmodulated enthusiasm as he says, "*That* is a *mystery*." He pauses to let the others consider what he's said before continuing.

"We cannot simply remove the caduceus. After it has been used in a join, removal of a caduceus will kill the host. Fortunately, we don't have to address the mysteries of Join in order to treat Leap. Instead, we focus on another curiosity. Once a flip is introduced to a network, you may euthanize all but one drive, but you never close the oscillating gate that is the source of the pathology. In a flip, the final gate is always the oscillating gate. So by euthanizing all but one drive, we can isolate and address the oscillating gate.

"I have had one success. A few years ago, I introduced a slight modification to an active caduceus and created what I think of as a complementary gate. It exists beside the flipped gate and is also both open and closed, but it does not move information. The coexistence of the flipped gate and the complementary gate appeared to resolve the flip."

Chance says slowly, "So far, gates have been unmanaged and fully open."

"Yes," agrees Hamish.

"You're combining an open and a closed gate."

"Yes."

"If they coexisted, could they be used to influence the flow of information?"

"Perhaps. The language we're using is very simple. The reality is not so simple."

"So that's how you get to a subnet," Chance says finally.

"Yes, that may be," Hamish says. "The Directorate believes that a complementary gate may be a key to understanding a so-called subnet join. A subnet would be a cluster of fewer than twenty drives, coordinated by a single mind. Each subnet would connect to the larger network through this different sort of gate.

"Many other questions would need to be answered, but I think we know enough about the nature of join to entertain this possibility."

Leap says slowly, "Excellence said that they're reducing licensing fees."

Hamish looks at Leap with undisguised surprise, as if Leap has just calmly plucked a bird from the air between them. "Why, yes, he did. I also connected that with my research on the complementary gate. I'm impressed that you put it together."

"I'm not sure I'm following," says Chance.

"What I think we're saying," Leap says, "is that they're reducing fees to encourage more joins, potentially because of this. Because they're preparing for the single network, the hive mind."

"'Hive mind' is an emotionally loaded metaphor," Hamish says. "The root issue is change. Why should we assume that what we believe to be fundamental about us is immune to change? What else in the universe is? And if the things we think of as fundamental to our essence are the things driving us toward our destruction, perhaps we should remain open to the possibility of changing them."

"But that is what you're saying, isn't it?" insists Leap. "That the reduced licensing fees are a way to move people toward accepting this goal."

"Of course, I don't know," Hamish says. "I drew that inference from our conversation with Excellence. And I do believe that it, Excellence, expected me to draw that inference when it talked about licensing."

Chance asks, "Why didn't he just come out and say it?"

"For Excellence, whose speech and actions can have far-reaching impact, implication is often the same as saying it. Certainly, the idea of a single vast mind connecting all of humanity would be more palatable to those among the populace who have already experienced join."

"And you want the Directorate to have that knowledge?" asks Leap.

"If it is possible to have it," says Hamish, "they will have it eventually, whether I help them acquire it or not." He sounds even more cautious than usual. "They know I've been successful with the complementary gate, so they know it's possible. They know what my interests are, my areas of expertise. The question for me is not whether I want them to have the knowledge; it's whether I want to be a part of their acquiring the knowledge. But I choose not to answer that question.

"I am interested in the knowledge for its own sake. I believe there is a universal, underlying principle that drives progressive discovery. I believe, without question, that science is actually in my very nature." He is watching Leap intently as he says, "As for this situation, what I want is peer review." He pauses and straightens in his chair, looking at each of them individually. "So the real question is for you," he says, "now that you are aware of the broader implications. Do you want to complete your join here, with us, or there, with them?"

The question lands in Chance's mind like a flash of light. Neither she nor Leap can find anything to say in response.

"You don't have to decide now," Hamish says. He glances at Chance and then turns to Leap. "And I don't know whether it will influence your decision, but you still need to find another individual willing to join."

"Okay," says Leap.

"Your treatment has three stages," Hamish continues. "First, we have to euthanize all but one of your drives. I'm very sorry. The choice of which drive survives will not affect the outcome. That is your choice.

"When you have only one active drive, I will make the required alteration to that drive's caduceus. This is a very delicate surgical procedure, but I have everything I need here, and I am very capable of it. After the caduceus has been modified, however, it must be used in a join. I believe that that has to happen within two weeks of the alteration of the caduceus, but the sooner it happens, the greater the likelihood of success."

. ●.

THE HOTEL IN BARCELONA IS old-style, simple elegance: weathered dark wooden furniture, hand smoothed from many decades of wear, oiled and rubbed to a high shine.

Chance Two has essentially been vacationing, and she has been a source of much-needed cycles as events developed in Arcadia. There's no hurry to return; no need to be back at work. Chance will stay at the hotel for as long as possible.

A yellow comforter is massed at the foot of the bed. Initially, the bed felt refreshing—a perfect fit the first night; but now it's starting to feel weak in the middle, as if the mattress is well past its best days. Chance Two had a slight lower backache this morning, which she worked out with a long walk and strong coffee. Now she's sitting at the modestly sized, dark mahogany desk, looking out the window at a handful of pigeons who are huddling on the rail of her fourth-floor terrace. One of them steps off the rail and falls out of sight.

The display that she has unfolded on the desktop in front of her shows images of the El Coahuilón Mountains. She started with the spire city Cordial before the storm. It was a new development, begun only thirty years ago with what were eventually classified as short spires. Five years later, during what has been called the first moment of true join architecture, the early spires went up.

Like many buildings of the period, the early spires emphasized long, cylindrical forms, but they were also varied, playful. Braided spires of multiple cylinders rose to an anemonelike crest. Spires that undulated horizontally before rising vertically. Spires the color of sunlight and moonlight, spires with the rich and varied green finish of kelp or that began in broad bulbs like bull kelp. The full effect, realized perhaps fifteen years after those first spires—and which Cordial became known for—was of a tangled underwater forest growing in clumps on the dry slopes of a low mountain range. Few spire communities emulated it. It was considered over the top, garish, to some, but also acknowledged as a showcase of architectural possibility.

The first video of the storm that she watched was taken on a sunny day from the height of one of the spires. It showed the glittering spread of the spire community under sunlight. In the distance, the horizon was black and fulminating. The video had no sound.

A follow-up was about eight minutes long. It showed a wall

of dark gray turmoil, as of a hurricane funnel, but massive, unimaginably broad. In the battering, crackling audio a voice called it, with ominous theatricality, *"La espada di Dios."* The sword of God.

As the video started, the edge of the storm was creeping forward over a slope, shattering short spires, swirling their pieces into a vortex, and tearing chunks out of the ground. As Chance watched, the storm consumed two full spires, one of which shivered into thousands of beautiful shards. The shards were quickly lost in the maelstrom. The other spire came apart in large chunks. It also disappeared.

There were videos that showed the hovering storm during the days when it squatted on top of the area where the spire community had been. As the storm slowly dissipated, people grew bolder and began to venture into the devastation in its wake.

Videos of the area after the storm showed a flattened and churned landscape, shocked rescue workers finding pieces of bodies in trees miles from the actual storm. There were interviews with solos who left before the storm arrived and somehow made their way to a hastily constructed refugee camp in the city of Saltillo. Several were crying as they talked of their losses. Their stories drowned Chance.

The short spires of Cordial were notorious for a thriving black market for mined commodities. Revolutions in the scale and efficiency of tunneling equipment had made the black market possible. The short spires throughout the El Coahuilón region were places where a small, enterprising team could purchase some mining tech, find a spot to mask the entrance of their operation, and, if they were fortunate, make good within a few years. Many of the solos in the videos were hard-bitten, grime-encrusted men and women who had been taking such risks for decades.

A join in Edinburgh had lost two drives in the storm. It was adamant in its demands of world governments, of the Directorate, of all the institutions who wield true power. "I was a nine. I'm now, because of inaction and apathy on the part of our authorities, a seven. Never mind how the feral, solo community of the area was affected. Their terrible losses."

Of course, like so many things happening in the past few decades, such a storm had not been contemplated or planned for. There were warnings about weather patterns; there were other freak occurrences. But after the storm hit, the majority opinion on the network was that a storm of such magnitude in such an unlikely location was both unprecedented and unforeseeable.

Associated with their storm coverage, several outlets revived coverage of the many global weather-management systems that had been proposed over the previous two decades. For the most part, they were deemed too large, too impractical, the science too uncertain, the needed research too expensive. And those systems did nothing to address myriad other environmental challenges such as detoxification or the resurrection and repopulation of wild species. Civ News reports concluded that the issues were systemic, the system complex, and that storms like El Coahuilón were simply anomalies.

Chance has some understanding of meteorology and has spent a career learning about the vagaries of known storm systems. When people in the videos she watched described the storm as impossible, she heard the word echo in her own heart, within the hollow chambers of her own fulsome certainty. She would also have said it was impossible. Now she'll have to learn why it was likely.

As Chance Two watches these videos, somewhere in North America, Hamish, Chance, and Leap have begun their conversation about what Excellence was actually saying during the conference and about how Leap might be treated. When Hamish is done talking, Chance Two goes back to bed.

.●.

HAMISH HAD SAID, "WHEN YOU have only one active drive, I will make the required alteration to that drive's caduceus."

When you have only one active drive. Leap Four lies on her back under a green wool blanket, facing the ceiling. Chance Four sits beside the bed, thinking about Leap Four's eyes. Right now, they appear to be dark brown, but the irises are usually slightly lighter, with a hint of orange, and are solid. They aren't flecked with other colors. Leap Four blinks and turns to look at Chance. It's clear that Leap wants to speak, but there's a slackness in her face that implies that speaking may be beyond her. Not knowing how to help Leap, Chance offers a restrained smile and puts a hand to Leap's forehead. Leap doesn't respond in any way, just looks dully into Chance's face.

As a join, Chance has gotten used to a sense of security. When Renee and Ashton—Chance One and Two—first joined, Chance practiced feeling safe. Chance would stand close enough to an electric transformer to hear the hum or walk at the edge of an aqueduct in New Denver or just look down from a pod's travel lane, and when the nagging, subtle sense of disastrous possibility made itself known, Chance would think: Even if this drive dies, I won't. There were moments when the insight took hold powerfully, making the world more vivid, richer. And there were more and more moments when the anxiety was simply not aroused. When there was no sense of risk.

Over time, Chance found that the body might still flinch: a drive's pulse might race, its heart pump adrenaline. But a join could manage a drive that was in peril, soothe it, smooth its responses, and direct it toward action. It became easier to face the prospect of a body dying.

That changed so many things. Throughout history, when solos engaged in ambitious projects, they might say something like "I'm working against the clock. I want to see this completed in my lifetime." Joins could spot the real risks of multigenerational projects—funding and irrelevance.

It also changed things at a personal level. After joining with Chance Four, Chance won every Jai Kido tournament that Chance Four entered except two. Speed was her weapon. Her body would never be where her opponents' expected it to be. Her hands would avoid her opponents' defenses. Chance Four would suddenly have a hold on their arms and bodies and would be forcing them to the floor. That was how she experienced it. Chance Four was clearly gifted, and Chance practiced endlessly. During tournaments, Chance focused on winning and trusted the drive.

In the second tournament she lost, Chance Four was slammed to the mat by another drive so suddenly that she had no memory of it happening. She was just down. She struck the mat at an odd angle and pulled a muscle in her neck.

It was a jarring impact, and Chance feared she might have been permanently hurt. That her spine might be injured. Losing Chance Four would be difficult but not *crippling*. Chance felt only the briefest intimation of mortality and quickly dismissed it.

Watching Leap lying in her near coma of grief and disorientation, Chance is acutely aware that all of Leap is lying on the bed. Leap has only a single perspective. In fact, at this moment, Leap has a gender.

It's a temporary state. But no matter how confident Hamish is of the surgery, the procedure will require opening the one cranium Leap has left. Chance glances at Elicia, sitting near the foot of the bed. Tall and slender, folded into a narrow wooden chair like a stick figure. She catches Chance's eye and smiles.

"How do you do it?" Chance asks.

"What?" Elicia asks.

"Live so close to the edge."

A look of annoyance flickers across Elicia's face, but she says, "You're thinking about Leap?"

"I've sometimes thought about what it would be like to go back to being solo. But I never believed it would happen. Not since I became Chance. I always assumed I would have more drives, a richer life, more choices, a broader perspective."

Chance appreciates how well Elicia hides her distaste for what Chance has said. Maybe it's not distaste; maybe Chance is just tired and paranoid and is mistaking how Elicia feels. Elicia smiles wanly. She says, "You were very respectful with Leap One."

Chance turns to Leap to see if the reference has hurt her, but Leap is looking at the ceiling again and appears impassive. Chance says, "That was difficult."

They had euthanized Leap Three first. He took a sleeping pill. Ernie, one of Arcadia's doctors, had strapped a mask to his face, then turned a valve that pumped in carbon monoxide. Hamish and Leap had agreed that killing both Leap Three and Leap One at the same time could be too traumatic for Leap.

But Hamish had first made the argument, energetically, that it might be the right thing to do. Leap had already lost Leap Two. Hamish was concerned that after Leap Three died, Leap would decide to face the flip rather than lose another drive.

When Leap did balk, Hamish reminded Leap of their agreement. "Remember, I told you how you were going to feel, and you chose to euthanize first one and then the other, rather than doing both at the same time. This next step is hard, but you must take it. Your fear is pushing you in the wrong direction."

"Oh," replied Leap One. "Oh, if you only knew how many people in my life have presumed to know more about what I wanted than I do."

Hamish accepted the rebuke, his lids lowering briefly, and a very slight nod demonstrating regret. "Yes, of course," he said. "I'm sorry."

"You can't know how I feel about this body. This isn't a drive. I gave birth to this."

"I am truly sorry."

And then something happened that Chance hadn't seen before. There was some discussion of it in the literature, where it was referred to as "simulated autonomy" or occasionally "facile autonomy"—an intense response to feelings of guilt, in which the join retreats from the reality of the union and attempts to simulate a reality in which one or more drives are still independent.

It was as if Leap had decided to let Leap One make the case for his own survival. Leap Four sat unmoving in one of the wooden chairs, like the one Elicia is sitting in now, and watched as Leap One advocated passionately and almost incoherently for changing Hamish's approach to the treatment.

"I know you think you understand all of this," Leap One began.

"I don't," Hamish replied.

Leap, clearly ramping toward an argument, stopped for a moment but then plunged ahead. "I mean the network connection, the flip."

"I know what you mean," said Hamish.

And Leap paused again before taking another deep breath and continuing. "There's evidence," he said, "that a bath of organic copolymers, such as polylactic acid and polyglycolic acid, stabilizing a matrix of silver-coated graphene nanotubes, will safely inhibit and then degrade the quantum properties of a caduceus without altering the mind's magnetic signature."

"That's meaningless nonsense," Hamish said sadly. "There is no such evidence. And if there were, would you want that solution applied inside your skull?"

"If it would save me. If it would save me, I would."

"You're going to be fine."

It went on. Leap Four watching with the same look she wore now while Leap One attempted to debate Hamish by drawing on the years that Leap studied alternative theories of join science. Chance was surprised by Leap's breadth and depth of knowledge, by the volume of loosely connected detail that Leap rushed through—manically and meticulously—while arriving at one unsupportable conclusion after another. At one point, Leap spent ten minutes cataloging famous cases of meme viruses with such rapidity and in such detail that Chance, with a professional's depth of knowledge, was left breathless. At the end of that magnificent and pitiable display, Chance felt the injustice of Hamish coolly dismissing both the detail Leap had produced and the question it led to with a single, simple judgment, "Nonsense."

After nearly an hour of barreling forward, Leap One began diving into an exploration of the possible quantum effects of meteorologic phenomena, and Hamish looked at Chance out of the corner of his eye, raising an eyebrow questioningly. Asking for help. Elicia had quietly entered the room fifteen minutes before. She stood listening from across the room.

"Elicia," Chance Four shouted the name, catching Leap's attention and interrupting the manic flow, "do you know if Ernie is ready?"

"He is," she said.

And then Chance Four turned to Leap One, who was standing very still and staring wide eyed at her. "You have to do this," Chance said calmly, "so that we can join. There is no other treatment that you, or I, can trust my life to."

Both of Leap's drives were quiet. Then Leap One took a deep breath, grimacing, his face reddening. He acknowledged with a slight tip of his head that Chance was right. Leap's fever had burned itself out.

Now Leap One is dead, and Chance and Leap are waiting for Hamish, who will arrive with an oral anesthetic for Leap Four, Leap's last drive. Twenty minutes after she swallows it, they'll wheel her into the operating theater, they'll apply the second- and third-tier anesthetics, and then Hamish will begin the adjustment to her caduceus.

·●.

CHANCE IS THINKING ABOUT TWO different songs. The first, "Petals of the Rose," is an up-tempo ballad:

> *the petals of the rose unfold*
> *revealing what the center holds*
> *an emptiness whose presence molds*
> *the petals of the rose*

It was a hit for Sky and Lick, fifteen years ago. Chance is overlaying a lyric Chance Five heard while waiting for a drug infusion:

> *so this song is*
> *what we can promise*
> *peace and justice*
> *if you trust us*
> *hope and freedom*
> *whenever you need 'em*
> *love and honor*
> *when you're a goner*

For the most part, joins filter out information they aren't interested in from the different environments surrounding their drives—sounds, smells, feels—just as solos do. But they also sometimes choose to pay attention to multiple things simultaneously. The interplay of sound heard simultaneously in different places inspired the genre of comusic, in which whole songs are overlaid on top of each other. It's not an enormously popular genre, but Chance likes it. Every once in a while, as a distraction, Chance tries to work out how two or more songs might sound as comusic. Where they'd fit together, where they wouldn't.

Chance is trying not to think about what will happen if the flip is not cured. Leap and Chance agreed to let the Directorate complete the join, though Chance is not sure whether Leap had really been paying attention. They made the final decision after the adjustment to Leap Four's caduceus, and Leap was still in shock. Hamish was clearly relieved when Chance told him.

For Chance, the decision was easy. Join should be an almost risk-free procedure. The Arcadians had failed two out of the eight times they'd tried it, killing both participants in each failure. Hamish had explained that there were particular complications with each of the eight cases that the Arcadians worked on. With a record like that, however, the Arcadians had no business even attempting joins. On the other hand, the team the Directorate had assembled was the very best.

The possibility of making a contribution to the understanding of exactly what was happening during a join was exciting. It might eventually lead to a fundamental change in the nature of the human species. Of course, that was only a theoretical possibility, subject to many dependencies. Whereas improved understanding and an increase in knowledge was a high likelihood. Considered on its own, that was a good thing.

So Chance Four and Leap had taken sleeping pills. They'd said goodbye to the Arcadians and then closed their eyes. They were fed intravenously for three days while they were unconscious.

Once, Chance Four jolted awake briefly. She was traveling in a pod, beside a drive that Chance didn't recognize. At that moment, Chance was mixing Chance One and Chance Two. Something about the upcoming procedure had made Chance sexually hungry. Chance Five wasn't healthy enough to participate, so One and Two were alone. The sex was particularly intense, and the combined orgasm broke Chance's concentration and sent a thrill through all four of Chance's drives. Afterward,

Chance Four quickly resumed her dreamless slumber. She eventually awoke in a Directorate hospital.

All of Chance's drives are lying down now, in anticipation of the join. Each of them fading into a gentle drug-induced rest. Chance will soon be completely unconscious. Each join procedure that Chance has undergone has felt unique. The wealth of experience gained during a join tended to reveal itself gradually over the course of the weeks, months, and years afterward. Memories or even skills often became evident only when events called them forth. That aspect of being a join was consistent.

But for Chance, memories of procedures—the time before and after a particular join—were more akin to a taste or a color, the quality of a touch or a specific time of day. They were core, sensual experiences, each unique, each requiring a new and different kind of language to adequately describe. Focusing on the memory of a procedure could shake Chance with a mixture of emotions that might leave one drive plastered with a silly grin and another weeping.

So Chance had some idea of what to expect, but this join would also be different. Leap was already a five, with mental resources reduced to that of a single drive. Even after Chance's years of personal experience and years of studying join science, this join felt like a dive into an unknown as profound and complete as Chance's imagination was capable of encompassing.

⠂⠢

CHANCE AND LEAP HAVE JOINED. A person is speaking, using Josette's voice. The complex of memories that Chance is experiencing has an acid-etched quality, as of things that have been worked endlessly, touched and returned to by a corrosive, anxious attention.

There is Mark Pearsun's office, elongated, filled with dark places that may be merely shadows or may not exist at all. A sense of panic and more than panic, an immense and unspecific emotional charge hangs in the air between Chance and a clear reading of what is happening.

Mark makes a dismissive gesture. He's sitting behind his desk, his face slightly aslant. The memory ripples as waves of anger and guilt break against one another.

And then a cyclone of conflicting emotion, a real and tangible pain that makes eyes clench shut, jaws freeze, makes muscles wooden so that no words can be formed and teeth cannot meet, even to grind together.

The world is decaying, and a wall of churning night rises around Chance. First, it is a memory of the join between Leap and Josette, stark and intrusive, unavoidably absorbing. Then there is a rushing outward from the boundaries of memory. It overwhelms. It consumes Chance.

TOMOHIRO, HIMIKO'S UNCLE, WAS A stubborn man. He had that, at least, to answer for.

After all of Josette's work, the years of unraveling risk while fending off her brother-in-law's idiotic attempts to run things, the flip has its roots in a single deal—a kind of financing Josette would normally never touch—mezzanine financing for a parts supplier for deep-water mineral extraction.

Everyone is enthusiastic. The company is exceeding milestones against an earlier round of secured debt. Their technology is state of the art. They're well positioned in a booming trade. If Josette's finance group supplies the money, she'll get a board seat and a detailed look inside the industry. A loss would be painful, but she could recover. Because they've already participated in an earlier round, they do quick diligence. Everyone else, already smitten, follows her lead.

Four months later, Mark tells her about a conversation with a line manager and a bitter comment about Monterey Bay. Monterey Bay, one of the few recovering coastal marine ecosystems. She brings it up with the CEO. "We're not concerned," he says. He won't say it isn't true.

She and Mark begin months of research. Their first real jolt is connecting company executives to a web of proxies and holding companies. From there, they go down a rabbit hole. The manufacturing company they've backed is at the public end of a long and live high-voltage wire.

An appointment with Tomohiro, her gardener, appears on her calendar. It's odd. They see each other regularly at the estate. But he has called her admin and scheduled a time. She's actually happy to see him, assuming it'll be a change of pace.

Tomohiro blindsides her. God knows how he got wind of it, but he's done his homework. It's almost eerie. He recites data—numbers, a précis of salient facts about the Monterey Bay and Monterey Canyon, lists of chemical compounds and their effects on living tissue. He gives her a history of complex changes in seawater composition, cumulative effects on various habitats, a long list of regulatory concerns. He's spellbinding. All of it delivered rapidly and with a quiet, unblinking certainty that leaves her weak with fury.

Into the silence that sweeps the room when he's done, she says simply, "Let me look into it."

If he did it on his own, as appears to be the case, Tomohiro would have had to have been working on that performance for months. But all he really has is an avalanche of correlations. It's extremely persuasive, but there is no smoking gun tying the company directly to the environmental damage. There are potentially arguable assumptions. She knows that might not matter.

As Mark says, when she tells him of Tomohiro's "project," "If this gets to the press, there'll be an investigation, and those guys are dirty. This is a black hole. Everything we have could be sucked in."

If they can reach Tomohiro and get him to listen, they might limit the damage.

.●.

CHANCE REMEMBERS A LARGE MAN lit from behind by strong sunlight. Chance is a small girl. Her name is Himiko. She is six years old. Everything is bigger than her. Quiet is her shield.

The man hits her face. She falls backward onto asphalt, her neck twisting so her cheek and forehead strike stone. She's scared for one of her eyes, but after a moment her vision clears again.

She doesn't know him. He had helped her, but when she asked someone else a question, he got angry.

He yells at her. His face is dark. His clothes are filthy and stained. There is blood on her cheek and on her hand. He turns. She stands and runs away as fast as she can.

That is one of Himiko's earliest memories as she traveled alone from Ulaanbaatar to her uncle Tomohiro's house. She spent the whole trip running away from that man.

The first time she sees Tomohiro, he reminds her of the man. But while the man was a darkness, she soon learns that Tomohiro lives in a world of vivid color. Tomohiro's tidy cottage is different than anything she has known before, filled with the braided fragrances of cut flowers and sharpened by a faint, acerbic scent of cleanser.

She wore a chain around her neck during her journey. Tomohiro told her it held a laminated card, explaining that her name was Himiko, and she was going to live with him. They don't know what happened to it, but Himiko likes the idea that she has been explained. Every so often, she gives Tomohiro a new explanation, written on a square of paper.

"I am Himiko. I am clure my hare. I am at house."

"My name is Himiko. I await for cake."

"I, Himiko, am good."

"I am Himiko, the girl who found the dog."

"Thank you for the lesson. I believe all nematodes are angry."

Among Chance's memories are these: A sprig of lemon peel that Tomohiro twisted into her tea. The light way he held his red coffee mug with both hands. The louse she found crawling through his black hair, trying to hide in the gray. The time he stood for twenty minutes at the school open house, in front of a drawing she had made. How he beamed cheerfully as he greeted the other parents. The month he taught her about stick bugs and beetles.

JOSETTE RECONCILED HERSELF TO THE facts. She had made a mistake. The bet had been too large, and she hadn't looked closely enough before committing her money. If that damaged her business, that was a price she would have to pay.

She meets Tomohiro at a popular barbecue place, Josette still feeling bruised from their previous encounter. As she sits across from him, a single word forms in her mind: "principled." From her years of working with him, she knows he is principled. And while she's always appreciated that about him, she also knows from experience that principles can be a source of the worst kind of havoc.

"I think perhaps your time here will be wasted," he says at the start. "I told you as a courtesy. I think there is nothing you can do."

She disagrees. She is open, direct, and respectful as she lays out the plan she and Mark have developed. Now that she has full control of the business, it's time for her to give back. They will create a foundation, with significant resources from the beginning, that can grow over time. It'll focus on cleaning up the bay. In time, it will also extend to related projects.

What's more, Tomohiro has made it abundantly clear that she hasn't been seeing his full potential. They'll build the foundation together, with him as a primary policy adviser.

"I appreciate what you're saying, of course," Tomohiro says. "And I know you are a good person. Though perhaps not good enough. I wish I could help you."

She presses on, but he resists her. Each variation, each concession—none of it means anything to him. At the end, after he has rebuffed a plea to simply wait for her to cut ties with the company, he asks, "What does Leap think of this business?"

She is desperately trying to imagine something that will interest him.

"I haven't told him," she admits.

Tomohiro draws in a hissing breath. He says, "Perhaps you should not be involved in a business that you cannot speak of with your child."

Josette recoils.

Tomohiro continues, "I can see your situation is difficult. I can see that you love your son and are trying to build a better life. I am not so different from you in that. But I think more broadly about what it means to make a good life."

⸙

"SANCTIMONIOUS SON OF A BITCH" is how the call with Mark begins, in a pod as she's flying away. Then there is a torrent of language that she remembers only as anger.

How could he judge her? He didn't really know her. She has fought with every fiber of her being against venality and stupidity. That's who she is.

Mark says, "It'll be the whole thing, Josette. All gone. I didn't tell you, but there's a trail. An employee complained, on a recorded call, and they didn't do anything."

Josette is high above the ground, falling. "You didn't tell me," she says numbly. Then "Who are these people?"

"It'll be everything," Mark says, "a financial blow, regulatory issues, the wrath of the press. Everything we . . . everything you and I have built. I'm talking about dissolution of the company. But I'm also talking about something else. I'm talking about a way to protect everything. And I'm saying I don't see other options. He may have to be removed."

This isn't her. This isn't Mark. It is her anger that moves her lips to say, "Go on."

"I did some digging," Mark says. "There are people who can make sure secrets are kept."

Then the memory stretches, wavers. Did he really say it that way? Is this really what happened? She says, "Do they know that he's come to us? Do they know what he has?"

"They won't know details. We just tell them what we need."

"Can they talk to him? Just scare him?"

"These aren't the kind of people who talk."

She already knows what she'll say. "Do it."

After a pause, Mark asks, "Does he have any dependents?"

Mark knows that he does. Tomohiro has a niece. Himiko.

"Don't hurt her."

"If he told her—"

"Mark, do what I said."

- ● ,

CHANCE SEES JOSETTE AS HIMIKO first saw her—powerful, beautiful, smart. Josette's feelings of guilt are initially expressed as interest, then as devotion, and then the guilt is hidden, and other feelings take root in fields that the guilt has cleared and plowed— a growing affection and eventually what Himiko and Josette both recognize as love. For Himiko, Josette is an aunt, a confidante and wise counselor, a role model. For Josette, Himiko is a companion who responds to her in ways Ian, a stubbornly independent child, never did.

But Himiko is also alone. Her uncle, her guardian, has gone. She is relying on people who have no ties to her.

Every teenager is encouraged to think about joining. By the time they're in their midtwenties, the majority have joined. Josette is against it. She tells Himiko that it's the two of them against the world. But Himiko knows that's not realistic. They can't be against the whole world and be a part of it. When she tells Josette that she's joining Leap, they don't fight; they just stop talking. Chance endures the pain of that separation from both of their perspectives, the inevitability and futility of it.

Tomohiro once told her, "No matter what you may wish from them, endings are always lies."

In retrospect, Chance is sure it was the arthritis, the constant, gnawing suffering, that eroded Josette's good judgment and left her vulnerable to that moment—asking to join Leap—that would effectively become a murder-suicide.

During their work with Oceanic, Josette wasn't able to tell Leap about Tomohiro. She tried twice, but both times, she thought about Himiko learning what she had done, and she couldn't say it. As she made the decision to join Leap, she convinced herself that what happened with Tomohiro could remain a secret. Her secret. And then, it did remain her secret, but what she was changed.

.●.

LEAP TWO WAS INTOXICATING. AT her best, she seemed almost more real than other people. People would often give up something of themselves in her presence, offer her their initiative, aspects of their independence that they would otherwise jealously guard. And seeing the world through five bodies had shown Leap the power of subtle differences in her interactions with others. It was natural for a join to use that power.

Weeks before Don Kim loaded all of Leap's drives into his truck, Leap Two called Mark Pearsun. They talked about the business, and as Leap expected, Mark quickly lost his derisive edge. Mark was more ready to listen and looked directly at Leap Two more often, and longer, than he had at Leap One.

They both knew that in whatever time she had left, they would have to work together. While they talked, Leap saw that she also had other purposes for speaking with Mark through Leap Two—which didn't surprise her, exactly.

Initially, they focused on business, but it was remarkable how quickly the two of them fell into old patterns. They had missed each other.

For Leap, the conversations with Mark required effort despite the familiarity she felt with him. Before and after their talks, Leap wrestled with a revulsion that almost subsided when they were actually in contact.

⚫

EARLY ON, LEAP TELLS MARK that she doesn't want to talk about the illness, the flip. When she talks with him, especially, she wants to pretend that it isn't going to happen. He says that isn't like her, and she tells him that she's fighting, but she needs one place where she doesn't have to.

After that, she begins calling him regularly, and he eventually tells her that he's happy she's calling so often. They both agree that they need to meet in person.

⚫

IT'S LATE AFTERNOON AND, AFTER a long shift, Leap Three is sleeping fitfully under light covers. Leap Two dresses in a pair of tidy gray slacks and a fine white blouse and adds a touch of perfume that Ian had given Aurora before they joined. It has become one of Leap's favorites. The perfume isn't for Mark Pearsun. It's a scent for special occasions.

Leap Two finds Leap One's old handgun, a Bersa Thunder 380 CC, and cinches the holster up to fit Leap Two's more petite frame. She doesn't wear a suit jacket because she wants Mark to see the gun.

Before leaving, she puts on her long, green tweed overcoat. A gift from Josette. Then she flashes through photos on her retinal display—low-resolution, mostly transparent reproductions—until she finds a picture of Tomohiro that she loves. He's unaware that he's being captured.

He's reaching out to touch phlox that's growing in a place he hadn't planted. "How did you get here?" she can hear him saying, the way he would when he was thinking about moving a plant. He was always gentle with the garden's volunteers.

MARK IS NERVOUS AND DOING a poor job of hiding it. He helps her out of her coat, a slightly awkward, old-fashioned thing to do. His hands linger on her shoulders. But she hears a *woof* of surprise when he sees the handgun.

"I'm sorry about that," she says, laughing it off. "I brought it for you."

"Oh, you came to kill me." He's making a joke.

"Mark," she says, as Josette would have.

"Yeah. I'm . . . this has all been moving very fast."

"What has?"

"The change. You. Everything. And our conversations, which I've enjoyed. I'm off-balance, I suppose."

He hangs up her coat but doesn't walk behind his desk. Instead, he sits in the guest chair beside her.

"Why *did* you bring the gun?" he asks.

"I guess I'm off-balance too, and frightened."

He waits for her to say more. When she doesn't, he says, "I understand."

"I'm glad we can talk," Leap Two says. She looks away and allows herself to show the embarrassment and uncertainty she feels. "Well," she says, "things really have changed, haven't they."

"Yeah," he says, "some things have."

They both start talking at the same time, then stop. She stays quiet longer than he does.

"It's just incredible to see you and hear you like this," he says. "Like the strangest dream."

"I get a do-over," she says. "I get to make things right."

"You're so young. I've seen other people do it, join, but . . . what is it like? How does it feel?"

He reaches a hand toward her face, and she leans into it, letting him touch her. From the narrowed distance she can see clearly how time is hastening the changes on his face, the roughening of his skin and spreading of lines engraved by years of tension and focus. She sees the stiffness of his neck and the unconscious forward tilt that his muscles are just beginning to surrender to.

"It's too confusing," she says. Almost a question.

"No," he says. "It's strange, but I'm very happy you're still here."

"And I'm glad you took my advice," she begins. Leap suddenly feels that she is speaking through resistance. Her voice roughens and lowers as she fights herself to say the words. The difficulty makes them sound more deeply felt. "I'm glad you took my advice, and you didn't join," she says at last. "I don't like to share."

Their kiss is tentative, slow, as if neither fully believes it. After they separate, she watches him.

"I'm not really sure what this is, Josette," he says. "I want to believe, but I'm not a dim schoolboy. I see what you're doing, that you're talking to me with this body."

"It's not like that. This *is* me, Mark. It is. And I couldn't close the gap between us before. But like I said, I can do things over, in the short time I have left. Make it right."

"Is it you—"

"Yes. It is me. I'm strong, Mark," Leap Two says, gently speaking over his voice, quieting him. "That's important in a join."

She leans toward him and runs a hand slowly up his arm. She is tense, her muscles flexed, but he relaxes and presses forward. Her hands are under his shirt, her nails wanting to cut, to dig into his skin. She pulls her hands down and begins loosening his belt. He's helping, and then his hands are on her back and shoulders.

"And Himiko," she says, feeling the conflict overtake her, whispering near his cheek. "Do you feel right making love to Himiko?"

He snaps backward in the chair, but she's already standing and not where he expects her to be. She takes a step away from him.

"I should take the gun off," she says, unholstering it.

"Josette—"

"Yes. Also here."

Mark tries to stand but hasn't positioned his feet well and

falls back into the chair. He tries to push away from her but almost tips.

"Whatever we did," he says.

"Yes."

"We had to. We both did it."

"But I'm already killing myself," she says. And she racks a round and points the gun barrel at his face.

"Josette . . . ," he says, almost a sigh. He tilts his head and closes his eyes.

"Who do you think is standing in front of you?" she asks.

When he opens his eyes again, one slender hand hangs softly at her side; the other holds the gun. "It would have gone to shit," he says. "The press would have eaten us." He's not pleading. He's describing his failure. He fades into himself, mouth slightly open.

She cocks the gun. But her hand is shaking. Her finger is pushing away from the trigger, pressing hard against the back of the trigger guard.

She finally uncocks the gun. Stares at it as she shakily reengages the safety.

Mark's body jerks with a caught breath. She walks cautiously around him to the hook where her coat is hanging.

"I do love you," she says, her back to him.

She holsters the gun, lifts her coat, finds her way to the door, and leaves.

SHE WALKS PAST THE ELEVATORS because she's forgotten what they do. When she gets to the fire door, she opens it. In the stairwell, she tries to catch her breath but finds herself gasping. She holds unsteadily to the rail and walks slowly down the stairs.

The evening looks warm and forgiving beyond the building's cramped lobby. She makes her way into it and crosses into the street, unsure of her destination. Then she stops. There's no traffic. It's late evening, and the area is deserted. A pod passes swiftly overhead.

Her jaw aches. She unclenches it, pulling against the muscles. Then she turns back toward the building.

She enters, goes to the elevator, and stabs the button for Mark's floor. She grunts from the sudden pain of stubbing her finger. When the elevator opens on Mark's floor, the gun is in her hand.

She walks to the door of his office and pounds on it, but he doesn't answer, so she's about to try and open it when it swings inward. Mark is pale and standing far away from the door, his eyes rimmed with red. He's not surprised to see her. At her waist, the gun is pointing at him.

His voice is hoarse, and it shivers as he says, "You know how I feel. I did what I had to do for you to survive."

"You know that I'm both Josette and Himiko?"

"Yes."

"I'm broken by this. You were wrong. We were wrong. I didn't survive."

Mark doesn't answer. She's holding the gun, but this time she hasn't even disengaged the safety.

Mark's office door remains open. He doesn't speak or step into the hall as she leaves.

.●.

AFTER WORKING SO CLOSELY TOGETHER for so many years, she had seen what he was thinking. At the critical moment, she had known with absolute certainty what he was willing to do for her. He was smart about it, as usual. Carbon monoxide poisoning wasn't as messy as a gun would have been.

.●.

ELEMENT—A JOIN OF FIFTEEN, FIVE of whom are surgeons— was the primary in the join procedure between Leap and Chance. Element shows them only one drive—a florid, heavyset join with a bald, bullet head and an infectious grin that complements Element's unceasingly positive tone.

By tradition, a drive's name is retired when the drive dies, memorializing its place in what is referred to as the "canon" of the join. Each of Leap's drives now has a place in Chance's canon, becoming Chance Six through Chance Ten. The drive that had been Leap Four—the only one of Leap's drives to survive—is now Chance Nine.

The day after their procedure is officially complete, Element arrives in Chance Nine's hospital room at the head of a large group of doctors. Element is beaming.

"Well," he says, "we've just come from the morning status meeting. As I mentioned to you yesterday, this was the meeting where the most important indicators were reviewed. I can now confirm what we have all thought to be the case: initial results are quite good. We are not completely out of the woods, but I think *we can say* at this point that your procedure, from the perspective purely of the research, has been an unqualified success. And with regard to your health, we don't see any indication of the flip persisting. We've never had a case like this before, so we aren't sure what to expect. But this is, to say the least, unprecedented and very encouraging."

A woman whom Chance does not recognize, who is standing beside Element, says, "One of the things that makes Element so essential is his optimism. In this case, I believe it may be warranted."

Element interjects, "I believe it is!"

"Yes," says the woman, "but, as he also said, this is completely new territory for us. We *can* say that the join procedure was without complication and that initial results regarding the flip are very encouraging."

"They are!" Element says. "They truly are." He moves closer to the head of the bed and peers into Chance Nine's face. "And you?" he asks. "How are you feeling?"

"Crowded," says Chance Nine.

"Ha!" says Element. "You've gone from two fives to one ten. No wonder! I think your recovery period will take quite a while. And I think that within the year, you should consider adding at least one more. You'll be able to use an additional drive, I believe, quite effectively. It will take many cycles before you feel fully yourself again."

"No," says Chance Nine. It's difficult to talk because her throat is dry. Her voice is crackly and halting. "I mean the room. This room is crowded."

"Ah!" Element says, with a broad smile. "Of course, of course. We can do something about that. And then I have good news about the treatment of your Five's cancer."

Element and the woman who had spoken sort out the rest of the medical staff. Six people leave. Only four, including Element and the woman, remain.

Element's team has been coordinating with Chance's

oncologist. Though Chance Five is still undergoing therapy, the join of Chance and Leap had to proceed quickly, so Chance had to deal with the effects of the drug regimens for both the chemotherapy and the join. Despite this, Five's cancer markers have actually improved. The cancer is greatly diminished, and Chance is almost hopeful. Whereas Five had been heavily drugged and a drain on all of Chance's resources, he's now becoming energetic and may be a source of some of the additional cycles that Chance needs to fully integrate a new identity.

"You have a background in the field," Element says to Chance Nine. Chance pushes herself up in her hospital bed and says, "Yes."

"You were a colleague, before the tragic events that ultimately led you here."

"Yes," says Chance.

"Then I think you may be interested in a more complete description of the contribution you are helping to shape. Do you have a few moments to discuss it?"

"I do," says Chance.

"Wonderful," says Element, "because this is potentially the most significant advance in join science since the breakthroughs of the original project. And while each of us has done our modest share here, if we do realize the promise of these new techniques, your name may be joined with the name of Hamish Lyons as one of the founders of an entirely new phase of human development."

Chance Nine's fatigue and Chance's suppressed resentment of Element's bonhomie are both gone. As Element begins a brief summary of Hamish's radical interpretation of the mind-network connection, Chance experiences a pure, adrenalized response to genuine discovery—a reaction that narrows awareness to the ephemeral diameter of insight and focuses the mind until the world is re-created.

⁙

"I WAS WEAK." "I CHOSE ignorance." "I want to give up." "I can't trust myself." "I am destroying things." "I'm useless." "Nothing has changed." "Nothing is meaningful."

The phrases surface relentlessly, at any time of day, a constant background of self-recrimination and defensiveness, interrupting other thoughts, demanding a moment to be heard. At their most insistent they color the world, turning it colder and more distant. Or they can burn with such force that they become a physical pain that spans drives.

Chance recognizes their irrationality, their injustice, but cannot suppress them. Even after long and substantive discussions with Element, Chance finds no real refuge from them. As Element has neatly summarized, you cannot be the sum total of all of the actions of both the transgressor and victim and not find yourself transfixed by the paradox. Though Chance's drives are no longer physically deteriorating, the truth of past events is unchanged.

In idle moments, Chance wishes that the people he had been would gather in a dream to discuss things. At times, Chance aches for it, but that mysterious internal messaging system seems to be offline. Perhaps, with the addition of Leap's psyche, it did get too crowded. Chance still has the memories of each of them but thinks less about the identities that made those memories.

⁙

A SHORT TIME AFTER CHANCE Nine is released from daily observation, Reason, an undersecretary of Join Affairs who is known to be a close lieutenant of Excellence, checks in via hologram. During their conversation, Reason casually reveals that the Directorate has known the location of Hamish's community for years. Jackson and Terry weren't meant to find Arcadia, but to report on activities within it.

Chance is stunned by the news. Don killed Leap Two to protect the secret of Arcadia's location, but the Directorate knew it all along. As Reason talks, Chance re-experiences the shock of losing Leap Two—sees Don's pistol gently touch her forehead, sees her head snap back from the shot, shudders at the prolonged and saturating ache of loss.

Chance realizes that the Directorate does not believe she will ever speak with Hamish again. Reason is saying they'll keep trying to place people inside Arcadia. Hamish is too important in the development of human potential to be left on his own, without institutional protection. And it will be critical for him to join soon, as the health of his current drive is becoming compromised by age.

"Your Nine," Reason says, "is young but has quite a promising future if you want to explore it. If you decide to train it for medicine, to follow in the footsteps of your Three, we hope you'll consider working with us at the Directorate. Hamish has told us how impressed he was by Leap, and we can always use good minds in our research arm."

"I may have picked up a little more of the independent solo perspective," says Chance, "than would be comfortable in that setting."

"Why would you think that wouldn't be welcome?" Reason asks. "We're searching for truth in our research. We'll need multiple perspectives to find it."

"But you're tracking solo communities, trying to infiltrate them, forcing them outside civilized areas."

"Oh," Reason says, "yes, I see your point. Although for ferals, the isolation is their own doing. We do have to track them, though. To keep an eye on them. You have very direct experience of how ferals react to anything that they perceive might be a threat. They're quick to resort to violence, with or without an understanding of its full effects. They think in relatively crude terms. We watch them to help them avoid hurting themselves or anyone else."

Chance says, "You knew Rope."

"Yes," Reason admits.

"What happened to Rope?"

"We are interested in understanding the twenty-drive limit. Hamish's technique appears to be supported by a promising line of theoretical inquiry. Rope's approach was not promising, and Rope had become destructive."

"Do you feel responsible for what Rope has done?"

"Chance, I know this experience has been difficult for you, but I honestly can't say anything more about Rope. I'll leave you now to rest and continue your recovery."

·◦·

FOR MONTHS AFTER THE COOLDOWN period, while adjusting to being a new join, a powerful paranoia inhibits Chance's activity on Civ Net. Knowing that the Directorate—and even the solo community Hamish lives in—might be interested in what the drives are doing makes Chance hesitant to research the "vanishing point" or the "final gate." Eventually, Chance works through it, reasoning that tracking is just one of the rules of the road while acting on the network. But Chance believes it's the paranoia, more than anything else, that inspires the decision to train Chance Five as an attorney.

There are still some licensing issues to be sorted out from the join with Leap. The Directorate waived the costs, but the unusual nature of the license has drawn attention from several low-level functionaries. Each inquiry has been taken care of quickly by referring whoever is asking questions directly to Reason's office.

At a point when Chance's paranoia is strongest, a request comes in for one of Chance's drives to visit a licensing office in the short spires of New Denver. The request is for a personal visit, and Chance, relishing the thought of having the requesting officer call the office of the undersecretary of Join Affairs directly, decides to honor it.

The licensing office is in a particularly rundown area. Chance brings a pod to rest on a narrow, old-world street, beside a curb that might once have been lined with wheeled vehicles, and approaches a boxlike eight-story building. The front, brick facade is blackened with soot, and many of the windows are cracked, plaster casements notched and crumbled. Inside, the purple-and-gray halls smell stale and moist.

After reporting to a distracted-looking woman at a small desk behind bulletproof glass, Chance Nine sits on the wilted and stained floral cushions of an old waiting room couch. A couple is sitting on an identical couch on the other side of the small room. The woman has thick eyeliner and a long, blond, greasy ponytail. Beside her is a large man with arms crossed, eyes closed, and his chin against his chest, apparently trying to nap.

They wait ten or fifteen minutes. Chance Nine is just about

to stand up and talk with the woman at the desk when the blond woman says to her shyly, "You're not solo?"

"No, I'm not," Chance says.

"We can't afford to join," the woman says.

The man opens his eyes, yawns, and stretches broadly. The woman leans forward to give him more room. The man says, "I wish they'd bring the price down. They already own everything." Then he folds his arms and closes his eyes again.

The woman's gaze is friendly but also tentative. Her shoulders are raised slightly, and she looks as if she's prepared to flinch. She asks, "What do you think?"

"I don't really know about it," Chance says.

"Oh"—the woman draws her fingers lightly along the underside of her chin as she watches Chance with a sad half smile—"Jason says if we still can't afford it, he'll leave me."

"I'm so sorry," Chance Nine says.

"I know there's nothing anyone can do. That's what he says, and I know it's true. It's just that the price is too high." The woman reaches into a large purse and finds a tissue to wipe her eyes and dab at her nose. "Other people, who could afford it, might join with us. But we love each other."

"You've still got a lot of time," Chance Nine offers.

"Thank you," the woman says.

Chance Nine looks away to respect the woman's attempt to maintain her composure.

"Do *you* think we should?" the woman says.

"What?" asks Chance Nine.

"Because it's too expensive, do you think we should join with other people?"

"I . . . I don't know," Chance says.

"I'm sorry. We're not that interesting."

"No, I'm sorry," Chance says. "I'm tired. I had a couple of medical procedures."

Chance Nine stands and walks to a water cooler.

A door next to the bulletproof glass opens, and a bored-looking man steps into the waiting room. "Carla and Jason Runfert?"

The large man seems to come to life again. "Come on," he says, and stands. He pulls up his baggy pants.

"Okay," the woman tries to keep her voice cheerful. She gathers up the personal display that had rested on her lap and slips it into her purse. She gives Chance an appreciative smile. "Bye," she says, and offers a half wave.

Chance Nine lifts a hand and nods back at her.

"Good luck," the woman says. "You did well."

And as she reaches the door, she says, "If you have to tell your other drives what I just told you, I guess it's okay. I wouldn't want you to lie."

She winks at Chance and passes through the door.

P A R T

Join addresses the challenges of over-population by turning the tables on mortality. We reduce the population by defying death.
— Excellence, CEO of Vitalcorp, Secretary of Join Affairs

All that I wanted was to be whole and know my purpose in the realm of my self.
— Joseph Rex, *Poe's Mission*, Book III

S I X

AS CHANCE EXITS THE JOIN-LICENSING office, a pod hisses into position outside the beige double doors. Chance Nine has just spent a useless hour and a half waiting for a meeting.

A drive who introduced herself as Ursa Three finally appeared and apologized profusely, walking through a tortured explanation about information firewalls, security requirements, and a regular rotation of positions meant to ensure no one got too comfortable in the office manager's job.

Everything is explained and sorted out now, she said, and there was no need to take any more of Chance's time. They were very sorry they had inconvenienced Chance.

That was it. There was no more conversation; there were no questions. "As far as this office is concerned," Ursa Three said, "your file is closed."

Chance doesn't mention the woman she ran into in the waiting area, who was an impostor, passing as a solo. What would be the point? The Directorate may have engineered the whole visit solely to let Chance know she's still of interest. Message received.

Chance Nine directs the pod to the spire apartment in New Denver, expecting to arrive about twenty minutes before Chance One, Four, and Five. One will be leaving work shortly.

Four and Five are shopping. Chance Two is sleeping off a long flight at the house in the Olympic Archipelago.

The last couple of weeks have been difficult, and Chance plans to spend the evening mixing the drives. Each has a dose of restless energy, and Chance is feeling a kind of irritability that sex often dispels. At least after a good mix, drives are more likely to sleep through the night.

The pod's low whine sounds almost companionable as Chance Nine rises to her lane and then accelerates toward home. The external lights on the spires are muted, tainted with color so that the whole of the cloud-darkened night is alive with a fusion of vaguely shifting blue, green, and orange hues.

Chance relaxes, concentrates on breathing—the long breaths of Chance Four and Five walking through the leafy shopping arcade, past the central waterfall—and the shallow breath of Nine in transit.

Chance Nine's pod arrives at the house, cruising to a stop with imperceptibly slight shifts in momentum. The stillness of the surrounding world rouses Chance, and Chance Nine steps out of the pod, onto the spire balcony and into faint, pooled light at the door of the apartment.

And then stops. The glass door is open.

"Please don't use comms." From inside, a familiar voice, frightening. "Really. It just wouldn't be a good idea."

Chance Nine stands motionless outside the door.

"C'mon in," the voice says. "It's your house."

All of Chance's drives become still. Chance Two, in the house in the Olympic Archipelago, is suddenly awake and listening.

"I know you're probably scared. Don't be. Come in."

It's the voice of the drive Chance last encountered as Apple One, the waitress. Which means that Rope is waiting inside.

Chance Nine steps slowly into the entryway. The interior lights come on, but only slightly, so that the room remains half in shadow. Rope is standing to the left of the door, leaning against the wall. Only one of Rope's drives is visible.

As Chance enters, Rope straightens, walks casually to a cushioned love seat in the adjoining living room, and sits down. She's holding a pistol in her left hand. With her right hand she motions toward the wooden chair across from her. An invitation for Chance to sit. Rope's face is half masked by shadow.

"Why are you here?" Chance asks.

"I'm joined with all of my other friends."

"Then you don't need me," Chance says.

The shadows around Rope shift. Her head turns slightly. "I think you still deserve an opportunity to play the game."

"I don't understand that. I never really have."

Rope says, "I'm talking about the place where a join and a death are the same thing."

Chance takes a step into the room. "That's you. You're the only one who's ever said that."

"Yeah," says Rope. "I know things no one else knows."

Rope sits forward, suddenly moving out of shadow as if responding to an internal cue. She turns and watches Chance. She says, "I never liked pods."

"What?"

"They seem vulnerable. The mass calculator for the energy translators is a ticking bomb. When I was killing my drives, I crashed quite a few."

Chance Four and Five had been about to summon a pod. They don't.

Chance asks, "Why are you here?"

"Just sit down," Rope says.

Chance Nine walks across the room and sits down slowly in the wooden chair. Rope says, "Thank you." Chance doesn't answer.

Rope leans back, into shadow. "I know it's uncomfortable, my existence. This vision of your future. You have to get past that. You don't get to decide whether light comes from the sun. You don't get to choose what happens when hundreds of minds join. I'm just a fact."

"But you choose to be who you are."

Rope's laugh is short and harsh. "Maybe. It doesn't always feel that way. An individual choice can seem independent, but if you look at a whole population, thousands, millions of individuals, the outcomes are always predictable. I'm like that. I make lots of choices, but in the end I'm completely predictable."

"I don't see the connection."

"Chance," Rope says, sounding disappointed. "I thought we were going to be honest with each other."

Chance Nine is breathing shallowly. Her hands are shaking. Her voice is unsteady as she says, "Your experiment was misconceived. Flawed from the start."

"Oh?"

"You assumed you could remove time. Hurry things forward, to solve the problem. Time is the solution."

"Chance, you're getting excited. You're not going to talk me out of here, so relax. I'm not going to go away just because you have an idea."

"When I join," Chance says, then she takes a moment and draws a short breath, trying to calm herself, "one plus one is two. I become two people. Psyches integrate quickly, but over time they *unify*. I'm *one* person. You didn't have the research then, but it should have been obvious. Over time, I become one person again, and I'm Chance. Then I join again. In ten thousand years, if I'm eight hundred people, that'll be okay. Those people will continue to be me, every one of them, because they'll have had the *time* needed to change—to change me and to become me. You're trying to force everyone together at once. That's what doesn't work. That's what's grotesque."

"I'm . . . you think I'm grotesque? Okay. That's fair. But as for your—of course, I've thought of that. Other people have said that before. Do you think you get to say that, and it's a new idea, and that just wastes all my work? Is that what you think this is, a dream of some kind where your ideas make everything right? You just . . . do you really believe that?"

"Do you?"

"You know, you kill me, Chance. And I probably mean that in a good way. I thought we were going to be friends and play the game. But you really don't believe that my work's been worthwhile. You don't think it's worthwhile to expose the violence that the very idea of Join does to us, to what we are. Let's say you're right, and your rehashed, third-tier objection handling has a sliver of truth. Because it does, doesn't it? What is that truth exactly? Each individual in a join gets twenty years of having an opinion? Eventually, each one is still just an observer. If you even exist, you're only along for the ride. Is it worth trading your identity for a sightseeing ticket into the future, as if life were an amusement park ride? So, no, you don't get to ignore my work. You don't get to dismiss it, unless there's no value in any individual life. Nothing important at all about any beautiful, whole, single thing with a beginning and an end. No need for any more of those. Chance, you don't get to ignore death and remain a person."

"That's not what I'm saying."

"Okay. That's not what I'm saying either, then."

"I want you to leave."

"You know, Hamish cured me."

"What?"

"I flipped, a couple of years ago. Hamish cured me."

Chance Nine's fingers are folded together. She squeezes them and then pulls her hands apart. She says, "He said he didn't."

"Hm. Chance, we're a kind of animal that lies. Even Hamish will lie. Don't hold it against him."

"But why?" Chance's throat is dry, her voice faded.

"Would he lie about that? Well, think about what I've been doing. I don't think Hamish wants to be associated with me."

"You had a flip?"

"Yes."

"And the flip was cured? You're okay?"

Rope laughs again, this time with warm, genuine amusement. "No one's said *that* to me for a while. If you mean physically healthy, then yes. That's the good news for you, isn't it. It worked." After a pause, she continues, "And I was offered the same deal you were—join in Arcadia, where they're, you know, still practicing, or get taken care of by the Directorate's best. I chose Arcadia. Actually, come to think of it, that join was with— well, at the end of it I had one of the drives you met, at breakfast that morning. The big male."

"Why did you choose Arcadia?"

"Yeah, I could have died, right? Even with Hamish, they're still not very good at joining there. But I didn't want to be part of giving subnet tech to the Directorate. Hamish, he's a little oblivious sometimes."

Chance flinches away from Rope. She almost stands, almost surrenders to an impulse to run, but then sees the gun resting on Rope's thigh, pointed at her, and settles back in the chair.

Rope says, "Oh, that stings, huh? Yes, your help has brought the whole world one step closer to my reality."

"Not to your reality," Chance whispers.

"No, that's true. The subnet is a little different. Close enough, though."

"You were doing it too, trying to remove the twenty-drive limit."

"Was I?"

"I want you to leave."

"I'm working on that."

Chance doesn't respond. Rope says, "Don't feel too bad. It would happen anyway. Every single join is eventually going to have hundreds of minds. Things get really tricky with that many people in your head."

Rope suddenly sounds frustrated, almost desperate, the edge gone from her voice. She leans forward, pulling the gun down beside her thigh. "Chance, I've been trying to make a difference. I thought you might want to help. Join can be wonderful, a miraculous experience. But we can't transcend death. We're all still part of the natural world. And subnets, the hive mind, me . . . it's all . . . just a different kind of death. The Directorate isn't listening. They want a single network. They want to colonize other planets. Chance, we've got a perfectly good planet."

The shadows are tightening. In an odd, petulant voice that surprises even Chance, Chance Nine says, "You're not dead."

Rope sits back again, and her face slackens. She closes her eyes and rolls her head. Then she hefts the gun, as if idly measuring its weight, and stands up. "I told you I was working on that."

"Look," Chance says quickly, "don't—you don't need to do anything right now. I'm talking, like you asked. I'm being honest. And if you want to know, do I want to help, then yes, I want to help. And I understand you, what you're *saying*. I just don't want to *be like you*, I don't want anyone to—"

"No. You're scared. You don't mean any of that."

Starting in her gut and chest, a touch of nausea and dizziness radiate through Chance. "Please," she says quietly, her voice cracking, "please don't. I'm not strong now, I'm—"

Rope's hand moves very quickly, coming out of shadow. Chance sees the gun in it, and as the barrel sweeps upward Chance looks for the briefest moment straight into it. Chance hears herself cry out.

Then Rope presses the gun under her own chin, and the report—a surprisingly quiet *pop*—sounds. Rope's head snaps back, and its body hits the floor.

＊

FOR FOUR AND A HALF years after that final encounter with Rope, Chance doesn't add any drives. Given the dramatic reduction in the price of licensing, the fact that Chance still maintains only five active drives occasionally raises eyebrows.

Many smaller joins have united, but there has also been a run on high-quality solos. They weren't too difficult to secure at first. A successful join could seal the deal with an "all this can be yours" sort of pitch, which actually went more like "I'm healthy, brilliant, immortal, have physical and intellectual capabilities beyond your wildest dreams, want for just about nothing, and am literally offering you my life." Eventually, the better-quality solos started realizing their value and becoming more selective about who they wanted to be for eternity.

＊

CHANCE NINE PAUSES AT AN observation portal where a starship floats before her. The Arc, white ribbed and gigantic, stretches into the starry distance like the mysterious bones of an interstellar whale, Earth visible between gaps in its frame.

In New Denver, Chance Five is playing football in an open-air night league. The timing of the game is purely coincidental, but it will make a credible cover if Chance is asked questions about a heightened stress response.

The goalie for Chance's side stops a kick, and Chance Five takes the opportunity to look up at the clear sky, where the stars are just beginning to show. What appears to be a large, wavering reddish star is actually light from the Derrick, a four-kilometer-square orbital way station and construction colony where the Arc is being built.

In addition to providing a platform for building the Arc, the Derrick is a stopover for most traffic to and from Earth. Space travel within the solar system has become almost routine, with three bleak but improving colonies on Mars and several auto-mated-mining operations on moons and large asteroids.

Chance Nine is up there looking down at the Earth as Chance Five looks up at the Derrick. Chance feels a very mild, almost pleasant, sense of vertigo.

Chance Nine trained in astrophysics. At times, the coursework was excruciatingly difficult, but Chance persevered and finally got to upper-level courses that were really interesting—a series of practicums on deep-space mechanics. There, Chance discovered that Chance Nine—who had been Himiko—had a talent for visualizing particularly complex mechanics, the interplay of stress and structure.

Chance asked Reason for help getting Chance Nine a job with the Arc Project. The Arc Project is a major international effort intended to begin the era of human colonization beyond Earth's solar system. The Arc is designed to travel indefinitely, undertaking a multigenerational, interstellar voyage.

Seven hundred joins will crew the Arc, each sending a single drive. Many famous joins are participating, including both Excellence and Advocate. Chance Nine was the five-hundred-thirtieth drive selected as crew.

After Chance One also started working on the Arc Project, as a predictive event modeler in the security subsection, Chance bought an apartment on the Derrick.

Chance's view of the Earth from the Derrick is always spectacular—a blue, radiant presence defined by a precise curve, the starting place of infinity. Over the last eighteen months, that view has become familiar but never routine, evoking a clear and haunting sense of the Earth's fragility.

Chance doesn't like to talk about that sense of fragility. There is a plan for many more interstellar vessels to be built after the Arc. For some, those vessels make the Earth's fragility less relevant. Chance gets angry when people express that perspective.

The Arc's mission is to find and occupy a habitable, Earth-class planet. Chance Nine almost flinches as Chance considers the term "Earth-class." She quickly turns away from the viewport, her face reddening and warming with a sudden, surprising shame.

A small man with body proportions that imply greater size is coming out of a teaming room to Chance's right. He sees Chance Nine and calls a greeting. The man is the seventh drive of a join named Gold. He is a biophysicist and member of the Arc's crew. Chance waits as he approaches.

"Are you going to help with the stress check in the hydro bays? You haven't confirmed yet, but Velocity said you're up."

"Yeah," Chance says. "Sorry, I thought I confirmed. I have valves."

"No, it's"—Gold Seven blinks—"oh, yeah, valves it is." Gold grunts while he considers something, then says, "I don't like late changes to the roster like that."

Chance Nine nods, avoiding looking directly at Gold, and turns to walk away.

"Uhh, see you there," Gold says, and Chance hears his frown in the tone of his voice. Chance Nine hurries, stepping quickly into a separate control corridor.

Even with Chance borrowing cycles to closely manage Nine's respiration and heart rate, that conversation was a disaster. Gold is going to remember it. Chance will need to do better at casual interactions.

IN NEW DENVER, GREENGROCER'S GOATS have just scored their third goal against Chance's football team, the Fourteeners, who are still scoreless near the end of the first half. Chance Five has been playing sluggishly as Chance prepares for what's happening on the Derrick. Bright Two, a Fourteeners midfielder who's running upfield, glances over at Chance.

"You want to sit out for a bit? Take a break, let someone else swing the pick for a while?"

Chance is taken aback. "What?"

"You seem distracted."

Chance Five says, in a what he hopes is a pointed but friendly way, "No, I'm good. That last one was you." Bright shakes his head and tosses Chance a noncommittal "Whatever" before turning and jogging away.

THE CONTROL CORRIDOR THAT CHANCE Nine is walking through extends in six regular well-lit segments toward a gate that leads into the Arc's superstructure. The Derrick's interior was designed to comfort the human mind and body. The corridor's walls are sheathed in a rich wood grain, the air infused with a loamy, slightly spicy scent of growing things. A subtle breeze stirs occasionally, and a quiet click, trill, or drip sounds at intervals in the distance. The whole effect simulates a passage through the semienclosed patio of a well-designed wooden manor on some supple alpine slope. The warmth of a late-morning sun shines on the back of Chance's neck.

An airlock at the end of the control corridor slides silently open. A mild, slightly moist gust of air riffles out of the Arc. Chance Nine steps across the threshold into the similarly designed interior of the Arc, and the door slides shut behind her.

It's a short walk to the hydro bay. She passes a couple of coworkers who greet her but barely look up from what they're doing. Once in the hydro bay, she opens comms and walks through a routine status check with Increase and Solve, the two joins with shift-oversight responsibility. Then she opens a pressure sensor panel and begins her visual inspection of valve circuitry. She engages her retinal overlay.

The germ of the idea had come to Chance during a Civ News report on the massive investment that would be required to make the planned Arc Project a reality. The report focused on the unprecedented marshaling of resources and level of international cooperation required to build the Arc. First, the Derrick would be enlarged to accommodate both its current missions and construction of the craft.

The Arc would be a grand symbol of humanity's ability to overcome differences and accomplish something that appeared to be almost impossible. Excellence had described Join as an enabling technology for multigenerational space travel. "As the ship explores the galaxy," he said, "Earth will receive continual first-person accounts of the voyage."

The Arc's primary systems, including energy, have been coming online during the last month. Today, as the energy translators and the hydro bays link up, their mutual fail-safes will be disengaged for three seconds. Chance One is part of the security team that modeled the event.

The Arc's energy translators rely on an incredibly precise mass calculator, similar to that used in pods. There have been a few issues with the mass calculator recently. Chance Nine has signed off on it, though. Because of the mass calculator, during the three seconds that the fail-safes are not engaged, a single body in an unexpected location could do serious damage.

Chance Nine moves to the next step in her inspection of the hydro-bay valves: *Observe the sealant condition on Valve C1.* Chance Nine straightens.

Chance is closely managing Nine's stress level, her pulse, and level of agitation. She'll appear normal on the hydro bay's bio-sensors. Someone across the bay swivels toward Chance Nine, and she nods a brief acknowledgment.

She walks toward a sealed bay door. On the other side of that door is Valve G1, which isn't part of today's inspection.

⁕

IN NEW DENVER, CHANCE FIVE is rushing an opposition striker who has control of the ball downfield. Chance Five's pulse is hammering. His vision blurs as he slides at the ball, knocking it sideways with the tip of a toe and forcing the striker to hop over him.

⋅●⋅

ON THE DERRICK, IN THE security subsection's open office, everyone is suddenly quiet. An alarm light is flashing on Chance One's monitor. A panicked voice shouts, "Shut it down!" Chance One flushes and rocks backward in his chair. Chance is momentarily blinded.

⋅●⋅

THERE HAS BEEN A SLOW and continual erosion in the size of the refuge that the Earth can offer. Chance has watched for years as its edges have crept inward and its center has weakened. Death is impatient, and suffering multiplies, but not yet for joins. They just don't notice it, as each successive catastrophe is quickly buried beneath the limitless weight of individual days and years. For now, Chance's fellow joins are comfortable, which seems to be enough for them to continue minutely examining the mysteries of life.

Chance does hear people saying the right things. And sees encouraging signs. But despite those, the fibers of the shroud that the race is weaving for itself continue to multiply and lengthen. And somehow Chance can see it all while others don't seem to be able to.

Then one day it dawns on Chance that the Arc Project itself is an affirmation of an argument Rope had been making. The Arc and the promise of interstellar travel give the human race an illusion of transcendence. As Join has.

Chance doesn't want to sabotage the Arc. Sabotage is an act of destruction, and bodies could be killed. Chance actually believes that the Arc would be a thrilling, inspiring accomplishment. But the world seems to be making a choice. Almost five years after Chance's video conversation with Excellence, Vitalcorp and the world's powers have offered nothing significant beyond the Arc Project and the reduction in licensing costs.

The irreversible past—Hawaii, Monterey Bay, all of the others—insists on action. Chance casts about for something that might be effective—that might provoke the needed changes—and ultimately targets the time line. There must be a time line. Any individual ship could meet with disaster, so for interstellar travel and colonization to be a viable choice, the Earth has to remain livable long enough for several colony ships to set out.

Simply slowing progress toward space travel might force those rushing toward colonization to concede that the Earth should remain a viable habitat indefinitely. If only as insurance against the unforeseeable. And if the same political will that was marshaled to build the Arc was applied to Earth's environmental problems, perhaps real progress could be made.

A plan begins to take shape, but as it's unfolding it just seems crazy. Even to Chance, who is conceiving it. Its assumptions seem crazy. Chance has all five remaining drives checked for a meme virus or cognitive degradation. But they're all healthy. The plan doesn't appear to be a figment of a pathology, at least not one that can be diagnosed.

Chance begins to suffer the burdens of a tyrannical conscience. Moving forward seems indefensible, while abandoning the plan is cowardice in the face of urgent need. There is no longer a safe choice. Indigestion afflicts many of the drives, night sweats, anxiety attacks.

If things go as Chance expects, there will be damage. Some drives will probably be killed. At least there are no solos working on the Arc. Joins can recover from the loss of a drive.

.●.

AS CHANCE NINE WALKED THE short gangway toward Valve G1 there were still many factors working against the plan. The fail-safes might engage and shut down the translators. Or the wobble created by the mass calculator might not result in a breach. That's what Chance was aiming for—a radioactive breach that would force a long delay in the project. Hopefully, it would be small enough that only a few drives would be hurt. The accident, and the delay in the project, could give opponents a reason to restart the debate around priorities and the allocation of resources.

But there was also a slight risk that heat from a breach would cause an explosion. And an even-smaller likelihood—an almost nonexistent likelihood—that that explosion would cascade through the whole bank of translators and then through the whole power infrastructure.

Many years later, a report on the incident will show that, at the moment of the initial breach, the recently engaged energy translators had been under temporary stress from a series of unusually large solar flares. Under normal circumstances, that wouldn't have been a problem.

.●.

WHEN CHANCE CAN SEE AND hear and breathe again through Chance One, he lies for a moment on the office floor, listening to the chaos erupting around him, the voices, the shouting, the sounds of panic. Chance Nine is gone.

Chance One's work space is inside the control structure on the Derrick. He props himself up on an elbow and peers around the room. A couple of his colleagues are also on the floor. Someone is bending solicitously over him. Someone is staring at a screen, moving her hands erratically and cursing loudly. Two bodies are standing in apparent shock in front of the large viewport, looking out into space in the direction of the Arc. Then they're using their arms to shield their eyes. Light is coming in from the viewport.

.◉.

CHANCE FIVE COMES TO ON the grass of the football pitch. There are faces in his peripheral vision. They're saying things he can't quite understand. He's watching the few stars visible in the night sky above them, searching until he finds one in particular. A red one that is brighter, angrier than it should be.

.◉.

CHANCE ONE ROLLS TO HIS side and then rises slowly. He walks to the viewport where the incoming light is diminishing but still flaring in small bursts. Others in the office walk there as well. There is crying, soft crying and loud sobbing. Someone is saying no, over and over. Those at the viewport are quiet.

As Chance's eyes adjust and process what he is seeing, he begins to perceive the things that are wrong. In the distance, a chain of bright explosions is lengthening across the structure of the Arc. Some are large, some smaller. Their combined effect is constant enough to create a pulsing light that burns multiple soft afterimages into his vision. The entire ship's structure rocks as the explosions shift it in its metal harnesses. The Derrick crackles and groans, and pieces of it that connect to the Arc are flung away into space. Someone says, "That's the last one."

Explosions continue along the Arc's length as it begins to move. At first, it drops very slowly away from the Derrick, toward the Earth, but as fires rake it, it picks up a little speed and a clear but subtle lateral trajectory, as if it has received instruction for a specific landing place and is moving under power. It noses to the edge of the viewport's range and then begins to exit the frame.

"Here," someone shouts. "The main screen."

Video from a high-orbit tracking satellite shows on the main office screen. On the right side of the screen, just within the Earth's shadow, are the blinking lights of a large portion of the damaged Derrick. Farther away, and floating gently toward the day-lit part of the globe, is the whole length of the Arc, small fires burning and bursting across its ribs.

The woman to Chance's left says, "I can't believe how fast it's moving."

And a man replies, "It's the starboard tanks, from the test yesterday. They're burning. You can see it there."

Eventually, as Chance One and his rapt colleagues watch, the Arc's acceleration sends it into distant atmosphere and brighter flames flare all along its length. It very quickly becomes consumed in a single ball of fire—all of it burning, hurtling downward, growing smaller, ever smaller in gravity's strengthening embrace. The fury and majesty of the fall is breathtaking but relentlessly diminishing, until in the Arc's final moment it appears to be only a tiny spark, like a single spark of consciousness, against the vast blue surface of the Earth.

ACKNOWLEDGMENTS

THIS BOOK WOULDN'T HAVE HAPPENED without David Vann's generous early interest and crucial comments. I cannot thank him enough. Many thanks also to my agent, the incomparable David Forrer, for believing in the book, for his essential insights, and for making things happen. Thanks to the whole team at InkWell Management for their effort and skill. Thanks to Bronwen Hruska, Meredith Barnes, Rachel Kowal, Janine Agro, Kapo Ng, and everyone at Soho Press, for taking a chance on *Join*, for making the novel a beautiful object, and for helping it find an audience. Profound thanks to Mark Doten, whose brilliant editorial contributions helped shape a novel from the story.

Thanks to Ilene, Leonard, Elsie, and most especially to Terri Linn, whose support and care helped make this story possible. Thanks to Charles Johnston. Many of his ideas inform *Join*. I don't know exactly how, or precisely which ones, but they are there. Thanks to KM Alexander, for thoughtful feedback and timely inspiration.

Thanks to each of the following people for their help with early drafts—it's hard to imagine this book without every one of them: Bob Shaw, Ruta Toutonghi, John Shaw, Carolee Bull, Geoff Pfander, Gary Knopp, Jack Hawkes, David Zitzewitz, Will Wagler, and Tom Richards.

Thanks to Pauls Toutonghi, my good and wise younger brother, for his smarts, eloquence, and informed perspective. Thanks to Annette Toutonghi and Bruce Oberg, for friendship and support, infinite awesome, and fundamentalist mac and cheese. Thanks to Gabrielle Toutonghi, for belief and commitment, and to Mike Toutonghi for the example of his daring and intelligence, and for the words.

Thanks to Mary and Joseph Toutonghi for their loving examples, and to Peyton Marshall, Alyona Toutonghi, John Greene, and the extended Toutonghi clan, and to Judi Linn and Leigh Anne Shaw, for unflagging encouragement. Thanks to Mason, Michael, Dan, Anna, Phin, and Bea for building a future and for not being too surprised that I'm proud of them beforehand.

Thanks to those colleagues whose collective efforts and goodwill allowed all of us to help our customers and to earn a living, making *Join* possible. Thanks to John Shaw (again), to Matt Boyle, Rob Ernst, Tok Thompson and Tollef Thompson, because the vorpal blade went snicker-snack.

And finally, thanks endlessly and most especially to my wife, Monique Shaw, who has made a welcome space in our home for each and every sentence.